★

As we near the end of the play, I launch into my big scene, the passionate monologue setting up the climax between mother and daughter. Suddenly, Queen Tut slaps her hands on the table and pushes herself up. Her face contorts into a snarling sneer.

Damn her. If she doesn't like my reading, she could at least have the common decency to talk to me later. Not that I'd listen.

I refuse to watch, continue my reading even though I feel everyone watching Diana. I hear Diana scrape back her chair, send it crashing to the floor. This time I do stop and look. I wish I hadn't. Diana claws her throat, staggers away from the table to the area Wexler chalked off as the stage.

We sit gaping as Diana, gone rigid as a tree, falls straight forward, her glasses making a sickening crunch as she crashes against the wood floor.

"My reading wasn't that bad," I say.

No one listens in their rush to where Diana sprawls, lifeless.

★

AUDITION for murder

Susan Sussman with Sarajane Avidon

WORLDWIDE.

TORONTO • NEW YORK • LONDON
AMSTERDAM • PARIS • SYDNEY • HAMBURG
STOCKHOLM • ATHENS • TOKYO • MILAN
MADRID • WARSAW • BUDAPEST • AUCKLAND

AUDITION FOR MURDER

A Worldwide Mystery/June 2000

First published by St. Martin's Press, Incorporated.

ISBN 0-373-26351-1

Printed in U.S.A.

Acknowledgments

Our thanks to those experts who so generously shared technical knowledge: humorist Belle Lyman, chemist Liz Doherty, theater expert Sy Sussman, Dr. Ann Ressetar, Detective Art Erzler, theater lighting maven Rob Nowicki, Susan and Arthur Goldner, Kenneth Denberg, the Multiple Sclerosis Society of Chicago, Dennis Nilsson, Evanston Police Department Commander—Support Services Division, Jonnie Ballis, literary agent Jane Jordan Browne, editor Kelley Ragland. And, of course, for Barry Sussman, magic-maker extraordinaire.

PROLOGUE

IT IS A SMALL theft. What harm, after all, in one purloined piece of fruit?

She picks her way through jagged backstage shadows, over rope coil and rusty scaffold, prop furniture and dusty scrim. Hamlet barks from the depths of her audition bag.

"Just one moment, precious," she says.

He barks again, offended by the intrusion of the giant grapefruit.

"We're almost there."

A bit more light would help. Her world has grown gray over the years, colors and shapes clouded by cataracts. A nuisance at times like this when dark shadows shift and unseen dangers lurk.

She isn't supposed to be mucking about back here. But she does so want to enjoy her little treat in private and soon there will be far too many Nosey Parkers primping in the lobby powder room.

She is too old for morning auditions, all this rush rush rush. She would never have agreed to this ungodly hour if Martin himself hadn't called. Begged her, *begged* her to read the Mother's part, "for old times' sake."

A dim light escapes under the door of the tiny backstage bathroom. She slips inside, glides past the pitted porcelain sink, and locks herself in the privacy of the single stall.

Hamlet yelps again.

"Hush, you naughty boy," she says, nuzzling the top of his head, turning him loose to explore the room.

She sets her canvas audition bag on the floor and lifts out the beautiful grapefruit, thick-skinned, laden with juice. Salivating, she sinks her teeth into the rind, greedily tears off strips. This is an altogether different species from the shriveled fruit she buys by the bag at her grocery. Quality will tell. Oh yes.

Crisp citrus smell fills the cubicle, teasing, tempting. The juicy sections separate easily. She eats the first, barely stopping to spit out the occasional seed. The second section nearly fills her and, by the third, she is sated.

Carefully wrapping the rest for later, she tests her voice. "Aaaaa - Eeeeeee - Iiiiiii - Oooooo - Uuuuuuuu." Lovely echoes in the small room. "Meee - mahhhhhh - mayyyyyy - mooooooo - muuuuuuuu." The citrus cuts a path through the morning dust, gracing her webby voice with vibrant tone. "Aaaaa-Eeeeee—"

A sharp pain shoots from navel to solar plexus. Just like clock-work. The nervous stomach before every audition arrives like a peevish old friend. As painful as it is, she will worry the day it doesn't come.

"Meee-mahhhhhh—" The pain again, sharper, more insistent. And again, striking like a jagged-edged knife, sawing up and around and down. By the time it occurs to her to call out, pain clogs her throat. The walls of her larynx constrict, shutting off air. Crumpling to the floor, she clutches her stomach, sucking in short sharp breaths, each a violent stab to the gut.

She falls back, her head wedging between toilet and wall, eyes staring up at the small overhead light. With each jolt of pain, the light grows dimmer and dimmer.

Until, at last, it goes out.

ONE

THE MURDERER'S WALK from cell to electric chair lacks the raw terror of an auditioning actor's walk across an empty stage.

I feel them watching from the safety of the darkened theater. Do I move like the character they're casting? Do I have Daughter's carefree gait, her ballsy humor, her irreverent take on life? She sucks in my stomach, lifts my chin, squares my shoulders.

Daughter has attitude.

Yeah.

Drives her sainted mother crazy.

Yeah.

And now Daughter and Mother will clash center stage in a knock-down-drag-out over Daughter's new boyfriend.

Problem is, Mother neglected to show for the audition.

An intern with hair shorn like a boxwood maze jogs onto the stage. He checks his clipboard. "Miss Ludwig?"

"No." I hand him my head shot and résumé. "Taylor. Morgan Taylor."

I point to my name at the top of his list. He frowns. "You were scheduled an hour ago, at nine."

"My partner never showed."

He checks my name off his list and disappears into the dark.

I stand naked. Exposed. Try to keep in character while waiting for Wexler's direction.

Damn you, Lily. Where *are* you?

Lily London's name and mine, paired first on the morning call sheet, crawled down and down while I let others go ahead. I stood, helpless, watching the parade of actresses who had no right auditioning, who'd actually *worked* in the last six months. Big fat juicy roles. Rent-paying, grocery-buying roles. They should step aside for other actors—me, to name a few—who have been shriveling in a Sahara of a dry spell. If not for my temp job, a few voice-overs, and a couple of TV commercial residuals, I'd have dried up and blown away by now. I need this job.

Papers rustle somewhere in the theater, the familiar sounds of my head shot and résumé being passed. Vague forms shift fifth row center. Martin Wexler, director extraordinaire, and his entourage.

Attitude.

Yeah.

Don't lose Daughter's edge. Stay tough.

I'd paced the lobby forty-five minutes waiting for Lily London to show. Finally rehearsed with the plaster cherub perched atop the drinking fountain. Even the monitor at the Equity desk took pity on me, giving me fancy fruit from a huge basket. No better way to tame crazed bears and frothing actors than to throw food at them. I took a banana and an orange, stowing them to eat after my audition, when my stomach wasn't inching nervously toward my throat. It would be bad form to toss my cookies all over the infamous Martin Wexler.

All right, so I'm not the first actress in history whose reading partner blew off an audition. It's not as if Lily London is such a prize. Still, with all her upstaging and overacting, she's a thousand times better than some stand-in stage manager who moves his lips while reading Walk/Don't Walk signs.

A sonorous voice arises from the dark.

"You are reading with...?"

"I was paired with Lily London."

"Lily's not here?" Wexler stands, his shock of silver hair glowing under muted house lights. At seventy, the man still has presence, the kind of Cary Grant leading-man looks audiences drool over. Rumor has it he and Johnnie Walker Black Label have been best friends since way back. He seems sober enough at the moment. "Where is she?"

"We were scheduled at nine, but she never showed."

"That's not the Lily I remember. She was punctual to a fault. Frank"—the intern snaps to—"see if you can track her down."

I am about to say I've tried calling. Several times. That I

plunked hard-earned shekels into the lobby pay phones trying to hustle Lily London's no-talent buns down to the theater. But I sense that Martin Wexler is a man who prefers finding out things for himself. Thorough. I've heard that. Determined. Genius. Demigod. One of America's great directors. If he wants to call Lily, who am I to say no?

"Should I wait until you find her?" I ask.

"No. Let's move on. Rob will feed you your lines."

A gorilla in high-top gym shoes and neon suspenders lumbers across the stage, knuckles scraping the ground. He comes to rest so close I can count the fleas jumping in his chest fur.

"When you're ready," says Wexler.

I am a professional. I am a professional. I am a professional.

"So, what is it now?" I ask.

The gorilla looks puzzled. "What is what?"

I AM A PROFESSIONAL.

"That is my line," I say, running my middle finger down his script to where it says "So, what is it now?"

"Oh, sorry."

"You're Mom."

"Right."

"We alternate lines."

"Got it."

"Ready?"

"Shoot."

Love to.

I steady myself, shifting back into character. "So, what is it now?"

"I. Want. To. Talk. To. You." No inflection, no vocal movement, no recognizable human emotion. He doles out words with all the passion of a brick.

It's hard to hear the gorilla through the sound of my blood boiling. The flip side is, I don't have to *act* angry. I'm all over the scene, erupting like Vesuvius, lashing out with force I would never have unleashed at frail Lily. I underplay my roles. It's my style. I'm a card-carrying devotee of the Clint Eastwood school of restrained rage.

All that is forgotten as I rant and rave at the lug, trying to shake loose a single sign of a *Homo sapiens* genetic link. If I've blown my shot at this role, at least I'll have a ripping good time. I blast through the reading, playing the scene as broad as vaudeville. When it's over, I bow low to the stunned silence.

Wexler's voice echoes from the dark. "Thank you for your time, Miss—ah—Taylor."

ONCE I VOMIT I'll feel better. My nervous ritual isn't something I care to share with the actresses crammed into the lobby ladies' room, making their last-minute adjustments to hair and makeup, stealing furtive drags off forbidden cigarettes.

I duck through the side door, around the rows of scrims, cables, and backstage detritus more precious to me than furs and jewels. I'd appeared at the Heartland, this grand dame of Chicago theaters, in five fabulous plays. I'd prayed today's audition would make it six. But after my overblown reading, there's not a chance in hell I'll get the part.

The power of my disappointment surprises me. Rejection is built into the profession. I know that. But this time it's more serious than usual. This was my last shot to work enough weeks to keep my Actors' Equity insurance in full force.

I close the door of the tiny backstage bathroom behind me. A dim bulb burns in the overhead fixture. The door to the stall is closed. Straps of a canvas bag trail out in the space under the door.

I grit my teeth against the nausea. "Will you be long?" I ask. No answer. I knock on the door. "Excuse me. Will you be much longer?" Nothing. I try the door. It is locked from the inside. "Are you all right?"

Something furry brushes my leg.

A rat!

I jump back, screaming, bashing against the paper towel dispenser. It crashes to the floor, scattering brown towels everywhere.

A large rat hovers in the shadows, backing away from me. Barking.

Rats don't bark.

I bend down for a closer look. It's not a rat at all. It is Lily London's little dog, the one she carries in her audition bag.

"Lily?" I say. "Lily?" No answer.

I reach under the stall, tugging at the handle of the bag. The dog yaps, running up and back, nipping my knuckles.

I work the bag partway out until I see the familiar gray-and-white-striped canvas. In all the years I've known Lily, she's never been far from this bag. I bend down, laying my cheek against the cold floor, looking under the stall.

Bits of grapefruit peel curl like dead leaves on the tile.

Just beyond, Lily's eyes stare back at me, wide and unblinking.

TWO

"I CAN'T BELIEVE she's dead," says Beth.

It is painful watching my best friend grieve.

"A heart attack..." her voice a whisper. "Lily looked so vibrant when I picked her up. So..." She burrows deeper into the corner of my lumpy sofa, cocooned in one of Grandma Ruth's afghans.

I putter around, straightening old magazines, fluffing pillows. What am I supposed to say? I want to comfort her, but don't know how.

The newly orphaned Hamlet nestles in her lap, sound asleep. "I wasn't even gone two hours." She goes over it yet again. "Dropped Lily at the theater, went back to my apartment to throw in a load of wash, ran a few errands, then came to pick her up. By then, she was...she was..."

She's crying again, adding soggy tissues to the pyramid on the end table. I become engrossed in neatening back issues of *People* and *Variety,* none of which mentions my name.

Beth's heart is as big as her talent. I tell her people take advantage of her. She says I'm too suspicious. Our unlikely but devoted friendship dates back to sixth grade, when we landed roles as two of the sisters Von Trapp in *The Sound of Music.* I was a street tough from Skokie, a multicultural village in Chicago's northern shadow. Beth was an innocent from Glen Ellyn, a far western suburb about as textured as white bread. Our opposites attracted and we stayed friends, appearing together through the years in plays, light operas, movies.

I freshen the chamomile in her cup, stifling my instinct to wisecrack. For some perverse reason, death brings out the smart-ass in me. It doesn't help that I always considered Lily London a royal pain, one of those perpetually helpless types who can't seem to do anything for themselves. Lily and Beth met on a movie shoot a couple of years before, and the old gal immediately latched on, calling Beth to do this or that little favor, pick something up, drop something off.

"The grandmother I never had," Beth had said.

"I have two grandmothers," I'd told her, "I'll sell you one." She thought I was joking.

I leave Beth to her tea and tissues while I take four messages off my answering machine.

Message One: "A Dr. Billy Roth will be calling," says my mother. "He's Gail Witlin's second cousin's son. Very bright, very good-looking, and the divorce is nearly final."

Who calls a grown doctor Billy?

Message Two: "Hello, Morgan? This is Dr. Billy Roth." His voice has the crackly static of an old crystal radio set. Either he's calling from a cheap car phone or he is a hundred and fifteen years old. He promises to call back. Oh joy.

Message Three: "Hi, sweetie." Grandma Belle. "Don't want to keep you. What do you call a father of twins?" She pauses a few seconds to let me work on this. "A pas de deux. Love you."

Message Four: "Morgan?" Mom, again, to see if the good doctor called and to ask why I'm never home. "What do you do with your time? Oh," as if an afterthought, "Sylvia called. Says she's tried to reach you but you still won't return her calls." I listen to the long pause, feel Mom wanting to say more but knowing better than to try to fight her children's fights. I'm grateful she hangs up without telling me how to deal with my back-stabbing baby sister.

I erase the messages, making room for more of the same, and curl onto the sofa next to Beth. Her nose and eyes are bright red from crying. Dear Beth. Although we're both hovering on the brink of (gulp) thirty, she looks closer to thirteen. Waiflike, she has the kind of pale skin, large eyes, and soft speech that makes total strangers want to take care of her. It drives her crazy. Which is why I am the only person Beth called last month when her new doctor diagnosed her long history of seemingly unrelated symptoms as multiple sclerosis.

"Lily looked wonderful," says Beth. "Had her hair and nails done yesterday. She was so excited about seeing the great director after all these years. Fluttery. Like a schoolgirl. She said Wexler once had a terrific crush on her but she was interested in someone else at the time. Do you think that was it? The excitement was too much for her heart?" She strokes Hamlet's silky coat. "Is there something I could have done? Maybe if I—"

"You can't second-guess the Grim Reaper," I say.

"She didn't complain of chest pain."

"Heart attacks don't always come with a warning."

"I mean, she'd get those scary palpitations now and then. Kept that vial of nitro pills in her bag."

"Death plays by its own rules." I cringe at my fortune-cookie dialogue.

"But this morning she was f-fine." Beth tears up again.

"Look at the bright side. She went fast. No pain, no lingering illness."

"I guess...."

"And she died in one of Chicago's grand old theaters, about to audition for a great director in a play she'd starred in forty years ago. If you gotta go—and we all gotta—it's not a bad way."

She nods, unconvinced. I know Beth, know her unlimited compassion for the aged and infirm. Probably explains why she hangs around me. She'll spend the next few weeks agonizing over what one small thing she could have done to save Lily's life.

The doorbell rings, startling Hamlet, who begins yapping and turning in circles, snagging his sharp little nails in Grandma Ruth's afghan. I dislike dogs in general, and this one in particular. He has all the appeal of a long-haired rat, and none of the personality. Beth, of course, thinks him adorable. I push the Talk button. The intercom crackles.

"Yes?"

"Miss Mfghrbuleyt?" I swear that's how it sounds. My intercom attracts static from a three-mile radius. Two tin cans with string would have more clarity.

"Yes?"

"This is Detective Rozzlittykq from the Chicago polizzzynnk."

Not for me, after all. "Who did you say you wanted?"

"Miss Morgan Taylor."

That's clear enough.

"And you are…?"

"Detective Roblings, Chicago polizzzce."

Polizzzce? For moi? Quickly scanning my larcenous life from birth to present, I come up empty. Oh, sure there's that ear of corn filched from an Iowa field, the box of tissues lifted from the Four Seasons ladies' room, and a bag of leftover candy liberated from the craft service table at my last movie job. All right, two bags. But certainly nothing serious enough to bring the Chicago polizzzce to my door.

"What do you want?" I say.

"May I come up?"

My finger hovers over the buzzer. Is he really the police? The building has already had three break-ins this year, all from strangers being buzzed in. Our last tenants' meeting, a knock-down-drag-out affair punctuated by energetic finger-pointings and loud accusations, ended with a clear description of the acceptable buzzing-in procedure. When in doubt, don't.

"What is this regarding?" I ask.

"The dpthrrst of Msskkffll Lnnnnaas."

"Could you repeat that, please?"

"The death, this morning, of Lily Londskyyg."

A burglar's not likely to use Lily's death as entrée. Besides, should I need help, I have the backup of Beth-the-waif and an attack-trained rat. I buzz him in, take my pepper spray from the hall desk, and slip it into my pocket before stationing myself at the open door.

THREE

THE GOOD DETECTIVE marches slow and even, landing by landing. I run up and down these same steps for half an hour every day, save myself a fortune by not joining some fancy health club. I'd have passed him seven times by now.

He rounds the last landing and pauses to look up. His face has been around a while, has visited some unsavory digs, witnessed the underbelly of man's inhumanity. Sweat glistens on his forehead, welling in furrows deep enough for planting. He nods my way, then lowers his head and trudges up the last flight.

The hand gripping the banister—meaty, flat knuckled, powerful—is not one I'd care to meet in a fight. I have a thing about hands. And feet. I didn't grow up the daughter of Skokie Sam the Shoe Shop Man without picking up a thing or three. These particular feet are large, housed in industrial-strength spit-shined oxfords, and walk with the toes pointing slightly out. Duck-footed men tend to be overweight, creatively intelligent, and wickedly funny. Zero Mostel. Alfred Hitchcock. Jackie Gleason. The good detective is trimmer than my usual favorites, more powerfully built. Probably just as well. I can't picture Zero sprinting after the bad guys.

"Miss Taylor?"

"Yes."

"I'm Detective Roblings." He pulls a white handkerchief from his pocket, blotting sweat from his forehead. A delicate gesture for such a lug of a man. "I'd like to ask you a few questions."

"May I see some identification?"

He reaches in his jacket pocket and I tighten my grip on the pepper spray. No victim, I.

Deft fingers flip open the ancient leather case to badge and ID. There is no mistaking the laminated face—sad-eyed, soft-lipped, broken-nosed. The photo does not capture the flecks of orange and green in his eyes, the glint of light when he looks directly at you. Which he does. And it misses the coiled energy fisted just below the surface. A young Brando could play this Detective Roblings. Yes, it would take that caliber of talent.

The Chicago city seal looks genuine enough. And the badge. I decide to assume his credentials are real. At some point I have to trust that people are being honest with me. Otherwise I'd never set foot outside the house. Like my Grandma Ruth.

"What can I do for you?" I ask.

"It's about Lily London."

The Potters' dog claws the door across the hall, which means Mrs. Potter has her good ear planted firmly against the thin wood.

"Maybe it would be better if we talk inside," says Roblings.

"Here is fine," I say. No need for Beth to hear the grim details of Lily's death.

He shrugs, exchanging his badge case for a small notebook. Flipping it open, he digs into another pocket for a pen. Harpo Marx did pockets this way, fumbling, looking, coming up with an endless supply of unlikely goodies. I wait for Roblings to pull out a rubber chicken, an Autoharp, the running board off a Model T.

"I understand you are the one who discovered Miss London's body."

"Yes."

"Tell me about it."

I do.

He checks his notes. "The ambulance driver says you accompanied Miss London's body to the hospital and took her belongings home with you."

"They're in a shopping bag in the kitchen."

"You were very close with Miss London?"

"Me? Oh, no. I brought her things to give to my friend. Beth is...was like a daughter to Lily."

I give him Beth's full name. I probably could mention that she is ten feet away, but I figure I can take care of whatever it is the good detective needs.

"You called Miss London this morning," he says.

"Yes. No. I mean I never actually talked to her. I was waiting for her at the theater—"

Mrs. Potter's dog begins barking, which starts Mrs. Potter shushing, which gets Mr. Potter yelling at both of them to shut the hell up.

Roblings raises his voice over the noise. "I didn't say you talked to her. I said—" The barking and scratching and yelling make it impossible to hear. I have no choice.

"You'd better come in."

I intend to talk to him quietly near the door, keep him away from Beth. But he strides past me into the room.

Hamlet leaps off the sofa, yapping in circles, nipping at Roblings's feet. These are not feet to fool with. Each shoe weighs twice as much as Hamlet, could crunch him like a roach. Hamlet's attack is an act of extreme bravery or abject stupidity, depending how you feel about dogs.

Beth makes a soft kissing sound. "Come here, sweetness. Come here, boy." Hamlet gives Roblings's right shoe one last nip then jumps back up to Beth's lap. "Good boy. That's a sweet boy. Yessss."

"Hello," says Roblings.

"Hello," says Beth.

"I'm Detective Roblings."

Beth looked puzzled. "Detective?"

"He's come about Lily," I say.

Beth's tear-ruined face and the mountain of wet tissues on the table obviously pique Roblings's finely honed detective instincts. "You must be Lily's friend Beth," he says.

One large tear and then another trickle down Beth's cheek. She barely manages a nod before the deluge.

"Detective Roblings," I say, standing behind him, forcing him to turn away from Beth to talk to me, "you said you have a few more questions?"

He nods, checking his notes. "You called Miss London's apartment this morning. Several times. Her answering machine logged your first call at eight forty-five."

"Oh, that. Yes. I was trying to find her. To rehearse before our audition."

"Why did you need Miss London for your audition?"

The question jars, a piece out of place. "What does this have to do with Lily's heart attack?"

Roblings shifts weight from one foot to the other. "I'm a little curious," he says. "I don't know much about theater, how it works. I'm trying to reconstruct Miss London's morning, and you were part of it."

"You mean I was supposed to be. The play's main characters are a mother and daughter. The director paired Lily and me so he could audition both roles at one time."

He flips to a new page in his notebook. "When Miss London failed to show, why didn't you just ask one of the other actresses to read with you?"

"I don't understand these questions," I say. He doesn't answer. Doesn't change expression. I try to read him but the man gives up nothing. "Actually, I did ask. Early on. There were a couple of actresses I would have loved to read with. The Equity monitor said she'd ask the director."

"Martin Wexler?"

I nod. "She asked. Wexler said no. I had to audition with the person I was paired with."

"Why?"

"Why?" I sigh. It's a pain when civilians try to apply logic to the theater. "Because Wexler ate bad shrimp last night. Because the taps fell off his dance shoes. Because he's depressed about global warming."

Roblings's face is not amused. "What happens when your partner doesn't show?"

"You wind up playing the scene with the drink concession kid, if you're lucky, the stage manager if you're not."

Do I detect a slight hoisting of the right lip, the faintest hint of a smile? But Roblings's voice remains all business. "You sounded pretty upset on Miss London's answering machine," he says.

Beth looks at me, questioning, her long lashes clumped with tears.

"We'd been scheduled for nine o'clock. I was checking to see if she'd overslept. Or forgotten."

"She wouldn't do that," says Beth. "You know how seriously she takes...she took her work."

"I know. That is, *intellectually* I knew Lily wouldn't be late. But I kept waiting and waiting. I mean, I *never* get first call. I'm usually slotted somewhere midday, which means rearranging my work schedule, rushing to the audition, then twiddling my thumbs because, by then, the auditions are backed up. So I was thrilled to be scheduled first. I didn't know until I got there that I'd been paired with Lily." And I hadn't been happy about it. But there is no need to say that. "I called and waited, called and waited. I had to let a long line of people go ahead of me. So yes, I guess I was pretty steamed when I left my messages."

Roblings jots notes, his powerful hands delicately flipping pages of the notebook.

"You should have known something was wrong," says Beth.

"Believe me, I ran through a whole checklist of things that could have happened to her. But being dead wasn't one of them."

"What time did you get to the theater?" asks Roblings.

"Eight-thirty."

"Did anyone see you come in? The janitor? Another actress?"

"What is this about?" He doesn't answer. Holds his pen poised, waiting. I try to think. "There were mobs of students going into the art school next door."

"Anyone in the theater who might know you?"

"No one. I walked into the entrance foyer, past the box office—"

"Anyone there?"

"It doesn't open until ten."

"But someone could have been there, getting tickets ready or whatever it is they do."

I think about that. "I doubt it. The curtain inside the box office was closed. I remember because, with the curtain drawn, the glass made a good mirror for me to check my hair and makeup before going downstairs to the theater.''

"So, no one saw you?"

"No."

"And if someone were inside the box office, you couldn't have seen them."

"Right."

Roblings glances at his notes. "You're sure of the time?"

"Excruciatingly sure. I was late leaving my apartment. Just missed the El. I was terrified I'd be late for the audition, watched the minutes tick off the whole ride down. By the time I ran the two blocks to the theater, I was a wreck. It was exactly eight-thirty."

"She was already there," says Beth, so soft I barely hear.

Roblings whirls toward Beth. "What's that?"

"I said," her voice a whisper, "she was there."

"Miss London?"

Beth blows her nose, nodding. "She had me drop her off around eight-fifteen so she—"

Roblings's left eyebrow hitches half a centimeter in what I suspect is a wild show of surprise. "You drove Lily London to the audition?"

"Why, yes, I—"

"Detective"—I try to gentle him away from Beth—"I'm sure I can tell you everything you need to know ab—"

The energy shift in the room is powerful and absolute. Roblings shuts me out, hones in on Beth like a hound on point. "I want you to tell me everything you can remember," he says, "from the moment you picked her up, until the last second you saw her."

Something strange is going on here. Everything about Roblings's demeanor—tensed body, faster speech, tightening of those Brando-esque lips—says this is no casual questioning. What is he not telling us about Lily's death? I study him for signs.

As Beth details her morning, Roblings takes off his jacket and folds it neatly over the back of Uncle Morrie's ancient La-Z-Boy recliner, the one Aunt Denise donated to my apartment without first clearing it with Uncle Morrie, thereby nearly ending forty-five years of wedded bliss. To his credit, Uncle Morrie recovered, developing a grudging attachment to the chair's replacement and a respectful wariness around Aunt Denise.

Roblings pours into the recliner with the sensual flow of molten lava. His body melds with the baggy cushions and sprung frame. I have a feeling it will be a long while before he flows back out.

FOUR

I AM SMOOTHING hot wax on my left upper lip between sips of wake-up coffee when the phone rings. I pick up to a lilting Irish brogue.

"Miss Morgan?"

"Yes?"

"This is Martin Wexler's casting assistant?"

Be still my heart. "Yes?"

"Mr. Wexler would like you to read again for him?"

"Yes?"

"Tomorrow? Ten o'clock? At the theater?"

"Yes?"

"See you then?"

"Yesh." The wax hardens. "Thanksh."

Yes! Huzzah! Fanfare, trumpets, bring on the elephants. Martin Wexler actually liked my overblown performance. Go figure. I tease up a corner of cooled wax, then rip it off, taking most of the hairs and a thin layer of skin.

My demons check in as I press an ice cube against the welting.

A callback is not a job.

It ain't over till it's over.

Don't count your chickens.

Wexler wants you to read again because he couldn't believe how amazingly awful you were the first time.

Begone! I flick the demons off my shoulder into a vat of boiling oil.

It's hard not to smile as I smooth hot wax on the right side. A callback! This tiny crumb of hope is more banquet than I've had in months. Part of me wants to jump up and down and celebrate. Another, the part that's learned to love macaroni dinners and twice-used coffee grounds, forces me to stay calm, realize there isn't a chance I'll get the role. I rip off hair and skin, press ice until the stinging stops.

Come on, Morgan, think positive. A callback is one step closer. I am going to land this job. Have to. It is possible to live without food but I refuse to live without insurance. I've watched too many of my uninsured friends and relatives, stricken by accidents or sudden illnesses, dragged through financial hell.

The trouble is, Actors' Equity reckons I should work every now and again if I want to qualify for its insurance plan. Its free insurance plan, as in *no charge*. Which is exactly what my budget allows. But my Equity jobs have been too few and too far between. I am dangerously near the cut-off zone. If I don't get this play, Equity will make me go on self-pay, which costs $3,000 a minute.

The overflowing laundry basket beckons. I left it blocking the front door as a reminder I'm out of clean everything. It will have to wait until I complete my deforestation. I bend over the magnifying mirror, attacking my left eyebrow with tweezers while I dial Beth. "Get any sleep?" I ask.

"Not much." A sharp yelp breaks in. "Shhhhhh," she says. "That's a sweet boy. Yessssss. Poor Hamlet. He's such a lost soul. Doesn't understand why I don't take him home to Lily. He paced all night. I think that detective scared him."

"Scared me," I say.

Beth drops her voice, hardening it to Roblings's West Side accent. "I just want to ask you ladies a couple questions."

I laugh. "I still can't figure out what he wanted."

"I swear, you are so dense sometimes. Here's a guy who lives in a world of muggers and gang-bangers, and he suddenly finds himself in the company of a couple of savvy dudettes. I'm surprised you got him to go home at all."

I can't quite conjure the image of the lumbering detective as come-on artist. Hamlet starts yapping again and, while Beth quiets him, I debate whether to drop the joy of my callback into the middle of her sorrow. But I have to tell someone. "Someone" used to be Adam, my first phone call in the morning, last call at night. That ended eight months ago, 'round about the same time

Sylvia—my back-stabbing boyfriend-stealing baby sister—discovered what a great listener Adam was.

Drop it. Just drop it.

Hamlet calms down, whimpering. "Poor baby," says Beth.

I'm going to burst if I don't tell. "I got a callback," I say, softly.

"Oh, Morgan, that's fabulous! When?"

"Tomorrow."

"You're going to be great!" She pauses. Sighs. Pauses.

"What?"

"I hate to ask—I'm afraid I already know the answer—but have you paid your Equity dues?"

"Shit."

"That's what I thought. Tomorrow's May first."

"I'd better get down there. Call you later."

I tear through the laundry basket in search of something wearable. Beth would never say "I told you so." But she has told me so, every week for the past month. Equity members must pay dues twice a year, October and May, to receive the current card. No card, no audition. And tomorrow is May first. May Day. Cinco de Mayo minus cuatro.

My slacks are hopeless, but I find a reasonably unwrinkled skirt and a passable knit top. The first pair of panty hose runs from toe to thigh. I scrounge another.

It isn't likely that I'll be asked to show my Equity card at tomorrow's callback. But I can't risk it. I once went on an important audition with an expired card. The Equity monitor, a Napoleonic nitwit aquiver with power, turned me away at the door. Wouldn't even let me plead my case to the director.

I call my boss at Junque and Stuffe while I tug on the hose. "Harold? I'm going to be a little late today. I have to stop at the Equity office."

"Not to worry, dearheart," he says. "I shan't need you until a positively humongous shipment arrives tomorrow."

"Oh. About tomorrow."

"Yes...?"

"I'll be in. Just maybe a little late. Depending. I have a callback for that Wexler audition."

"Dearheart, how lovely for you."

"I'm scheduled early. I expect to be in on time."

He sighs. "Well, I shall just have to manage until you arrive. Break a leg."

Beth calls back as I'm flying out the door and asks me to track some Equity insurance information for her while I'm at the office. "I'd do it myself," her voice shaky, "but I'm not feeling up to making calls just yet."

"Stop apologizing. It's okay to ask a favor. I owe you about five hundred."

Why is it that Beth, who loves doing things for other people— the Late Great Lily London, me, every hard-luck Harry with a sob story—finds it so difficult to ask favors for herself? As I head out, I liberate a rubber band from the stash on the front doorknob and put it around my wrist. A reminder not to forget.

FIVE

THE EQUITY OFFICE looks like a convention of Who's Who in Chicago Theater. The Atlanta Shakespeare Theatre is holding auditions in the Library. Anyone who can pronounce "Shakespeare," and too many who can't, wait to try out.

I plow through the thespian throng and head down the hallway. A few actors pore over the audition book, jotting down dates and addresses. Others wait to sign up with the person making audition appointments. A neon-clad messenger pushes through to the out-of-towners' table and drops a package among the piles of flowers, packages, letters, and telegrams. He holds out his clipboard to me.

"Not me," I say, leading him through the crowd to Rosie. "Her."

Moving at lightning speed behind the massive counter, Rosie fields ten frantic requests at once, calming, cajoling. Short and wide as a fire plug, wispy white hair flying in all directions, she takes one look at us, dispatches the messenger in two seconds, then congratulates me.

"Not many catch Wexler's eye, I can tell you. Well done. Hold on, hold on." She riffles through a stack of scripts. I don't bother asking how Rosie knows about my callback. Her Equity antenna picks up the slightest vibration. "Here you go," she says, pulling a packet from the middle of the pile. "Your sides."

A chill goes through me as I take the half-dozen pages Wexler selected from the script. Receiving sides is a giant step forward in the audition process. These pages are tangible proof that I am a heartbeat away from being cast. Sides give me something concrete to work on, words to breathe life into, a key to plumbing the depths of my character.

Excited, I flip through the sides, scan the snippits of unrelated scenes, each calling for a different emotion. There is meat here.

I can do something with this role. I am ready to run home and begin working on my lines when I hear someone ask about renewing her Equity membership. Thank goodness. I would have forgotten.

I move to the end of the counter to fill out my check, helping myself to a couple of mints from Rosie's never-ending candy jar. Industry gossip flows around me, and I eavesdrop to see who is cast in what role, which play is rumored to be coming to town. An elderly man mentions Lily's death at the theater. "That's how I want to go," he says. "In the saddle."

I am handing Rosie my check when the rubber band around my wrist reminds me. "A friend has MS," I say. "She's heard the disease might be made worse by an allergic reaction to the old silver fillings in her teeth."

Rosie snorts. "Sounds like an old wives' tale."

"Might be. But she's desperate. Needs to know if Equity insurance covers the cost of replacing her old fillings with some newer material."

"We'll take a look-see." Rosie snaps her fingers, dispatching one of her interns to check it out. I step aside to wait.

"*Mor*-gan." Diana Tuttle's voice axes the back of my neck. She floats toward me through the crowd. I pull up my shoulders to ward off the next blow. "How *won*-derful you look." She kisses the air next to my cheeks. "What-*ever* have you been up to? It's been ages. Simply ages."

It appears as if she's speaking to me. But Queen Tut never plays to an audience of one. Even her stage whisper projects across entire time zones.

"I still can't believe the Rep cast that dweeb Louisa instead of you in *As You Like It*. And wasn't that audition for *Under Milkwood* the most *dreadful* thing? Honestly, sometimes we actors are treated like *such* cattle. Why, you should consider yourself lucky you didn't get the part. You didn't have to work in that abysmal theater. The heat conked out opening night and every one of us in the cast about died of pneumonia."

She is doing it to me again. Sweet as sugar substitute—and as genuine—Queen Tut is announcing to all present that I haven't worked in a while—and she has. I try not to notice her perfectly coifed hair, starched linen suit, unscuffed shoes, and manicured nails as she rattles off the long list of auditions she's been on. Even though we're about the same age, I always feel like a little girl around her. A poorly dressed, wrong-side-of-the-tracks little girl. Queen Tut's one of those focused, humorless, annoyingly adult people who seem to have been born old.

I'm thinking how to cut off her oh-so-concerned inquiry as to why I wasn't at this or that audition, her "you would have been so perfect for" such-and-so role, when she offers up the ideal cue.

"And," she says, "you really should have auditioned for Martin Wexler. That man is—"

"I did," I say.

"You...?"

"Did. Audition."

"Oh. Really?"

"And," projecting my voice across the assemblage, "I have a callback."

"Oh? How nice for you."

"Tomorrow."

"Wonderful. Well, wonderful. Really. Which role?"

"The Daughter."

Her smile freezes. "Me too. A callback, that is. Tomorrow. I expect, that is, I may see you there."

She becomes suddenly engrossed in writing her dues check. "So sad about poor Lily," she says to Rosie. "I hear the police are concerned about some irregularities."

First I've heard. "What kind of irregularities?"

"I'm just repeating," says Diana, "what a friend of mine overheard at the theater."

"If anything's irregular, it's those police," says Rosie. "One of them—looks like a cross between a bear and a basset—came nosing around yesterday."

Detective Roblings no doubt. That man does get around. "Do you know why the police are so interested?" I ask.

Rosie waves a dismissive hand. "It's no biggie," she says. "They can't find any next of kin for Lily so they're hoping to get a line on her through this office." She peers at us over the tops of her glasses. "I tell you, that man was into everything, bothering us with questions, wanting files looked up, copies made. As if we don't have enough to do."

Queen Tut, bored by any conversation not about her, projects her voice to the last seat in the third balcony. "I was in the theater when Lily died." She shudders prettily. "If only I'd known she was having her heart attack. I could have used the CPR I learned for my role in *Stat!*"

That does it. I feel my weak-willed self sucked into Diana's relentless game of one-upmanship, and—heaven help me—I am powerless against it.

My voice rises from the depths of my diaphragm. "I found the body."

Wonderful effect. All the room goes quiet. Then, slight murmurs swell to a barrage of questions hurled at me from all directions. And, as I cast pearls of information before inquiring minds, I feel a twinge of shame for using Lily's death to boost my miserable ego.

"Who wanted this info on multiple sclerosis?" shouts the intern, waving a sheaf of papers.

"Here," I say, grateful for the distraction.

"This is all I could find"—he hands me two pages—"and here's the section on dental care."

I leaf through. There is nothing about removing old fillings. Beth will have to contact the insurance company directly.

I am halfway down the hall when Diana sings out, "See you at the callback tomorrow. I'm so glad things are finally looking up for you."

SIX

BEAUTY AND THE BEAST stop by the next morning as I tear apart the apartment searching for the exact same clothes I wore to the audition.

Beth holds out a Dunkin' Donuts bag. "We come bearing gifts," she says.

"Just in the nick." I dash toward the bathroom, Hamlet chasing after me. "Coffee's ready. Pour us a cup?"

I find the skirt hiding on a bathroom hook under my kimono, the shoes kicked into opposite corners of the hall closet. But the blouse…where did I put the blouse? Maybe my bedroom. I search my drawers, the closet floor, the random piles of stuff littering the room. It is imperative that I wear the same outfit.

"Superstitious," Lester-the-attorney used to say, when Lester was still around. "You actors are so superstitious."

That isn't it, isn't it at all. What if it isn't me the director remembers, but "the gal in the pink blouse"? I once nearly lost a part because I wore a striped blouse to the callback. Who knew the director had fallen in love with my gray fuzzy audition sweater? I had to promise to let the costumer copy it. That's why I wear the same clothes for a callback. It has nothing whatever to do with superstition. Sure.

Blouse searching is hard work with Hamlet yapping around my ankles. I flip through my closet, hanger by hanger, in case, in a rare fit of tidiness, I actually hung the damn thing.

Hamlet finds the pink blouse before I do, dragging it from under the chair last inhabited by Detective Roblings. I wrestle the blouse away—wrinkles wrinkles everywhere—wiping dog spittle and dark smudges off the sleeves. The smudges don't wipe. I work a damp cloth over them. Old stains. Set. They must have happened when I found Lily's body, when I bent down on the dirty tile floor to look under the bathroom stall. Lily's eyes, that empty stare. I shudder.

Breathe deep. Let all things go. Relax shoulders. Roll eyes. Waggle jaw. Feel the world fall away. There is only the audition and me. Slow breaths. Slow.

Beth brings coffee and a chocolate doughnut, settling on the bed as I finish dressing. Lily's death has hit her hard. She looks tired, pale, her bright eyes dull. The ready smile folds down. Oh, the pain of losing someone you love. However it happens, through death, distance, or a sister's betrayal, they're gone from your life, forever.

I hand her the MS information. "I don't think Equity will pay to have your fillings replaced," I say, pulling on my last good pair of panty hose.

"I know. It's a long shot. Probably won't help, anyway. But, at this point, I'll try anything. My energy level is next to zero."

"That's because you're depressed over Lily's death."

"Even before, I was draggin' my wagon." She tries a smile. Doesn't quite make it.

Hamlet zooms into the room, grabs hold of one leg of my stockings and starts pulling.

"No!" I yell. "Let go. Don't—"

Beth makes a clicking sound and Hamlet releases my stocking, jumps up onto the bed, and rolls over for a tummy tickle.

I check for runs. "Listen up, you little rodent," I say—Edward G. doing *Silence of the Lambs*—"I am going to roast you slowly over hot coals. Serve you up with fava beans and a nice Chianti."

Hamlet growls.

"No she won't," says Beth. "Don't you worry."

"You're spoiling him."

"It's not his fault. Lily was a fastidious housekeeper. She never left things lying around." Beth nuzzles his neck. "This place is just one huge playground, isn't it, you sweet thing."

"Just because I'm from the hurricane school of housekeeping..." I pack my audition bag with tissues, comb, hair spray, breath mints, makeup, extra head shots, and other exotic tools of my trade. Beth stands to walk me to the door and falls back onto the bed.

"What's the matter?"

"Dizzy…" Her breath comes in short bursts. "Stood too fast. Nothing serious."

"Something."

Her skin is waxy white. A small twitch jerks her right eyelid.

"A little flare-up," she says.

"MS?"

She nods. " 'Tis the nature of the beast. I'll be all right."

"You're staying right here. Don't move until I get back. There should be something moderately edible in the fridge."

"I'm fine."

"You're staying."

"Come on, Morgan, you can't stand sick people."

"Just the goldbrickers and complainers. You don't qualify. Besides, if you stay a few days, I can coach you for your industrial and you can help me with my lines."

She manages a half-smile. "You know you'll get the part, don't you?"

No. "Sure."

She promises to think about staying.

On my way to the theater, I wonder if all my acting jobs until now have been flukes, if I was ever any good. The demons have returned with a vengeance.

SEVEN

I SHOULD ZERO right in on the blue-and-whites parked akimbo on the theater walk, but I don't. I don't even question why I have to flash ID to Security at the door.

On a normal day, I might assume there's been a terrorist threat from an obscure fringe group. Barely a play opens without offending someone with obscenity, nudity, politics. Lately it seems every play has at least one character urinating onstage. Heck, even *Snow White* has its detractors.

But this glorious day is anything but normal. I have a callback! I'm totally concentrated on the audition. By the time I reach the theater, I've shuffled off this mortal coil and fallen into the world of the play. I enter the theater, oblivious.

If my first go-round was the audition from hell, the second is pure heaven. A dynamo with a wild frizz of red hair replaces the flea-infested stage manager. Too young to be cast as Mother, too old for Daughter, the woman is nonetheless wonderful, feeding me lines with brilliant tone and tempo. Her performance empowers me. Instead of drowning in audition sweat, I stride around the stage, easily becoming the tough-talking character Wexler responded to the first time.

After a couple of read-throughs, Wexler comes onstage, giving us crude blocking, suggesting things to think about as we go through the scene again. "The Wexler genius," they call it. He has an eye, all right. There is the hawk about him, tense watchfulness, sure movements. He is at once opinionated and innovative. The kind of director who would be off-putting if his instincts weren't so perfect.

I'd missed the fun of it. The excitement of layering art form upon art form—playwright's words spoken through actor's interpretation shaped by director's eye. And all this before the set designer, costumer, lighting director, and sound engineer work their magic. Add audience and shake well. Ah, the exhilaration, the tension, the creation of a world where none existed. I become not someone other, but a heightened part of myself.

As Wexler moves us around the stage, I sense an intimacy between him and the redhead. She's imported from New York, that much is clear from her accent and style. Wife? Mistress? An old friend helping out until he casts Mother? Maybe he doesn't want to appear insensitive by auditioning for Mother so soon after Lily's death. Whatever his reasons, I am grateful. This woman brings out the best in me.

The rear exit doors open and close. Two policemen station themselves like sentinels.

"Damn," says Wexler.

He hops off the stage and strides up the aisle. I can't make out the words, but Wexler's body language says he's not happy the cops are here. His voice rises and falls, his arms gesture wildly. The cops don't move.

I tighten. It's one thing to be observed by theater people who understand the ragged edges of an audition. It's quite another to have rank amateurs look on, seeing only half-played scenes and interrupted movements, unformed characters repeating the same lines five different ways.

Wexler storms back. Great. An angry director. Every auditioning actor's nightmare. I redouble my efforts: breathe in the role, breathe out the tension. Erase the cops completely. Luckily, the actress playing the mother is so good she sweeps me out of this world into the one on stage.

We hit the climactic scene full tilt, Mother raging about the sacrifices she's made so her children can enjoy the sort of life she's only been able to dream about, Daughter refusing to accept guilt any longer. I finish, drenched in sweat, my heart beating a thousand times a second, my character vindicated, liberated, triumphant.

Wexler lets the delicious silence play itself out before saying, "Thank you, Miss—ah—Taylor." He waits as I come down from the stage and gather my things. "I'm curious," he says. "Your mother, is she anything like this mother?"

"My mother?" I laugh. "Mom would chew this woman up and spit her out."

"Why is that?"

"This character nails herself to the cross with solid gold nails."

"So?"

"My mother hates martyrs. Can't stand people who blame everyone but themselves for their unhappiness."

Wexler smiles. "Unfortunately," he says, "well-balanced mothers make for boring drama." He asks me a few questions about my professional and personal life, then says, "Thank you very much. We'll call you."

I walk toward the exit, agonizing. Did he love my performance? Hate my performance?

"Miss Taylor?"

His voice stops me cold, raises goose bumps. *You're hired. You have the role. We'll pay you triple the going rate.*

I turn. "Yes?"

"Is it true you're the person who found Lily London's body?"

"Yes."

He nods, turns away. Dismissed. Don't call us…

I push past the cops to the lobby, practically mowing down Queen Tut. Diana is a spring vision in a pale salmon linen ensemble and meticulous makeup. We force smiles as she walks past me into the theater for her audition. Old dressing-room shtick pops into my head. "To be a good actress you must have a good lip line." If there is even a modicum of truth to that, Diana is one of the truly gifted actresses of all time.

I AM ABOUT to leave the theater when I am overwhelmed by the need to revisit the bathroom where I discovered Lily's body. It is critical that I re-create the moment, isolate my exact feelings, recall every detail of my reaction. "Everything is copy," says my mother the journalist. It would be criminal to let the experience of discovering my first dead person go to waste. I duck backstage.

The area looks less cluttered and brighter than on the day Lily died. Yellow police tape cordons off the area. A couple of cops wander around. Crime investigation signs are posted on the door. What crime?

"Miss Taylor." Detective Roblings emerges from the shadows. "Just the person I want to see."

"What's going on?"

"Exactly what the signs say."

A crime scene? It takes a moment to sink in. "Y-you think Lily was murdered?"

Roblings stays silent, waiting, watching. He studies my face for reaction. Suddenly, Roblings's interview at my apartment, his odd questions to me and Beth, make perfect sense.

"But I was here when the paramedics tried to resuscitate Lily. She died of a heart attack. Everyone said so." I stare past the police tape into the small bathroom. And then it hits me. "I may have been nose-to-nose with a murder victim? Inches away from her murderer?"

My legs go rubbery. I try to pretend I misstepped, but my legs won't hold. Roblings slides a strong hand under my elbow, supporting me without making a show of it.

"I'd like you to accompany me downtown," he says.

"Why do you think Lily was murdered?"

"I have a few matters I'd like to discuss."

He is leading me out, past the blue-and-whites pulled up on the lawn. Cops and onlookers turn as we pass. It is not the sort of audience I crave. "Do I need an attorney?"

Roblings looks both surprised and amused. "I don't know, do you think you need an attorney?"

"Don't you ever answer a question?"

"Don't I?"

On the ride downtown, I curse my perpetually lousy timing. I broke up with Mel, proud owner of a forty-five-foot luxury sailboat, the month before they invented the seasick patch. I broke up with Barry, Vogue Fabrics mogul, the night before my upstairs neighbor's bathtub overflowed, raining bubble bath over my uninsured drapes and slipcovers. And now I split with Lester-the-attorney just before the police invite me downtown to discuss the body I happened to find.

A quick mental scan of friends and relatives comes up empty for an attorney type who might be willing to help pro bono. My racquetball buddy Walter once played a lawyer on *All My Children,* but I doubt that qualifies. Why didn't my parents force at least one of their children to become a lawyer? Or doctor or plumber or carpenter or *anything* useful?

The police station is a scary place. We pass through metal-detector portals and ride an elevator surrounded by too many people wearing guns. I decide to swallow my pride, bite the bullet, and any other cliché I can think of, and call Lester. Roblings directs me to a pay phone down the hall from his office.

Lester's secretary, a romantic who had hopes of standing up at our wedding, is genuinely happy to hear from me. "He's on the phone," she says. "I know he'd love to talk to you. Can you hold?"

"Three more dimes' worth."

Elevator music clicks on, soft violins creating a surreal background for the parade of drunks and hookers marching past. Lester, a perfectly nice estate planning attorney, had been sent with impeccable references by way of Mother's poker club. They'd intended him as balm to soothe the pain of losing Adam. Ha!

I worked at creating a relationship with Lester, truly I did. Listened for hours to his scratchy collection of Count Basie, Duke Ellington, and other royalty of the swing era, all the while trying to convince myself that Lester was the strong silent type. Boring as mud was the truth of it. When the boredom became unbearable, I made up some excuse, sent him and his toothbrush packing.

Two dimes later, he picks up. I talk as fast as I can, give him the short version before my money runs out.

"Where are you?" he asks.

"Eleventh and State."

"I'll be there in fifteen minutes."

No questions, no excuses, no third degree. Just a simple "I'll be there." Now, I ask you, why would any sane woman, especially one on the verge of spinsterhood and starvation, break up with a gent like that? Must be out of her everlovin' mind. I'll have to give Lester another good hard look. Maybe I'd been too hasty. Believe it or not, I've been wrong before.

EIGHT

I SIT ON THE hardwood bench outside Roblings's office, wedged between Boris Karloff and Vincent Price. A gaggle of homicide detectives argue sports around a battered coffeepot. They pause as an elderly woman, bent enough to remind me to eat more yogurt, is led past by a solicitous young officer.

"Whacked her husband," says one detective.

"You're shittin' me."

"Married sixty years. This morning she ups and cracks him on the head with a cast-iron skillet."

I wonder how someone so frail can hoist a cast-iron anything. I also wonder what her husband did today that was so different from anything he'd done the last sixty years.

Boris snores softly, his body sagging against mine. Smells waft, an exotic mix of onions, mothballs, urine. I lean toward Vincent, who coughs delicately into a nail-bitten hand. It occurs to me that, if Roblings thinks I killed Lily, he wouldn't leave me alone where I could amble out. Maybe he really does just want to ask a few questions.

Why did I call Lester? Dragging in a high-powered attorney makes me look guilty of something. My whole life I've put things off, been a veritable pinnacle of procrastination. Why, today, did I have to be Little Miss Efficient? Maybe it isn't too late to call him back and—

Lester strides in. Fit, handsome, impeccably dressed, he exudes the kind of natural authority that turns heads and hushes voices. Homicide's polluted sea of humanity parts before him. Even the coffee-klatch cops show mild interest as Lester reaches out, says "Morgan," helping me up from the bench, embracing. None of the other attorneys moving through the place look remotely like

Lester and, the whole time I've been here, nary a one has hugged a client. "Where can we talk?"

"This is your turf," I say.

"Never been here."

Of course not. Death and Taxes may be sure, but they inhabit separate courthouses. "There's a stairwell over there," I say. "Might give us a little privacy."

The enclosed space reeks of cigarette smoke. Ghost whispers echo from floors above and below, other attorneys, other clients. We huddle on the landing while I tell Lester what I know.

"It doesn't sound serious," he says. "You discovered the body. The police want your statement on file. Not to worry."

"I shouldn't have bothered you with this."

"I'm glad you did." He squeezes my arm gently. "It's good to see you again." I brace for his "Let's get back together," but he guides me toward Roblings's office.

LESTER STANDS behind my chair tapping impatient fingers as Roblings shuffles papers on his desk. The office smells faintly of aftershave. There are no photos on desk or wall, no personal items to indicate hobbies or family. From where I sit, I can see the bent old woman in the office across the hall. She seems calm, composed, with none of the nervous fidgets I would use to play an accused murderess.

"Is my client under investigation?" asks Lester.

"Why would you think your client is under investigation?"

"You won't tell her why she was brought down."

"Invited down."

"Then she is free to go."

"There is some information…."

I watch them dance. For all his lumbering and stumbling at my apartment, Roblings moves with animal grace on his own turf. By contrast, Lester seems stiff and deliberate.

Roblings begins by taking me back over the questions he'd asked me and Beth in my apartment. Lester rests a reassuring hand on my shoulder. "You don't have to answer anything you're uncomfortable with."

"Do you have a problem with these questions?" asks Roblings.

"I have a problem," I say, "with why you think Lily was murdered."

"Oh?"

"Wouldn't the paramedics have noticed if something was wrong? They're the ones who said Lily had a heart attack."

"That's because everyone at the theater *told* them she had a heart attack."

I shake my head, recalling the scene. "There was no blood, no sign of violence." Just pale white skin and staring eyes. "She was locked inside a toilet stall. Her money was still in her bag. Her jewelry was still on."

Roblings leans forward, his eyes intent on my face. "This is one of those deaths that can skate through. An old woman with a history of a bad heart is found dead. Who's going to think anything about it?"

"Exactly."

"Except..."

"Except what?"

"Homicide received a call suggesting perhaps Miss London didn't die of a heart attack."

"What do you mean?" I ask. "Who called?"

"Didn't leave a name."

"Don't you have caller I.D.?"

"They used a gas station pay phone."

"Did they say she was murdered?" asks Lester.

"They weren't in a chatty mood. I've had the medical examiner pick up the body from the funeral home to run an autopsy."

I groan. "This will kill Beth. To think of Lily... What they do to the body when...I'd better call her. Break the news."

"You can use my phone when we're through," says Roblings. "But first I need to fill in some background information."

An officer walks into the room across the hall carrying a large cast-iron skillet wrapped in a plastic evidence bag. The old woman looks at it with affection.

Roblings asks questions about Lily and I tell him what little I know. "I don't like to speak ill of the dead," I say, "but the truth is Lily was a terrible actress."

"She couldn't have been all that bad," says Roblings. "We found boxes of press clippings in her apartment."

"Lily was a gifted self-promoter who knew how to get her name in the columns."

"Isn't that good?"

"I would have killed for that kind of press." I wince. Bad choice of words. "But if you check those clippings, you'll find more gossip columns than theater reviews. Half the information Lily leaked was grossly exaggerated and the other half was out-and-out lies. All that mattered was to get her name in print. It's an art form all its own. I don't know how to do that."

"But you wish you did?"

"Yes."

He's quiet a moment, then leans back in his chair, rocking slightly. "Had Lily ever been threatened?"

"Not that I know of."

"Did she have bad business dealings?"

"I wouldn't know."

"Had she been bothered by prowlers?"

"Look, most of what I know about Lily are things Beth told me."

"Like?"

"Like Lily's weak heart. Like some great tragedy in Lily's life."

"What?"

"Beth never said. That's one of the great things about Beth. When you confide a secret, it stays a secret. Personally, I always thought Lily laid the Camille routine on a bit thick. Especially around Beth, who is much too trusting."

"Unlike you," says Roblings.

"Exactly."

He shuffles through some papers, setting one on the top of the stack. "Do you know that Beth is Lily's sole beneficiary?"

I laugh. "Of what? Old scrapbooks? Lavender bath salts?"

"She seems to have left an estate of some value."

This doesn't compute. Lily never had money. Lived a frugal life. Roblings waits for me to say something.

"I'm happy Beth will get something out of this. I never thought Lily appreciated her, the errands she ran, chauffeuring Lily to and from auditions, doctors, grocery stores."

"If there's nothing more," says Lester, "I should get back to my office."

"And I'd better call Beth, break the news about the autopsy. I'd rather she hear it from me than..."

"Just one more thing." Roblings sets a tape recorder on his desk and presses Play.

My recorded voice booms across the room. "Lily, it's Morgan Taylor. I'm at the Heartland Theater." The tape from Lily's answering machine. "You and I audition in fifteen minutes. I sincerely hope you're not still home to hear this, that you will show up any second."

Click, beep.

"Lily, you once told me if you miss an audition you must be dead at the side of the road. I trust you were joking. Where are you?"

Lester fidgets behind me. I feel myself splitting in two—half of me cringing at my flippant messages, the other half critiquing my voice. Evidently, when I'm nervous or anxious or whatever the hell I was when I called Lily that morning, hard Chicago edges creep back into my speech. I'll have to work on filing them down.

Click, beep.

"Lily, I swear I'm going to kill you if you don't get down here right now."

Lester's left eyebrow twitches. "These messages are obviously Morgan's little joke," he says. "We're hearing them out of context." He shoots Roblings a guy-to-guy smile. "I can vouch for the fact that Morgan has a rather, I would say, unconventional sense of humor. Macabre for a woman."

I clench my teeth and force my big mouth to stay shut as Lester explains me to Roblings. Lester's turn-of-the-century solicitousness is one turn of the century too late. The gentility so admired by Mother's poker club gives me cramps. Lester never understood why I refused to attend parties at his exclusive country club, the club that denies women equal membership, that segregates wives and daughters to a separate golf course. This same man who won't set foot inside private clubs discriminating against a particular race or religion, who genuinely considers himself a champion of human rights, doesn't have the slightest problem relegating women to second-class citizenship. I could never fit into his world, couldn't trust myself to be civil around its inhabitants. Why had I called him today? It was a mistake.

Roblings rewinds the tape.

"If I were going to kill Lily," I say, "I certainly wouldn't broadcast my intentions."

"Unless you want to establish an alibi." Roblings leans forward on his desk, his stare hard and unblinking. "You pretend to look for Lily, pretend to be upset that she's late for your audition, all the time knowing she's dead."

The sheer absurdity of that stuns me to silence.

"That's enough," says Lester, fairly pulling me out of my chair. "My client has no involvement with this murder. If, in fact, that's what this is."

Roblings watches us leave but doesn't move. "I'll be in touch," he says.

WE STEP INTO blinding sunlight and fresh spring air. The fear of confinement, no matter how remote, makes freedom all the sweeter.

"You think Lily was murdered?" I ask.

"From what they're saying, it does seem to be a possibility."

"They can't think I did it."

"You really shouldn't have said those things on the phone."

"But that hardly makes me a killer."

"I don't get the feeling they think you're involved." Lester brushes imaginary lint from his lapel. "I'm not so sure about Beth."

"Oh, come on. You know Beth couldn't hurt anyone."

"Yes, I know. And you know. But the police are looking for

motive." He chews his bottom lip thoughtfully. "Evidently, Beth stands to inherit a good-sized estate."

"Beth doesn't know that."

He hesitates, weighing his words. "What if she does know? What if she just never said anything to you about it? Take it from an old estate planner. The promise of a large inheritance often brings out the worst in people. Especially people unwilling to wait." I must look forlorn because Lester puts a comforting arm around me. "How about I buy you lunch?"

On cue my stomach growls. It takes great strength to refuse what I know would be a fine restaurant with as many courses as I care to order. But as my much-married Grandma Belle often says, "The Krumpke diamond comes with the Krumpke curse: Mr. Krumpke." And though I feel indebted to Lester for rushing to the police station, I don't feel strong enough to sit through an entire lunch with him and his stories of the big band leaders of the forties.

"You're a doll," I say, "and I can't thank you enough for helping me out, but I've got to get to work if I hope to pay my rent sometime this millennium."

Lester flashes one of his boyish smiles, content to be cast as my knight in shining armor. He kisses me on the cheek, hops into his trusty cab, and rides off into the sunset. My stomach growls again. "Hush," I say, "I'll buy you a Snickers."

NINE

MY BOSS, Harold, is a spats-and-cane kind of guy, forever frozen in the 1920s. A trim gent who admits to being "seventy-two and change," he sports a pencil-thin black mustache dyed to match his slicked-back hair. For all his bluster and bravado, he is at heart a fragile sort. At the moment, he seems more hyper than usual. I decide to hold off telling him about my command performance at Eleventh and State.

He darts like a ferret through the narrow aisles of Junque and Stuffe, fussing over several huge crates. Their layers of ancient grime and dust have turned his hands coal black. He unwraps yellowed newspaper from a lamp. "Tiffany. Oh—" He gasps, presses a hand to his chest, leaves a black print on his once immaculate white shirt. "Oh, dear."

I whistle. "What is this stuff?"

"A fortuitous happenstance, my dear," he says. "Positively." He sets the lamp reverently on the counter. "Three Winnetka sisters—all in their nineties would you believe?—never married, not a one, lived their whole lives in the house where they were born. Where their *father* was born. Died of pneumonia last month, all three. What are the odds? I mean, really. Dame Fortune has truly smiled upon me." He digs into the crate, unwrapping the next treasure.

"Where do you want me to start?" I ask.

"Be a love and open that last crate. No, no, no. That other last crate. Yes."

Balancing an armload of old hats, he climbs into the display window. I toss my coat and audition bag on a counter, find the crowbar, and start prying up aged pine planks. Nail heads break, wood splinters. My hands and clothes turn black with dust.

"How old is this stuff?" I ask.

"Lord knows. These crates were found stacked in the old coal room." I swear he seems about to cry. Harold, who has seen it all, rarely effuses over people's family treasures. That Ming vase in your family for generations? A copy. That painting by someone you thought might be Someone? A rank amateur. Aunt Sophie's mismatched candlesticks hand-carried from Russia? Richer in sentiment than marketable value. Not the sort of appraisals people like to hear. But Harold knows his stuff and doesn't bandy about when it comes to setting a realistic price. Inevitably, it is people who lug in mildewed boxes bound with frayed twine, the ones who tell Harold they'll take whatever he can get for the damned stuff, who provide the real treasures.

I pry up the last board. The items inside are lovingly wrapped in yellowed newspaper. I scan the ancient headlines: BREAD, FIVE CENTS A LOAF. STEEL-TOED WORK BOOTS, THREE DOLLARS. My fingers itch to unwrap, but this is Harold's party. "Ready," I say.

Harold clambers from the window, nearly trips in his rush to the crate. He begins unwrapping crystal, a cut-glass creamer, sugar bowl. "Oh, oh, oh. Lovely."

An incredible collection. Sylvia would go crazy if she saw it, which she won't since I'm not going to tell her. I push away niggling guilt. Even as a toddler, my baby sister loved glassware. I'd bought her a piece every birthday. First, penny stuff from garage sales and flea markets, then better goods from dealers. On her twenty-first birthday, I hit up the rest of our siblings to pitch in for a Waterford vase. That was before she walked off with Adam. Now she can damn well buy her own glass.

A woman clicks the front window with a coin and points to her watch.

"Time to open," I say.

"Away. Send them away."

"If you don't sell something you won't be able to afford my exorbitant salary." The woman clicks again. Two more women walk up. An elderly gent. A decorator and client. "Want me to wait on customers while you finish here?"

Harold glances up at the madding crowd. The coin lady clicks harder. "No, no, that's all right. That's Mrs. Thistler come to see the hat-pin collection. The old girl's rich as Rockefeller but won't part with a penny unless I fawn and grovel." He wipes the dirt from his hands on a neatly pressed kerchief and runs a knuckle across his mustache. "You may unwrap. Careful, mind. Windex the glass, dust the china. I'll be back to help you price."

There is joy in a mindless task. I spend half an hour unwrapping, sorting, dusting while I rehearse ways to break the news to Beth.

Direct: "The police say Lily may have been murdered."

Indirect: "Remember the other night, all those questions Detective Roblings asked..."

Beth is so weak, physically and emotionally. When I tell her Lily may have been murdered, how will she bear the shock? But this needs to be done. I walk back to the office, dreading having to make the call. Mrs. Thistler has commandeered the phone, loudly rearranging a dressmaker's appointment. A reprieve.

The unpacking goes quickly. The crate smells as musty as an old man's closet. My grandfather's smell. He'd moved in when I was eight, claiming he was too ill to care for himself after Grandma Belle divorced him. Grandma Belle tried to warn my parents. They ignored her, gave Grandpa my room, and fixed a corner of the basement for me, slapping white paint on crumbling brick.

I hated that dank, dark netherworld, crawling with demons and spiders and things that went slither in the night. A wrong place for a young girl with a vivid imagination. My grandfather died with us for years, always complaining that I didn't appreciate how sick he was. A week after I left for college, he did die—hit by a car while crossing the street to place a bet with his barber-bookie. I've hated illness since, hold it suspect, not believing when people complain. Beth is the one exception. She developed MS after we were already best friends forever.

I empty the last items from the crate. Mrs. Thistler is long off the phone. All right, Morgan. Quit stalling. I force myself back to the office, warding off the image of Lily laid out on the autopsy table. I have to tell Beth as gently as possible, have to do it before some insensitive stranger botches the job. I dial my apartment, still uncertain what I'll say. Beth picks up immediately.

"Morgan. Thank God. They've stolen Lily's body."

"It's not—"

"Right out of the funeral parlor. She's at the morgue. The *morgue!*" Her voice jerks and jumps. "The police say she was murdered. Murdered! What an idea. Who would kill Lily?"

"They're not sure about anything, yet," I say. "They're investigating."

"What could they possibly—"

"Someone called the police, hinted it might not have been a heart attack."

"That's dreadful. Who would do something like that?"

"Probably some nut cake getting his jollies. You mustn't worry. It will all sort itself out."

"They, the police, asked all sorts of questions about Lily, about our relationship, as if I had something to do with her death. How could they think that?"

"It's not you," I reassure her. "The police asked me the same sorts of questions. They're just trying to piece things together and you're the one person who knew Lily best. You can be a great help to them."

Harold keeps glancing at me from the other room. I know the look. It means: How can you chat on the phone when we have so much work to do?

"Let me call you later," I say. "Will you be all right?"

"I'm drained. Can't seem to force my limbs to move. I want to take Hamlet for his walk but my legs are in spasm."

"That sounds awful."

"It's more annoying than painful. But Hamlet—"

"Don't worry about him," I say. "Toss the newspaper in a corner, let him do his business on that. You need to relax. Watch the soaps, take a nap. I'll call after work, maybe cook up one of my famous spaghetti dinners."

THE LAST CUSTOMER leaves around six. Harold and I work together, marking items from the crate. Usually he has all the juicy gossip. Tonight it's my turn. Harold is wide-eyed as I describe Lily's death, how I discovered her body, how the police are hinting that Lily may have been murdered.

"Terrible. Horrible." His delicate hand trembles as it pats mine. "Why, you might have been the one murdered had you, and not Lily, visited that washroom before the audition."

"I've thought of that."

He sighs. His eyes glisten with tears. "It is such a thin line, between life and death. A mere instant, an inch, the taking of one small step left instead of right."

I am touched by his concern. For all his theatrics, Harold rarely seems deeply affected by the human drama. We finish our work and he settles into a Queen Anne chair, pours us each a glass of brandy.

"If you ask me," he says, "that play's the problem. Jinxed, one might say."

"How do you remember that old chestnut? It's been in mothballs for years."

"You know I have a fabulous memory for all things theater. Names, dates, who did what to whom and when."

"Still…"

He swigs half his drink. Most unlike Harold the sipper. "It is," he says, "quite a mediocre play. I assure you, if this weren't Heartland Theater's fortieth anniversary celebration, neither the play nor Wexler would have been dug up from under their respective rocks."

"He's a famous director."

"*Was,*" says Harold. "Martin hasn't had a hit since bellbottoms were in."

"You have to admit the play is an interesting period piece."

"The play, my dear, attracts death and controversy."

I snap to. "Death?"

"When the play premiered, a young intern died under mysterious circumstances."

"What do you mean mysterious?"

"Oh, to be sure, the witch doctors spouted some medical mumbo jumbo, but I've always suspected there were darker forces at work." He refills his glass. "As for the play's controversy, you should have seen the costumes. Exquisite beyond belief, to be sure. But also outrageous, absolutely indecent for the times. The more Chicago's civic and religious groups blasted the play's immorality, the more the public fought to come." The ends of his mustache twitch up into a smile. "There was actually a fistfight at the box office over the last two seats for a Saturday night performance. Of course, the press played all of this up. You can be sure it was their titillating publicity rather than the quality of the play that filled the house every night."

"The play seems so tame."

"Think of the times, my dear. You must remember things in context."

A horn honks and Harold waves out the window. "My ride," he says. "We'll finish tomorrow. My love to Beth. Tell her how sorry I am about Lily. Wait. Wait."

He dives into the retro jewelry display, rummaging furiously. Most of my theater friends, including Beth, have worked for Harold from time to time. He is one of those angels who understands our need for jobs flexible enough to accommodate auditions and the occasional role.

"Here." He hands me a Bakelite brooch. "For Beth. She's always been one of my favorites. A great talent, with a kind heart and modest soul. Would there were more like her."

We raise our glasses to Beth, kill the last of our brandy. I think it best not to mention that the police are interrogating Beth about Lily's death. Harold has delicate sensibilities. He tends to dwell on things, to work himself into an agitated state over perceived injustices.

The horn honks again and we hurry out. Maybe, when this whole ugly business passes, I'll pump him for gruesome details about the play's dark history. In exchange, I'll regale him with stories about basset-faced detectives and cast-iron murders. We will sip brandy from heated snifters and discuss life and theater into the wee hours.

TEN

THE INSTANT I unlock my front door I feel the stillness inside. Absolute. Complete. Where is Beth? Where is the yapping little beastie? Cold silence fills the space where the warmth of living creatures should be. Fear prickles my spine, radiates out to fingers and toes. All this chitchat about murder has made me just the slightest tad paranoid.

"Beth?"

Nothing.

"Hamlet?"

I leave the door open behind me, move cautiously into the apartment. It's one thing to walk into an empty house when you expect it to be empty. But this void sucks energy like a black hole. I lift the sofa skirt. Dust balls and an old *TV Guide*. I press against the wall next to the tiny coat closet. Slowly twisting the knob, I yank the door open. The cramped mess inside—out-of-season clothes, rusty golf clubs, boxes not yet unpacked since my last move two years ago—is exactly as I left it. All right, the living room is clear.

I tiptoe along the edges of the hall floor, avoiding creaks as I head for the bedroom. Bring up the scary music. My heart's chugging worse than when I jog the front stairs. What am I doing? If I think there's the faintest chance something's wrong, why don't I get the hell out? I hate those movies where the heroine, ignoring a zillion warning signs, goes alone at midnight into the house/factory/attic. I mean, if I'm scared enough to leave the front door open in case I need to flee an attacker... I hear the audience scream warnings at me, beg me to go across the hall and call the police.

The bedroom is clear. Everything in place. Neater, in fact, than when I left. That leaves the kitchen. I move noiselessly, holding my breath, listening against the silence for any telltale sound. The reason the frightened movie heroines don't call the police is because they're embarrassed by their fear. *It's probably nothing. It's probably all in my mind.* Better to risk a mad attacker than public embarrassment.

I don't draw an easy breath until I spot a note propped on an exquisite bowl of fruit, the pieces so perfect they look more wax than real. Beth's normally flowing handwriting jerks at odd places: *Thanks for being such a good friend. Lyle (Yes, the Lyle! I'll tell you later) drove me to Lily's apartment to pick up Hamlet's food and toys. I brought you this fruit and a few other goodies (see foil bag in fridge) from Lily's to help stave off starvation. May I have a rain check for the spaghetti dinner? P.S. Should you feel the need of canine companionship, I'll be happy to share custody of Hamlet.*

Fat chance.

I bite gratefully into a tart Granny Smith, savoring it as I close and double-lock the front door. Exhausted, I run a hot tub, ignite the forest of scented candles lining the ledge. It's nice that Lyle's back in the picture. He's a sweet guy, a lighting genius in demand by theaters around the country. That's what broke them up, the two of them traveling so much for work. They drifted apart. Looks like they've drifted back together.

I pick up messages as I soak.

Message One: "This is Betsy again, from Steven's Dry Cleaners. *Please* pick up your order." Love to. As soon as I have money.

Message Two: "I met an overbearing woman today," says Grandma Belle. *(Beat.)* "She has eleven children." She leaves space for my laugh. "Love you. I'm off to Vegas with a nice gentleman. Not to worry. *Gentleman* is the operative word. I'll call when I'm back. Love you."

No wonder some women never find a man. My grandmother has used up their share.

End of messages. Wexler hasn't called.

I dial my mother. "I think the audition went well," I say, even though optimism is usually the kiss of death. It's the auditions I think I've loused up that turn out to be winners.

"I'll keep my toes crossed," she says.

I tell her about Queen Tut in her crisp linen suit with matching shoes and purse. "Maybe I should have gone for the irony of a tough-talking daughter dressed like a Sunday school teacher."

She makes soothing mother noises. "At least if Diana does get the role, you'll know it's because of that outfit."

"It sure won't be because of her acting."

"You did your best, Miriam, now let it go." Sometimes she forgets, calls me by my birth name. A sweet name, Miriam, no edge to it. I let it pass. "Life's too short to walk around second-guessing yourself," she says. Lets it hang, knowing I'll read in volumes about sister Sylvia and Adam and how the three of us might have played our triangle better. It is killing Mom to have two of her daughters estranged, two children ailing from jealousy and betrayal and perhaps a dollop of pride.

I hang up without mentioning the possibility that Lily was murdered. There are some things one doesn't tell one's mother if one doesn't want to listen to lectures on safety the rest of one's life.

Sensually soaked and perfectly powdered, I wrap myself in my Chinese robe and pad to the kitchen to heat water for spaghetti. Drizzling double virgin olive oil into a pan, I chop a mélange of fresh veggies and slide them in. Pasta primavera, la spécialité de la maison. The sizzle is so loud I barely hear the doorbell. I turn down the fire, press the intercom. "Yes?"

"Detective Roblings." His voice comes loud and clear. I buzz him in, quickly finger-fluffing my wet hair as I race to the bathroom to brush blush on my winter-pale cheeks. A flick of mascara. Spritz of Opium—damn. A gift from Sylvia I vowed never to use again. No time to wash it off. Quick brush of tooth and gum, spray of Binaca, small gold-hoop earrings. Pull on jeans, shrug on a tank top. I make it back to the door before he mounts the last flight.

"I was…passing by on the…way home," he says.

Not only is he out of shape, he's an appallingly terrible liar. We actors know bad acting. Roblings wasn't just "passing by."

"I have a few more questions...for you and your friend."

"Beth?"

"If you don't mind."

"She's not here."

His disappointment is genuine. "When do you expect her?"

"She's probably at her place."

He hoists his left eyebrow. A small scar bisects the end of it. "She doesn't live here?"

"Here?"

"I thought you were roommates."

"I live alone."

Somehow he has moved into the apartment. I close the door behind him. "I assumed..." He clears his throat. "Your friend seemed so at home the last time I was here. And she answered the phone today when I called."

"You're the one who told her about Lily?"

He looks contrite. "I'd assumed you'd already broken the news. In my office, you said you were going to call."

"You're—the one who told her Lily's body's at the morgue?"

He winces. "She didn't take it well."

I explode. "What did you expect? Beth loved Lily. How would you feel if they yanked your grandmother's body from the funeral home and dumped it on a cold morgue slab?"

Roblings doesn't move, takes everything I throw at him. My intellect tells me he is just doing his job. My emotions tell my intellect to shut up. Emotions usually win these little conflicts, but this time logic reminds me that Roblings came here alone. Wouldn't he bring along another warm body if he intended to interrogate/arrest/torture someone? I reckon it is a friendly enough visit.

"You're steaming," he says.

"You'd be angry too if—"

He nods toward a large cloud pouring out of the kitchen. The spaghetti water and I have come to a boil at the same time. Roblings follows me into the kitchen, leans against the counter.

"Don't let me interfere with your dinner," he says, handing me the pasta. I slide it into the pot, bring the vegetables back to sauté. He breaks a piece of celery off the stalk and munches thoughtfully. "I interviewed the Equity monitor this afternoon," he says. "The one on duty at the theater the day Lily died. She says she gave you a couple of pieces of fruit from a gift basket."

I'd forgotten the banana and orange. "She felt sorry for me, pacing the lobby waiting for Lily, having to let so many other people audition ahead of me."

"Did you eat the fruit?"

I have to think. Between the audition and finding Lily's body, that was one hectic morning. "I think they're still in my bag."

"Could you bring me the bag?"

"The fruit?"

"No, don't touch the fruit. I want the whole bag."

I lower the flame and go to the bedroom, liberating my audition bag from under my audition clothes. By the time I return to the kitchen, Roblings is adding oil to the spaghetti water with one hand and expertly stirring the vegetables with the other. I'd pegged him as a frozen-TV-dinner kind of guy. Which is why I'm the actress and he's the cop.

He relinquishes the cooking tools and takes a plastic bag from his jacket pocket. Pulling on plastic gloves, he carefully sifts through my collection: spare stockings, scripts, makeup bags, hairbrush, magazines, tissues, tapes, glossies, toothbrush, toothpaste, waxed floss, breath spray, spray cologne, deodorant, one half-eaten stick of beef jerky, pens, scratch pad. Watching his large hands pick through my most personal possessions strikes me as unspeakably funny. I manage to suppress a laugh. Death is serious business, after all.

When he concentrates, he develops deep furrows from eyebrow to widow's peak. He does something wickedly sexy with his lower jaw. I'll have to study this face a while. There are nuances to be learned.

He lifts out the fruit. The once perfect banana is bruised and brown, the orange shriveled, their pretty gold stickers lost somewhere in the wilds of my bag. As he places them carefully into the plastic bag, I remember the grapefruit peelings on the bathroom floor around Lily's body. My stomach lurches.

"The grapefruit," I say. "You think someone poisoned it?"

"I won't know until I get the ME's report. It's entirely possible Lily died of natural causes."

"Like a heart attack."

He studies me a moment, debating something, deciding. "Lily didn't have a heart attack. Whatever else she might have died from, her heart was healthy."

"That's wrong. She had a history of heart disease."

"Not according to her doctor's records."

"She carried nitro pills in a vial in her bag. I've seen them."

"Little silver round ones?"

"Yes."

"Candy."

"Candy!"

"Like you use to decorate cakes. It seems she fabricated her 'heart problems.'"

A sympathy ploy. Why doesn't that surprise me?

He picks a mushroom out of the pan and pops it into his mouth. "Mmmmm," he says, reaching for another.

I slap the back of his hand. "You can check the spaghetti."

He lifts a strand out of the pot, throws it against the wall. It hits, drops to the floor. A little too al dente. "You didn't tell me about the fruit when I interviewed you yesterday," he says.

"I forgot about it."

"Anything else you might have forgotten to mention?"

He makes it sound like I intentionally forgot. I feel my hackles rise. "I also didn't mention I went to the bathroom five times—audition nerves. Or that I back-combed my hair to make it look wild. Or that the cigarette smoke in the lobby ladies' room made my clothes reek. How was I supposed to know what information you wanted?"

"If you'd like to call your attorney—"

"Do I need my attorney?"

He shrugs, an almost playful gesture. Then it hits me: Roblings is flirting. Although, with his face, it's hard to tell. Its features are not given to the subtleties of seduction. He tests another strand of spaghetti. This one sticks to the wall.

"Ready," he says, grabbing a towel, wrapping it around the pot handles, carrying the pasta to the sink.

I pop the garlic bread under the preheated broiler, then hold the colander steady while Roblings drains the spaghetti.

"If you ever do need an attorney," he says, "I can give you a few names."

So he spotted Lester as a lightweight in the crime arena. And he didn't even have to date him.

The phone rings. It's the Irish brogue. "Miss Taylor? This is Mr. Wexler's assistant calling? We are pleased to tell you you have the role."

My fingers shake as I jot the rehearsal time and place, gripping the receiver long after the assistant hangs up. I close my eyes, offer silent thanks.

"Something wrong?" asks Roblings.

"I got it," I whisper. "I got the part."

"You sound surprised."

"Stunned."

"Shouldn't you jump up and down, scream or something?"

"Not my style. But I'm doing somersaults inside."

"Well, congratulations."

I smile, grateful he is here, a live person to share this exhilarating moment. "Stay for dinner," I say, "help me celebrate."

"You sure you have enough?"

"I shopped for two but my dinner date ditched me." No need to mention Beth's name. Let Roblings think I mean some man. "Besides, you helped cook."

There are times when I enjoy living alone. And there are times when I love having someone around. Roblings is the perfect person at the perfect time. We carry dinner to the table.

"Talk to me about actors," he says, tossing the salad while I cut the garlic bread.

"What kinds of things do you want to know?"

"I'm having problems with Lily London."

"Like?"

"Like there's a bright beautiful bathroom in the theater lobby. Right?"

"Right."

He pulls out a chair. "So why does this frail old lady with bad eyesight walk through dark backstage clutter to get to a dingy hole-in-the-wall bathroom? And why would someone that fastidious want to *eat* anything in there?"

It takes a second for me to understand he is holding the chair for me. Luckily, I have moved past early feminist rancor, learned to accept kindly gestures in the spirit offered. I thank him and sit, opening my napkin daintily on my lap.

"I have no idea why Lily picked that bathroom," I say. "But I can tell you about the grapefruit. Most actors perform some kind of personal ritual before an audition or performance. Voice and mouth exercises are pretty common, but there's a fair share of quirky things. They help us prepare mentally and physically."

"And Lily's ritual was eating grapefruit?"

"A few sections, before every audition and performance. She said the acid cleared the 'groggies' from her throat, left her voice clear."

He serves the salad, neatly dividing the portions in half. "But why that bathroom? It almost looked as if she were hiding. Is this ritual something she did in private?"

"Hardly. She made a show of it, the way she did everything. Lily adored being the center of attention."

"So you'd seen her do this?"

"Every time we worked together. Although I don't remember her ever taking out a whole grapefruit and peeling it. She usually brought a few sections in a little plastic bag."

"We found sections like that in her audition bag," says Roblings.

"Why bring both?" I bite into the garlic bread. "Unless she didn't get the whole grapefruit until after she left the house?"

"It's a possibility."

I twirl my fork slowly, wrapping spaghetti around. "Ah. You think that grapefruit came from that same basket my fruit came from?"

"We're looking into it."

We eat, exchanging growing-up stories, a Miles Davis tape

cushioning the space around us. Roblings has impeccable table manners, his large hands precise and delicate. This is one elegant book you can't tell by its rough-hewn cover. He helps clear the dishes and I set Beth's bowl of fruit on the table by way of dessert.

"My local store never carries produce this beautiful," he says.

"Mine either. Beth brought it from Lily's this afternoon."

"That's not possible. My men cleared all the food out of the apartment."

"They must have left this."

He shakes his head. "All foodstuffs were brought to headquarters for testing. There was an open bag of grapefruits in the fridge. Small, thin-skinned, sold ten to the bag. Nothing like this. This kind—the kind Lily was eating when she died—comes from designer food shops."

I watch him pack Beth's gift into a bag. "You're wrong about this," I say. "This fruit has nothing to do with Lily's death or anything like that."

"Then why did Beth lie to you? Why did she tell you she brought this from Lily's house?"

I have no answer. I think about the Granny Smith I ate. My stomach's been churning, cramping, but I thought it was from the excitement of getting the role in the play. What if it's the apple? What if—

Stop it. Beth couldn't poison anyone. Roblings might not know that, but I sure do.

The second he leaves, I call Beth to find out what's going on. Her phone rings until the answering machine clicks on.

I hang up without leaving a message. I don't trust answering machines anymore. Things you say into them have a way of coming back to haunt you.

ELEVEN

IT'S A PITY Lily's dead. She'd love her funeral. At long last, she's the full-blown Center of Attention, Queen for a Day, the raison d'être for an industry circus.

Chicago's theater world has turned out in force for one of its own. It's one part our desire to pay final respects, one part our constant hunger for community and—I admit—one part the faint possibility of making contacts.

Lily's funeral has an added edge. In the week since her death, word of a Murder Investigation has somehow leaked to the press. Lily's mysterious exit in a city of mostly shoot-'em-up murders is the stuff of front-page news. The smell of Story brings members of the fourth estate sniffing like bloodhounds. Newspaper, radio, and television reporters snake through the mob seeking pabulum to feed an insatiable public.

Crowds loiter on the church steps, the best place to see and be seen. I squeeze through, passing actors giving heartfelt interviews about their dear friend Lily. Never mind that some of them never met her.

Strands of whispered conversations tighten around me.

"There's the one who found the body." "That's her." "Discovered Lily's body."

I pretend not to hear as I inch my way up. I don't want this kind of attention. Still…

When I was ten, already craving stardom so much I got cramps, I assumed everyone sought the spotlight. Until, one day, leaving the planetarium with my family, Sylvia ran out the revolving door just as a tourist aimed his camera. Sylvia ducked out of his way. I whisked out the door behind her and, seeing a camera pointed at me, smiled broadly as I walked directly toward it.

A pivotal moment. I immediately understood the innate difference between me and the rest of the world. Most people duck. Sylvia and I didn't grow up and decide to become Actress and Writer. We were cast in the womb. I to seek the light, she to dart among the shadows.

I think of that childhood moment from time to time. We actors are often labeled difficult, moody, unpredictable. But I've learned it's the quiet ones you have to watch for, the ones who creep from behind, grab what they want, steal away silent in the night.

"If only I had stayed with poor Lily." Queen Tut's voice grates my nerves. I skirt the church stairs around Diana and the reporter, feel her voice crawl up my spine. "I held the door to the theater for her.... She was so very frail. But I needed to prepare for my audition and I left her...." She dabs a hanky. Best tears-on-demand in the business.

I keep moving. "That's Morgan Taylor..." Voices all around. "...found Lily's body..." At the top, I squeeze through the thick crowd blocking the church doors. I am out of breath by the time I join Beth and Lyle in the front pew.

In the week since I've seen Beth, the one-two punch of illness and sorrow have drawn dark circles around her eyes, dulled her vibrant skin ash gray.

"You gotta come early if you want a good seat," she says, patting the space next to her.

These seats are much too close to Lily's body. Beth honored Lily's death directive, which specified an oak coffin, pink satin lining, and open casket. I risk a quick look, bracing myself for a gash of Frankenstein-style autopsy stitches bisecting Lily's forehead. She appears remarkably unremarkable. Whoever did makeup applied the too-dark foundation with a trowel, the too-bright lipstick with palsied hand. But, if the pathologist left any telltale marks, they've been hidden by makeup and covered by a silk scarf bowed at Lily's neck.

I take Beth's hand, try to warm the icy flesh. My feet brush the cane hidden under the pew. Beth and Lyle arrived early so they could sit before anyone saw how difficult it is for her to walk. For the hundredth time I want to ask about the beautiful fruit she left in my apartment. Why did she say it was from Lily's place? For the hundredth time, I back off. It hurts that Beth lied to me. But I won't push the issue until she's stronger. One thing is sure: Beth wouldn't lie without good reason. I just can't imagine what that reason is.

A young minister paces in front of us, hugging his Bible like a shield against the animated conversations, wild outbursts of laughter. This is not his usual crowd. No one seems in need of comforting words. I feel a twinge of pity. We actors are a tough house, no doubt about it.

It is a relief when mourners parade past the casket, blocking our view. Of the many familiar faces—actors and union people, theater staff and board members—precious few are visibly saddened by Lily's death. Even Lily's agent seems more interested in chatting up the young actor in line behind her.

Harold, dressed much snappier than his usual Junque and Stuffe work clothes, passes the casket escorting a costume designer older than God. I thought she'd died years before. A crony of Lily's, no doubt. Her silk floral dress is hot off the Junque and Stuffe vintage designer rack and her shoes, hat, and gloves are from our better stock. Dear Harold probably liberated the woman from her nursing home and dolled her up for the occasion. What a love he is.

Beth cries softly throughout the service. Lyle rubs her back. I am grateful for him, for the easy way he deals with her pain. While checking the house, I spot Detective Roblings in the back pew. My protective instincts snap to and I brace myself, ready to head him off if he dares make a move toward Beth. She said he's been phoning her all week, going over and over her relationship with Lily. He has to back off, has to.

Luckily for him, he keeps his distance.

Near the end, a few people share stories about Lily, some tempered, some wildly overblown. I think of the truth behind the fictions. From what I saw, Lily London was a selfish woman who devoted her life to pleasing herself. But that would never be said today. This Lily London is without fault, a sainted woman taken before her time.

What harm? If you can't star at your own funeral, why bother going?

During the closing prayers, Beth leans over, whispering, "Did you see Lily's obit in the morning paper?"

"No."

"They put in her age," she says. She lowers her head, her shoulders shake. "Her real age." I think Beth is crying until she says, "She'd die if she saw it. She'd just die."

That sets us off. We bow our heads together, covering our mouths to stifle laughter, struggling mightily to maintain some semblance of decorum. A kindly soul behind us pats our backs comfortingly.

Martin Wexler walks to the front of the church, "Lily London was an actress," he says, his strong voice booming over the assemblage. "She paid her dues and then some. You all know what a long and distinguished career she had. Some of you appreciate the great personal hardships she overcame to continue this work she loved more than life itself. Lily always found time to mentor young actors, was available day and night to lend advice and comfort."

As he drones on, I am thinking, *this is one huge crock of stuff.* But the tender-hearted actors around me buy into it. Sniffing breaks out, tears flow freely. Beth's hand trembles on my shoulder, and her mournful sobs remind me not everyone shares my view.

"And now," says Wexler, "she is gone. Her passing has left a great void in our world. What suitable homage can we offer one of our own? How do we bid farewell to a valued friend? Ladies and gentlemen, Lily London was an actress. Let us all rise and give her a standing ovation."

The casket is carried down the aisle to the applause of the traditional actor's farewell. I rise and follow as the mourners file out. Beth stays behind. She will visit the cemetery to say her good-byes at a more private time. She can't risk letting anyone in the business see her in such poor condition.

Roblings stops me on my way down the stairs. His large hands worry the rim of a hat. "The fruit I took from your house checked out okay."

"I told you. I trust this means you'll leave Beth alone."

He tries to say something but I stride off, shoulders squared in righteous indignation. No one accuses my friend of trying to poison me.

Cars form a funeral line. I, who have no stomach for sickness, death, or cemeteries, decide to put in a couple of hours at Junque and Stuffe, shoot over to my folks' house for dinner, then go home and work on my words for tomorrow's rehearsal.

TWELVE

THANK YOU THANK YOU thank you thank you.

I chant hosannas to the theater gods as I make my way from the El to the old loft building owned by the Heartland. It would be so much better if we could rehearse in the theater, but there's a play in production. Alternate space is never as good as the real thing. The proportions and size are different. Blocking doesn't translate correctly to the main stage. Actors go bumping into props, get in each other's way, pacing is off, exits and entrances mis-cue.

Thank you thank you thank you.

Forgive me, oh fickle gods of Gielgud. I don't mean to sound ungrateful. I will gladly rehearse in a closet if it means a chance to perform. Truly. I am most deeply and humbly grateful.

An arctic blast hits me as I turn the corner. Head down, shoulders hunched, I struggle against the wind whipping off the Chicago River. Small whitecaps dance on murky water. Clouds vie with sun. Winter never leaves this town without a fight. My Ethel Merman gene kicks in, launches my mezzo-soprano clear across the river, "Let's go on with the show." The last note echoes long and loud down concrete pilings. A flock of pigeons flies off and settles on the far bank. Everyone's a critic.

The rehearsal building, an aging brick fortress scarred by a century of battling river weather, cowers between spiffy urban renewal condos. I jog the steep flight of stairs wondering if Old World charm will translate into ancient plumbing, poor heating, no air conditioning.

Thank you thank you thank you thank you. One can never be too careful.

Activity in the loft is a P. T. Barnum wet dream. Actors, director, producers, artistic and producing directors, manager, stage manager, assistant stage manager, box office, publicity, lighting, sound set, costume, music director, union representatives, assorted assistants—a Cast of Thousands—all vie for center ring.

A small room has been set aside for stuff that would otherwise clutter the rehearsal space. I drop my coat and bag in a corner, then join the crowd in the main room. I spy a comforting number of familiar faces, smile. They smile back. We are preparing alliances, lining up cliques, some of which will shift in the weeks ahead, while others will remain constant to closing night.

Lyle spots me and waves me over.

"Beth said to tell you she's feeling better," he says.

"And I'm the Queen of England."

He laughs. "No, really. She says—"

"I *saw* Beth at the funeral. Lily looked healthier, and she'd been dead a week."

Lyle does a one-eighty: happy to sad, invincible to vulnerable. I have that effect on men. "Well, she has been crying," he says. "It's really not like her."

"I'll call her later. Try to cheer her up."

His cheeks and ears turn bright red. "Sh-she's at my house." He's embarrassed. I'd forgotten how shy he is. "I—I've managed to convince her to stay with me until she gets her strength back."

There is a sudden push of activity around us as we prepare to begin. Lyle's tech assistant calls him over and he turns to leave.

"Hold it!" I grab him. "Where did you get that fruit you and Beth left at my apartment?"

He looks like a cornered squirrel. "W-what do you mean?"

"Her note said you brought it from Lily's apartment."

"Y-yes."

"Lyle, Lily's cupboard was bare. The cops took all her food for testing."

Tiny beads of sweat dot his forehead. "Beth will kill me if she finds out I told."

"I'll kill you if you don't. And I'm a hell of a lot tougher."

"We bought it on Oak Street."

"At the Fruit Boutique!"

"See? She knew you'd be upset. That's exactly why she didn't—"

"Three dollars an apple? You bet I'm upset. What kind of—"

"She wanted to do something nice, to thank you."

"For what?"

"Everything. Finding Lily, staying with her body when they took her to the hospital, bringing Hamlet home with you, offering Beth your place to stay. She figured you couldn't be angry if we said we found the fruit at Lily's." His eyes go all puppy-cute. Not my type, but he makes Beth happy enough. "Don't tell her I told?"

"Yeah, sure."

"Promise?"

"Right."

I'm furious with Beth for forking out a fortune she can't afford, but I'm relieved to know why she lied. Lyle is right. I would have gone ballistic.

The actors gather around the long rehearsal table. I settle between Brenda Moore, who is teasing her hennaed hair to amazing heights, and the very laid-back Murray Banks. I am delighted Murray landed the role as my brother. He's a good solid bread-and-butter actor who gives lovely gifts onstage. He also has a deliciously biting wit.

"Hey, sis," he says.

"Yo, bro. 'S'up?"

"What it *is*."

We high-five, and I follow his easy lead into a convoluted hand-jive, which ends with a triple-clinking of elbows. Brenda Moore stares, open-mouthed. "Are we doing this black?" she asks.

"Purple," says Murray, pushing up from the table. "Coffee?"

"Love some," I say. "Milk, no sugar."

"You got it."

Brenda, totally confounded, watches him go. "Purple?"

"It's a joke," I say.

She turns her back on me. Brenda doesn't like jokes and takes offense when people make light of our profession. She is, she once told me, a Serious Actress. Dumb as a brick is more like it. Still, this rat-haired wonder manages to work twice as much as I do. She has a way of ingratiating herself with management, producers, promoters. Unlike me, she follows direction to the letter. The more direction, the better she likes it. I once worked a job where she pressed the director to tell her how he wanted her lines presented, then tape-recorded his reading to get them exactly right. Is it acting or is it Memorex? Murray brings my coffee. It should go well with sour grapes.

While Wexler and his assistant work at one end of the loft, chalking off an area to serve as a stage, Rosie from Equity gives the usual "You know your insurance will come in force…" union spiel, then answers our questions.

"When do we get paid?"

"Friday."

"Will we get out of rehearsals in time to get our check to the bank?"

"I'll ask."

Petty trifles? Perhaps to people who eat on a regular basis. But it's serious business for those of us who, while playing kings and queens and scions of industry, exist hand-to-mouth. My father, who should know better, sends me clippings about the latest multibillion-dollar deal just signed by yet another moderately talented, highly connected Hollywood actor. He means them as signs of hope, but has no idea how painful such astronomical figures are for those of us struggling in the trenches.

"While I ask Mr. Wexler about your checks," says Rosie, "why don't you go ahead and elect the Equity deputy?" She leaves, ignoring our groans.

We all slide down in our chairs, avoid eye contact, try to become invisible. One of us must become the Equity deputy, responsible for taking our fellow actors' complaints and passing them on to management. It is a horrible, thankless job. Still, the union says rehearsal can't begin until we elect someone. I once saw the process drag on for an hour.

"Oh, what the hell," says Murray. "I'll do it." We applaud

his sacrifice. He holds up his hands for quiet. "And I'll buy a beer for every single one of you who goes through the entire run of the play without once griping to me." This gets a laugh, since complaining is something we actors have honed to a fine art. "Okay, Rosie," he booms, "coast is clear."

While she gives him the weekly forms he'll need to fill out, conversations about our production weave around the table.

"The production is haunted...."

"...mysterious accidents, illnesses..."

"...jinxed..."

I toss Harold's bit of gossip into the pot. "A young intern died," I say, "during the play's premiere."

"How?"

What had Harold said? "Mysterious circumstances."

"Like Lily."

That quiets us.

As soon as Rosie leaves, Wexler joins us at the head of the table. "I want to welcome you all," he says. "We have a superb cast, a fabulous script, and the best theater in Chicago." Applause, applause. I settle into the cozy comfort of family all around. He introduces the various trades, shows a mock-up of the set, allows a couple of the designers to explain their vision for our production. He then thanks them for their time and we are alone, actors with their director. Excitement twists my gut.

"Lily London's death is a great loss to Chicago's theater community," he says. A lovely beginning. "She will be missed. I had hoped... I haven't found anyone I like for Mother, the role I hoped Lily might play. For today, I'll—"

"Sorry I'm late." Queen Tut rushes in. What is she doing here?

Wexler motions her to a place at the table. "Diana Tuttle," he explains, "will be understudying the role of Daughter."

On fire. My face, my hands. The other actors shoot sidelong glances my way. I burn with humiliation, affect a benign expression before it shows. No one else at the table has an understudy. Why me? Does Wexler think I'm so weak I need to be covered? I glance at Diana. She flashes a smile. I know that smile. She is up to something sneaky. I become suddenly busy opening my script, digging through my purse for a pen, yellow highlighter.

"All right, ladies and gentlemen," says Wexler. "Shall we? Diana, why don't you read Mother today?"

Scripts open around the table as my heart thuds double-time. If Diana reads Mother too well, Wexler might reconsider, cast her as Daughter.

"Let's take it once through beginning to end, then we'll break for lunch."

Brenda gasps. "Aren't we going to discuss it first?"

"I prefer to begin with the read-through."

Thank you thank you thank you thank you.

Bless Wexler for getting right to it, meeting our dread of the first reading head-on. Some directors, trained in the Marquis de Sade school of theater, lead all-day discussions about the play before ever opening a script. The Agony and the Agony. There will be time enough for all that later, if we survive.

But my relief doesn't overcome the sheer terror of a first read-through. Like my comrades around the table, I'm convinced I'll be found out as a no-talent wanna-be. If this reading is out of joint, it will be because of me. If there is no energy, it will be because of me. If the words stay dead on the page, it will be because of me. I believe that. Every actor at the table believes that about him- or herself. Good old actors' paranoia. Except, today, mine is worse than usual. I have Diana the understudy sitting here as proof positive Wexler doesn't think I'm up to the job.

The read-through, done at breakneck speed without a tinge of ensemble, is every bit as awful as I expect. The best I can say is Wexler doesn't jump up and fire me. We don't quite make it through the whole way.

"We'll finish after lunch," says Wexler.

All of us heave a communal sigh as we push away from the table, the condemned given a last-minute reprieve. We manage weak smiles and weaker jokes as we break for lunch. I follow the masses to the back room, half of them rummaging in bags and pockets for the cigarettes banned in the rehearsal room. They race downstairs to light up.

I search the mess of coats and bags for my particular pile of stuff. Famished, I open my rehearsal bag and take out my lunch. A piece of noodle kugel is missing. I comb through the bag, take everything out, double-check. Gone. Last night Mom sent me home with four pieces of her kugel, thick noodles languishing in cinnamon-sugary cottage cheese, sour cream and raisins, each piece carefully wrapped in silver foil. I'd brought two to rehearsal. And then there was one.

"Hey, little sister." Murray, a pristine Camel dangling from his lips, has his lighter primed and ready.

"Hey, bro," I say.

He disappears before I can complain about the theft. I join a small group eating around the table. Should I say anything? I mean, it's a theater truth that food left backstage is fair game. But I've never heard of someone filching food the very first day of rehearsal. I scan the group for suspects. Brenda cracks a hard-boiled egg on a piece of waxed paper, delicately peels away the shell. A carrot stick, two celery sticks, and a rye crisp complete her meal. Not a kugel kind of gal.

Where is Queen Tut? Anyone who would try stealing my role isn't above copping my kugel. I bet she was late to rehearsal because she was rifling bags in search of sustenance. I don't see her anywhere. Probably hiding out enjoying my lunch. From now on I'll keep my bag with me.

When I finish, I find a pay phone out on the street and call Beth at Lyle's place. I can tell from the remaining tremor in her voice that the last MS flare-up hit her hard. Not that she'd admit it.

"I think the strength is returning to my arms and legs," she says. "Enough for me to work on the industrial."

"Can you walk without the cane?"

"I've told everyone I twisted my ankle."

"What about your voice?"

A long pause. "You hear the difference?"

"Of course."

"That's because you know me so well. No one else has noticed."

I doubt that, but don't say. "Should you push yourself so hard?"

"I'm taking it slow. Pampering myself. I'll stay at Lyle's a while."

"He told me."

She sighs. "What else did he say?"

"Just that you're staying until you're stronger."

"He isn't reading anything more into it, is he?"

I laugh. "That man's been crazy about you since forever. And now you've moved in. What could he possibly read into that?"

"Come on, Morgan. It's not like that."

"Sure."

"I'm going back to my own place as soon as I get my strength back."

"Methinks the lady doth protest too much."

"Don't you go making something out of nothing."

"Moi?"

A FEW MINUTES into the afternoon rehearsal, I get the uncomfortable feeling that Wexler and his staff are watching me. Closely. Are they still weighing my performance against Queen Tut's? Am I on some sort of secret probation? One bad reading, one misspoken line, and—Shazam!—Wexler switches me with Diana?

I try to flick the demons off my shoulder. When does an actress become sure enough of her talent to stop worrying? Never, that's when. I should give it up, sell aluminum siding, marry Lester, join the ladies on their segregated golf course. Now, there's a lifestyle devoutly to be wished.

As we near the end of the play, I launch into my big scene, the passionate monologue setting up the climax between Mother and Daughter. Suddenly, Queen Tut slaps her hands on the table and pushes herself up. Her face contorts into a snarling sneer.

Damn her. If she doesn't like my reading, she could at least have the common decency to talk to me later. Not that I'd listen.

Not that any actor with a modicum of professionalism would dare give another actor notes. How can she upstage me so blatantly?

I refuse to watch, continue my reading even though I feel everyone watching Diana. I hear Diana scrape back her chair, send it crashing to the floor. This time I do stop and look. I wish I hadn't. Diana claws her throat, staggers away from the table to the area Wexler chalked off as the stage.

We sit gaping as Diana, gone rigid as a tree, falls straight forward, her glasses making a sickening crunch as she crashes against the wood floor.

"My reading wasn't that bad," I say.

No one listens in their rush to where Diana sprawls, lifeless.

THIRTEEN

AN EERIE STILLNESS becalms a group when one among them is freshly dead. Silence blankets sound. Inertia cripples movement. Small warning pulses scuttle along arms, legs, necks.

Unfortunately, only Diana, star of *Stat!*, knew CPR.

"She should be on her stomach."

"On her back."

"Check if she swallowed her tongue."

"I'll push down, you blow in her mouth."

"*You* blow in her mouth."

"Pinch her nose shut."

A couple of cast members valiantly apply what they can recall from high school Red Cross life-saving classes. But it's obvious to one and all that Diana won't be coming back for any encores.

The group separates, half escaping to the coat room, the rest choosing to keep Diana company until the police arrive. I opt to stay with the body. Considering how many people die every day in this world, how often do we witness the actual moment? There is life and then there isn't. An eye blink, no more. What passes in that instant? How do we capture the essence? I've heard that the heart stops before the brain. I've left careful instructions that my family is to keep talking to me at least fifteen minutes after I'm "gone." Hate to be abandoned on my way out.

Diana's body draws us down into a circle around her. I sit to her left, watching for the lift of breath in body, the throb of blood through vein. Nothing. I push aside thoughts of my own mortality. Brush away feelings of unfinished business between me and my sister Sylvia. Think of my grandmothers, alive and well, too ornery to die.

Wexler paces. The only one of us up and about, he seems nervous, charged, like a wild animal suddenly caged. I remember

Harold saying that Wexler loves sensationalism, used it to create box-office excitement. If so, Diana's demise is made to order. Gossip about sudden deaths and ancient ghosts makes for lively ticket sales.

Occasional crying seeps from the other room, from those faint hearts who prefer death at a distance. Those of us willing to cozy up to the corpse sit dry-eyed, speak in hushed tones. What a fine time for a séance. Got the people, the body, fresh spirits. I have the good sense not to mention this. My macabre take on death isn't to everyone's taste.

The revivers give up. Murray drapes his coat over Diana's body.

"You're disturbing the evidence," says Brenda.

"Evidence?" I say. It takes a second to register. "You think she's been murdered?"

I glance around the circle. The others quickly look away. Tag, I'm it. First I discovered Lily's body, and now here I am again. Just a walking death-meister. I've been too busy analyzing my reaction to her death to wonder why it happened.

The police arrive and it takes them about two seconds to determine that Diana might have shuffled off her mortal coil a tad early. They declare the loft a crime scene and invite all of us to headquarters. We watch each other the whole ride down. It's a creepy feeling knowing the person next to you, the perfectly ordinary-looking chap with the oh-so-pleasant smile and spot of dried egg on his lapel, might cheerfully do you in.

Police stations are strange places. I know I didn't kill Diana, yet I can't help but feel guilty of *something*. They've separated our troupe, members tucked away on benches and chairs, so we can't talk to one another.

A stone-faced policewoman takes my fingerprints. "Why this?" I ask.

She shrugs. "No big thing. We want all your prints on file. In case the investigators need to compare them with prints at the scene."

The press arrives en masse, darting through the building like a school of fish, first one way then another. How did they hear so soon? I slouch on my bench, dropping my head in my hands, cringing at the thought of lurid jailhouse photos splashed across tomorrow's papers. Not to worry. The reporters hurry past, massing at the end of the hall, recorders on, notepads out, cameras clicking. I crane to see the Chosen One. Wexler. Of course. I bet he tipped them off to the story. Bought himself and the play a frenzy of free publicity.

After forty minutes, I'm led to a drab room decorated in early Formica. The one small window, set high on the wall, is protected by a metal grid bolted to concrete. Waning afternoon sunlight glows red through the filthy glass. Minutes pass as I watch the grid's shadows crawl along the table. How would it be to mark a lifetime like this, endless days spent watching shadows of prison bars crawl across a cell floor? The weight of the thought overwhelms me. I turn my eyes to the rest of the room, have time to commit an entire wall of particularly uninspired graffiti to memory before the door opens.

"Hello, Morgan." Roblings walks in, notepad in hand, slides into the chair across from me. I study my cuticles, still angry with him for suspecting Beth of killing Lily. I tend to hold grudges. "We really have to stop meeting like this," he says. When I don't answer, he sighs and flips his notebook to a clean page. "We'd like you to go over your morning, everything you can remember."

When Lily died, Roblings accused me of giving him incomplete information. I won't make the same mistake this time. I recount every detail of my day: the brushing of my teeth, the washing of my face, the eternal search for something clean to wear. This seems to amuse the good detective.

"I left my apartment at eight thirty, stopped at Junque and Stuffe to pick up my check—"

"Anyone there?"

He doesn't add "who might have seen you." But I know he's thinking alibi. I don't like it.

"The shop doesn't open until noon. Harold, the owner, is a night owl, rarely comes in more than a few minutes before the shop opens. I usually let myself in with my own key on the days

I work. Monday mornings, I pick up my check, which Harold writes out Sunday night and leaves on his desk."

"And after you left the shop?"

"I went straight to rehearsal." I take him through the rehearsal to our lunch break. Which is when I remember. "Someone stole food from my bag."

He doesn't appear to move, yet everything about him shifts subtly, a hunting dog going on point.

"What kind of food?"

"Noodle kugel."

"From?"

"From my audition bag."

"No, I mean where did you buy it?"

"I didn't. My mother made it."

"Was anyone else's food stolen?"

"No one said anything. But then, neither did I."

"Why not?"

I study Roblings. Mistake. His is a remarkable face. Powerful. Intelligent. Battle scarred. Bright. Stop! This is neither the time nor the man. He is looking at me. I've forgotten the question.

He asks again. "Why didn't you tell anyone your food was stolen?"

"Sometimes, too often, things get tight for actors, food becomes an issue. I've been there. I didn't feel the need to embarrass whoever took it."

"Wait here." He leaves the room, returning with a clear plastic evidence bag. He tosses it onto the table in front of me. "Look familiar?"

Inside is a wrinkled piece of aluminum foil soiled with bits of noodles and raisins.

"That's the foil my kugel was wrapped in."

"We found it balled up in Diana's bag."

So she did steal from me. He watches me closely.

"You think it was poisoned?" I say. "That's ridiculous. I ate the other piece and I'm perfectly fine."

"The other piece?"

"I brought two."

"Do you have more?"

"At home."

This seems to catch his interest. He checks his watch, stands. "Let's go," he says.

"Where?"

He picks up the evidence bag, hefts the enclosed foil in one meaty palm. "To pick up the rest of this."

"Mom always said her kugel was to die for." He doesn't smile. "C'mon, Roblings, that was a joke." He holds the door open. "What? You think my mother killed Diana?"

"Humor me," he says. I hear him tell someone in the hall he's leaving for the day then he looks at me and takes out his car keys, waiting. An exit cue, if ever I saw one.

I WONDER, sitting next to him in the intimacy of his small car, if he is using the kugel as an excuse to spend time with me. It is not an altogether unwelcome thought. I sneak a few glances, feel his cologne getting to me. Damn. If the good detective would leave Beth in peace, I might consider becoming interested.

Halfway to my apartment he casually asks if Beth was at the rehearsal.

"Beth? Why would she be there?"

He shrugs. "Just wondering."

"Let it go. Beth never hurt anyone."

He doesn't mention Lyle, so why should I? So what if Beth's boyfriend is our lighting designer and just happened to be at the loft this morning? I have to be careful not to make any connection, no matter how thin, between Beth and this latest murder. She has enough trouble in her life without Roblings nosing around.

It is a relief when he shifts the conversation to Diana. What kind of person was she? Was she well liked? What do I know about her private life? Who might have wanted to kill her? I nearly say "Me!" Stop myself in time. I'm learning you don't joke about murder to the cops, unless you're hell-bent on becoming a prime suspect.

FOURTEEN

THE KUGEL IS buried in my freshly stocked fridge behind five thousand pounds of Mom's beer-cooked brisket. Roblings helps me juggle the pans, which leads to his asking about the brisket, which leads to me inviting him to stay and eat some, if he isn't afraid it's poisoned.

"You can be my taster," he says.

He sets the table and pours the wine while I nuke the food. I am thankful Mom forced a shopping bag full of home cooking on me last night.

This is our second meal together. Each unplanned, each delicious. He is good company, this Roblings. The Chianti, sipped against a backdrop of soft jazz, relaxes us enough to take measure of each other. He has wit and a self-confidence that doesn't come off as arrogance. All right, so his questions keep winding back to Beth. Wouldn't I do the same, if I were in his size-eleven-D oxfords? Beth was at the center of Lily's life. It's a natural enough place to begin an investigation.

What I really want to do is tear a piece of challah and dunk it in the rich brisket gravy. But this is not how Edie and Sam Tiersky raised their daughter to eat in polite company. One of the very best things about living alone is eating exactly the way I want. Dunking, wiping, sipping, slurping. Emily Post positively corkscrews in her grave.

I distract myself by pushing a drip of Chianti into patterns around the base of my glass. "Did you ever find out what killed Lily?" I ask.

"Now, that's interesting." He adds wine to our glasses. "The ME's report shows an overdose of crystodigin."

"Is that a poison?"

"It's a common heart medication."

"I thought the autopsy showed Lily didn't have a heart condition."

"She didn't."

He tilts his goblet side to side. Blood-red Chianti coats the glass, runs down in smooth waves. My, what big hands you have.

"The crystodigin was injected into the grapefruit she was eating when she died," he says. "We're pretty certain the grapefruit came from that gift basket delivered to the theater that morning."

"The one sent to Wexler?" He nods. "Did you find this crysto-crysti—"

"Crystodigin."

"—in any of the other fruit?"

"None that we've recovered."

"Including the banana and orange I gave you?"

"The grapefruit was the only tainted piece."

"So"—I clear my throat—"that anonymous phone call you received was right: Lily's death was anything but natural."

"Looks that way."

I try but can't compute this information. Someone I knew, had spoken to, had seen on and off over many years of my life, had been murdered. "It's so easy on television," I say.

"Sorry?"

"Murder. Gunfights, knifings. I don't even notice them anymore. But this...actually knowing someone..." I swig the wine. "Was that grapefruit meant for Lily?"

"Ah." He runs a finger around the rim of his glass. Be still my heart. "That's the big question. It's just as likely the grapefruit was sitting in the basket for anyone who happened to pick it out."

"Like those people who tamper with drugstore medications?"

"Exactly. It's a scattershot approach to murder. The killer gets his kicks watching us run around in circles on the evening news."

"So maybe this creep poisoned the grapefruit, waited to see who keeled over, then called the police to be sure they knew the death was no accident."

"I was sort of leaning that way," he says, "until this afternoon."

"Diana's murder?"

"Suddenly the killings don't look so random. What I don't know is who the killer meant to kill. Diana or you."

I wait for the punch line. There is none. A cold hard thing knots in my gut. "I haven't had an enemy since high school."

"Some people hold grudges a long time."

"High school wasn't that long ago."

He smiles. "What happened?"

"It was one month before the prom. My best friend's boyfriend dumped her, so she just turned around and stole mine. If anything, I'm the one who'd be holding the grudge."

"And you're not?"

"I ran into him a few years back. She did me a favor." I don't mention my anger at my boyfriend-stealing sister. But Sylvia does cross my mind.

My mother doesn't do desserts. I dig out a box of stale Snack-well's and set them on the table.

"How about," says Roblings, "we go in search of a cappuccino and something chocolate."

"Oh, twist my arm."

A SURPRISING NUMBER of people are out on the streets enjoying one of our first springlike nights. Sometimes I forget there is a world around me free for the taking. I tend to hole up, turn hermit. It is lovely to stroll in the comfortable company of an interesting man. With very little effort, I am able to block out the murderous events that brought us together. Fate will have her little joke.

We wind up at Ennui, hangout of Northwestern and Loyola students, professors, neighborhood intellectuals. While Roblings orders at the counter, I liberate a corner table, shoveling off remnants of Sunday's *New York Times,* a chess set, scraps of paper scrawled with mathematical formulas. He sets a plate of chocolate biscotti in the middle of the table, returns with two cappuccinos.

"What can you tell me about Wexler?" he asks.

"I barely know him."

"What you've heard."

"Just rumors."

"Fine by me."

I stir my coffee, sorting through the gossip. "I've heard talk of alcoholism, but he seems sober enough. He is, or at least was, a brilliant director, depending on whom you talk to." I think about what Harold told me. "Some think he was a wunderkind, made a big splash very young, then disappeared."

"What do you think?"

"Too early to tell. Our first rehearsal was today."

"I've heard he has an abrasive personality."

"I haven't seen that."

A young couple takes the table next to us. Something in the way she looks at him is so pure, so clear. Is it the eyes? The soft parting of the lips? Her love is palpable. Encases her in an impenetrable rosy shell. Nothing can hurt her. Nothing of the real world can make its way in. If I ever play a character in the throes of love, this is the look I'll want. I try to mimic the shape of her mouth, the droop of her eyes.

Roblings clears his throat. "I've also heard," he says, trying to make me focus, "Wexler is sometimes volatile and egocentric."

"I haven't seen that, either." The coffee goes down smooth. Ah, the delicious decadence of fresh grounds and a new filter. "You think he made someone angry enough to want to kill him?"

"The fruit basket was sent to Wexler. That makes him the likely target."

"Was my kugel intended for him, too?"

He graces me with a slight smile. "Did you lace it with poison," he asks, "and plan to serve it to Wexler for lunch?"

I offer the plate of biscotti. "A little arsenic?" I ask.

He takes one, dunking it, sucking the coffee from the sweet biscuit. So, he is not altogether rigid about proper table etiquette. I relax a notch.

When he excuses himself to the bathroom, I take our cups to the counter and order refills. I feel wonderfully lithe. Haven't felt this particular buzz since Adam. As in Adam and Sylvia. Anger rush. Okay, I hold grudges. I have the right. No harm wallowing in righteous indignation a while longer.

The lovers at the next table haven't moved since they sat down.

They evidently can stare into each other's eyes for hours. Sweet. Young. Unspoiled. She with the doe eyes, he with the soft, boyish face. Round cheeks, soft skin. Like Adam. Roblings is rougher around the edges. More textured.

Ho!—a bit of a spark. Great. That's all I need. A cop in my life. It's the one occupation with hours worse than an actor's. Besides, it's exhausting trying to guess what Roblings is thinking. Much easier to be with uncomplicated men, more pulp fiction than *Ulysses*. It's also infinitely more boring. I push thoughts of Roblings-as-lover aside.

Halfway into our second cups, Roblings asks for a crash course in theater.

"My favorite subject," I say. As I talk, I watch for signs of come-on. The good detective keeps his distance. I regale him with witty, charming, pithy stories. He is more amused than ardent. I pith harder. By the time I run out of steam, Ennui is closing.

On the walk home, an idea occurs. "What if Lily and Diana's deaths aren't about killing a particular person?" I ask. "What if they're about perpetuating the myth of the jinxed play?"

"Murder as publicity stunt?" He mulls it over. "I doubt it. Outside of gang-bangers and TV wiseguys, people don't engage in murder lightly. Especially murders like these, which take advance planning. I'd be much happier if we could link the two deaths, find a reason someone specifically wanted to kill Lily and Diana."

I try to think of connections. "They were both actresses, Chicagoans...." An uneasy feeling nags. "What if it's not the person?"

"What, then?"

"What if it's the role? Lily played the daughter forty years ago. I'm playing it now. Diana was my understudy. Maybe I was supposed to die today. Diana might have saved my life by stealing my food."

"Why would anyone want to kill off the daughter?"

I can't think of a single reason.

He opens the door to my building, walks me into the lobby, waits while I unlock the inner door.

"I'd like to read the play," he says. "May I borrow your copy?"

"I only have one and I need it. I'm sure Wexler has extra—"

"I'd like to read it tonight."

"I can't let you take it."

"I can read it here."

Ah. Once again I look for signs he's on the make. But Roblings seems all business, not at all attracted to me. Not that I want him to be, not particularly. Although it would be interesting.

I set him up on the sofa with the script and a pot of coffee. "I'm beat," I say, yawning, stretching. "Not used to getting up before the crack of noon. It's been a rough day all in all."

He says good night with barely a glance my way. "I'll let myself out," he says.

The next morning, I find his note on top of the script. In a strong, clear handwriting, Roblings thanks me for the coffee and says my mother called to say she'd seen an old friend of mine on *The Late Show*. She wants me to call. Great. Now I have to face Mom's questions about some strange man answering the phone in my apartment while I was sleeping. That was no man, Mom, that was a cop. Wonderful.

I drag myself into the kitchen to make coffee. Before leaving, Roblings washed out the coffeepot and cup, stacking them neatly on the sideboard. While he was at it, he washed the week's worth of dishes in the sink.

I once dated a fastidious man, the kind who triple-folds his guest towels after guests wash up. The kind who *owns* guest towels. Our relationship was a disaster. If Roblings is a neatnik, there isn't a prayer the two of us will ever get together. Not that I want that. Not at all.

FIFTEEN

I'M A FEW MINUTES late to rehearsal, which for me is early. Trouble is, the other actors have already selected their seats, severely limiting my options. I circle the long table, trying to decide where to sit without being obvious about it. Yes, I know some actors better than others. Is that any guarantee of safety? Aren't most people murdered by family or friends?

Gone is the friendly banter of our first rehearsal. We've grown wary, fearful. Who is the murderer? Where is the murderer? When will the murderer strike again? Backpacks and rehearsal bags, usually tossed carelessly around a rehearsal space, sit clutched on laps or snuggled safely under chairs. If someone wants to kill us, they'll have to use something more direct than poison.

Murray waves me to the chair next to him and I slide in as Wexler arrives. Hunched, pale, he looks as if he's taken a blow to the gut. He is followed by the talented red-haired woman I'd read with at my callback.

"Who's that?" Murray whispers out the side of his mouth.

"Don't know. But she's good."

An uneasy thought niggles. Maybe, since Queen Tut bit the dust, Wexler imported another understudy for Daughter. This one is a bit long in the tooth, but a little stage makeup and the right lighting could take care of that. She pulls up a chair next to Wexler.

"Let's begin," Wexler says, fingers trembling as he opens his script. "Evelyn," he says, nodding at the redhead, "will read Mother until the role is cast."

This reading moves more slowly than the first, people occasionally interrupting for line clarification, scene interpretation. The mood remains subdued. I wonder if we will ever crawl out from under the murder pall.

During the break, I walk down the block to the corner to call home for messages. I can go months without work but it seems as soon as I land one job, another pops up. Feast or famine. A teen boy hunches over the phone. Gang-banger. His pants sit low on his hips, the brim of his baseball cap angles to the left. I wait, keep one eye out for drive-bys as I turn my face to the sun, breathe in the cool air—a welcome respite from the tension in the rehearsal room.

It occurs to me that the boy isn't talking. I open one eye and see his finger holding down the receiver. He's hogging the phone, waiting for an incoming call. Drug deal, most likely. The phone rings. He picks up. Ten seconds later, he hangs up and disappears around the corner. I drop in my coins and dial my voice-mail code, listen hopefully for job offers. One phone message, from Beth.

"I'm at police headquarters." Is she crying? "They've brought me and Lyle in for questioning." Damn Roblings. "I told them I barely knew Diana, but they seem determined to connect me to her murder." Her voice breaks. The thought of my fragile friend adrift in that sea of human scum turns my stomach. "I...should never have told them Lyle...was at the rehearsal loft the morning Diana died. Now they think he had something to do with it."

I assume Beth called to ask me to come down and bail her out. I assume wrong.

"I need you to take care of Hamlet," she says. No, no, not that. "Lyle is desperately allergic to dogs so I've kept Hamlet at my apartment while I've been staying at Lyle's. It's been hard, what with the MS flare-up, going over twice a day to walk and feed him, but he makes Lyle deathly ill." I know the feeling. "Please, just until I come home? I've asked Mrs. Hamu in Four-o-one to let you in. Please call my machine, let me know you got this message and that you'll take care of Hamlet. Thanks."

How long ago had she called? Is she still at the police station? I dig more coins out of my wallet, dial Detective Roblings. I need to know what's going on. He's not in. Beating Beth with a rubber hose, no doubt. I leave a message asking him to call.

Another teen in oversized pants, the crotch seam riding somewhere around his knees, pimp-rolls my way. He's aiming for the phone. But I need to make one more call. I violently shake my purse, coaxing loose coins to the bottom, shoving them into the phone slots, pushing Lester's all-too-familiar number. Just because Beth didn't ask for my help doesn't mean I can't do something. She would help me if the situation were reversed. Lester's secretary immediately puts me through. I tell him what's going on.

"Can you do anything to help?" I ask.

"I'll check into it."

I know, I know. I promised to stop taking advantage of Lester's good nature. I can't keep stringing him along, making him think there is even a microscopic chance we'll get back together. He hasn't said anything. Yet. He will. I suspect even Lester has his limits.

I call Beth's machine and tell her yes, I'll walk and feed the furry beast. Not to worry. And, by the by, Lester the Constant might ride by police headquarters. He'll be the attorney on the white horse.

Wexler starts the afternoon rehearsal. It is no more satisfying than the morning. The specter of Diana's death dries up all creative juice. It isn't fair. We go so long between jobs—some of us longer than others—that we are desperate to savor every drop of the experience. But this is hopelessly cut and dried. Where is the fun? The games? The reason we put up with lousy pay, horrible hours, and cruel and unusual treatment?

The afternoon drags on. From time to time, Evelyn whispers to Wexler, touching him lightly on the arm. She seems to have a calming effect. Wexler's assistant? Lover? There is a certain intimacy between them I can't quite read. I haven't heard any juicy tidbits from the actors' rumor mill. Of course the rumor mill's not always accurate. And what is it saying about me, finder of Lily's body, supplier of Diana's killer kugel? I'd rather not know.

It isn't until the end of rehearsal that Wexler explains. "Evelyn will be handling publicity, arranging radio, TV, and print ads, setting up your interviews and otherwise generating interest in our production."

Evelyn smiles. "Please," she says, "if any of you have personal contacts in the media, I encourage you to share them with me. I'm from New York so I can use all the help you can give."

"Why doesn't he use someone local?" Brenda sniffs. I'm certain she doesn't intend her voice to be so loud.

"Evelyn is also my daughter," says Wexler. "I am a great proponent of blatant nepotism."

Brenda's creamy skin glows red. She mumbles something as she hurries out. I, on the other hand, feel a thousand-pound weight lift. Evelyn's not an understudy, *my* understudy, at all. Begone, ye demons of self-doubt and paranoia! This is my role fair and square.

I float down the loft steps, light enough to fly all the way to Beth's building.

MRS. HAMU opens her door on a short chain and peers out. I have to shout my name a couple of times before it registers.

"Beth said as how you'd be coming." She slams the door on me, disappears for a year, returns with Beth's key and mail. She feeds everything to me through the narrow opening. "Slide the key under the door when you leave," she says. The door slams, two dead bolts click into place. Reminds me of Grandma Ruth. Hasn't stepped out of the house since I was ten.

Hamlet starts barking as soon as I key the lock. I ease open the door and he wriggles through.

"Down, Fang!" I yell as he jumps all over me, yipping and yapping. "Leash?" He stops, cocks his head. "Leash?" He dashes back into the apartment. I follow.

What a mess. He's pulled all the pillows off the sofa. Chewed a stack of magazines. Unrolled balls of yarn. Knocked the large bowl of keys off the entry-hall table.

I don't understand the appeal of dogs. I swear I don't. The guy who invented the Pet Rock had the right idea.

"Bad dog," I say, tossing my gear in a pile on the floor, trying to straighten things so Beth won't come home to this mess. I scoop the keys back into the bowl, including the large daisy key chain with my house and mailbox keys. Beth and I exchange services, bringing in mail and watering plants for each other when we have out-of-town jobs.

I retrieve a diamond-studded Big Ben key chain from under the table. *Lily London* is etched in the plastic. The unexpected name jolts me back to the dingy backstage bathroom, Lily's wide unseeing eyes. I shudder. She would have been mortified at such an undignified death. I may not have liked her, but I'm sorry she died the way she did.

Hamlet races up, clamps his rabid little teeth on the pieces of mail I'd set on the floor, then tears off down the hall. Rats! I run after, following the trail of dropped letters to the bedroom. "Where are you, you little thief?" No answer. "I know you're here." I find him under the bed, happily chewing a manila envelope. "Let me have it," I say, reaching under the bed. He growls, snaps at my hand. "Oh no you don't, you mangy mutt." I manage to grip a corner of the envelope and wrestle it away. Hamlet comes out barking.

"Leash!" I command again. He barks twice then takes off down the hall. I sit on the bed, checking the envelope. Rissman, Gordon, Kanter, and Denberg Attorneys at Law. I turn it over and over, debating. The last time I read something I shouldn't was half a year ago. My chronically tidy little sister *just happened* to leave her diary on top of an otherwise immaculate desk. Granted, I'd broken up with Adam two months before. Still, reading about Sylvia's love for him and his for her turned my life inside out. I had no business reading that diary, and I have no business reading Beth's mail.

But the envelope is badly torn. I slip out the contents, just to be sure Hamlet hasn't damaged anything. And I should check to see that there's nothing upsetting inside, something that can wait until Beth is stronger. It is a copy of Lily's will. I fan the pages, scanning paragraphs of legalese until I come to the list of Lily's sizable estate: jewelry, property, investments. All willed to Beth.

I whistle as I reread the list. Does Beth know she inherits all this? Roblings asked me that, Lester asked. No. I can't believe Beth has any idea.

Hamlet races in, drops his leash at my feet, jumps and yaps

until I hook him up and take him out. I let him drag me around the block while he sniffs trees, fences, flowers.

What a con artist Lily had been. She never carried more than a couple of dollars. We all assumed she was scraping by, like the rest of us. Felt sorry because she was so much older. At rehearsals, we'd share food with her, pick up the tab if we went out to dinner. When Beth ran errands, she often paid for Lily's laundry, groceries, other things. Maybe that's where all Lily's money came from. From not spending any.

"All right, class. How do we spell 'opportunistic'?"

"L-i-l-y."

"Excellent."

I wait while Hamlet leaves a deposit at the base of a large oak. A woman trimming her hedge across the street watches with interest. I didn't think to take a pooper-scooper. No matter. I couldn't bring myself to use one. The idea of cleaning up after a dog repulses me. When Hamlet finishes, we walk off. I think I hear the woman shout "Hey!" but I don't turn.

Back at the apartment, Hamlet follows me around as I freshen his water, fill his food dish, and gather my things. "Don't give me that look," I say, trying not to feel guilty about leaving him alone. "Beth will be back soon."

But what if she isn't? What if the police detain her? Or if all this trauma makes her MS flare so badly she can't take care of herself, let alone Hamlet? I'd have to run back and forth to walk and feed him. I don't have that kind of time. Hamlet blinks at me, waiting. Damn.

"If I take you home," I say, "you'll live by my rules. Understood?"

He tilts his head to one side, flips up his ears until the tips flop over.

"You think you're cute," I say. "But that stuff won't work with me. I'm warning you, you tear up one thing of mine and I'll freeze-dry your sorry self and use you for a paperweight."

I go to pack his food. Two cans left. I'll have to stop at the grocery store, a chore only slightly less appealing than total tooth extraction. I pat my pockets for money. Shake my purse on end.

Pathetic pickings. A dollar and change and my undeposited Junque and Stuffe paycheck. Certainly not enough to actually buy something.

Then I remember: Beth once complained that Lily bought dog food by the case, heavy cases, difficult for Beth to carry. There are probably tons of tins at Lily's. Her apartment is on my way home. I take Lily's diamond-studded key ring from the bowl. I'll stop and pick up food for Hamlet.

And maybe, while I'm there, I'll take a little look around. The police may know about murder, but I know about actors. Maybe there is something in Lily's apartment the police missed. Something that will set them on the trail of the real killer, make them leave poor Beth alone.

SIXTEEN

THE AGING BRICK three-flat overlooks Indian Boundary Park.
Benches of old women and men guard the playground. I wedge
my car into a space in front of a large fenced enclosure and am
locking the door when Hamlet yanks the leash from my hand and
races away, barking.

"Hamlet!" I yell, running after. "Stop. Heel. Come back."
Lily obviously never invested in obedience school.

By the time I reach him, he is trying to wedge through a small
opening at the base of the enclosure. "Bad dog," I say, stepping
on the end of the leash, wrapping it around my hand. An animal
roars in my ear. I shriek. Jump back.

A bear! A large, moth-eaten bear lives in the park, its stinking
fur mangier than Grandma Ruth's old mink stole. Another roar.
It flashes yellow teeth against dark fur. Its nose glistens, wet and
runny. What idiot puts a vicious animal where children play? It
roars again, swatting the cage with a huge paw. Hamlet barks,
bearing tiny teeth. "That's smart," I say, picking him up. "Pick
a fight. Make him good and mad. Way to go."

Nothing about Lily's building hints at the wealth she's socked
away. Paint peels from wood window frames and too many seasons have passed between tuck-pointings. Hamlet wriggles as I
unwedge mail from the lobby box.

"Hold on, hold on," I say, unlocking the inner door, pushing
it open. "Go on." Once inside I drop the leash and he races
upstairs. The second I open the apartment door, Hamlet flies
through the apartment, tearing in and out of rooms. He darts back
to me several times, cocks his head, then takes off again.

Lily. The poor mutt's looking for Lily. It never occurred to me
how confusing a trip home might be for him. I feel a twinge of
pity. He can't understand that Lily is dead. All he knows is that

the one person who loved him most has disappeared from his life. Hamlet might be annoying, but he is also a creature capable of feeling love and affection—and pain. He curls on the sofa, whimpering. I sit next to him, petting him gently as I look around the room.

Roblings told me the police were here, but there are no signs of anything disrupted. Beth must have come and straightened up after them. As weak as she is, it couldn't have been easy. But it's pure Beth. What a loving gesture to honor the memory of a fastidious old friend.

A battered green fishing tackle box, Lily's name stenciled on one side, sits like a piece of sculpture on a pedestal end table. I open the metal clasp and lift the lid, unfolding rusty trays crammed with theatrical makeup: half-squeezed tubes of greasepaint, stained sponges, blunted pencils, brushes, shadows, powders, emery boards, opening-night telegrams flaking at the edges, a St. Genesius medal *and* a St. Christopher's, needle and thread, glue, spirit gum, a small knife. Flesh-tone face powder coats everything. I poke through the smeared tubes. We haven't used grease in years. Why on earth did she keep these? They wrench my heart. Of all an actor's tools, makeup is the most intimate. These should have been buried with Lily the way favorite oils and fragrances were buried with Egyptian queens. Didn't they also bury the queen's pets? Hamlet growls softly. A mind-reading dog. Swell.

I get up and roam the living room. It is a shrine to Lily. The walls chronicle her career: posters from plays, playbills, a Spanish fan, a rhinestone bracelet, ruby slippers, kindly reviews, fan letters.

The one thing Lily spent money on, lavishly, was framing. Some items are encapsulated in huge frames with tri-cut mats, displaying a photo in one, a play program in another, and a prop of some sort in the third. I've seen memorabilia framed like this for Abraham Lincoln, Babe Ruth, Marilyn Monroe. None of the actors I know can afford such framing. Even if they could, they'd be embarrassed by this scale of self-accolade.

Only two photos don't include Lily. Centered on one wall is a professional studio portrait of a perfectly groomed Hamlet perched on a satin pillow. The other is Beth's most recent head shot, autographed, *To Lily, a gifted actress and treasured friend, with love, Beth.*

Hamlet whimpers at my feet. I pick him up. He's trembling. "It's all right," I say, stroking his coat, making soothing sounds.

"Will you look at this?" The original cast of my play poses for a photo on an empty stage, striking attitudes of their characters. I find Lily London, forty years younger, a wispy young woman with delicate features and regal posture. I don't get it. I'm more the Judy Jock type. How could Wexler have cast Lily and me in the same role?

I scan the photo. A gorgeous young Wexler, an imposing presence even then, sits in his director's chair surrounded by the company. He couldn't have been much more than in his late twenties, early thirties.

And the crew! They look like babies with their close-cropped hair and fresh-scrubbed faces. I never see such young kids in companies anymore, not since unions became strong and insurance went through the roof. No, this photo dates back to simpler days when a starstruck kid could hang around a company running errands, make himself useful, plant a foot in the stage door.

Matted next to the photo is the program. I scan the actors' names, looking for anyone who might have survived forty years in Chicago theater. A couple ring faint bells, but no one I've worked with. Then I read the crew list. Harold Shaw—Wardrobe Assistant. Harold? My Harold?

I take the photo off the wall, turn on the reading lamp. It takes a while to pick out the young man in the back row. His hair was thicker then, naturally black, and he didn't wear glasses or mustache. But it is Harold, all right. Proprietor of Junque and Stuffe, mentor, financial savior, and costumer to Chicago stars.

Harold was there forty years ago.

Why didn't he say so? Why hasn't Harold, a dedicated gossip, bragged about knowing Lily and Wexler? I pack the photo and stage bill in my bag. I will ask about this at work tomorrow. Indeed I will. Mr. Harold has some explaining to do.

I wander through the rest of Lily's apartment. The back bedroom closet is filled with theatrical garments, boas, sequined dresses, gowns and furs, a harem girl's jeweled pants, World War II fatigues, a fringed cowgirl jacket. I recognize a milkmaid's outfit from one of the living room photos. How did Lily get these? I've never been allowed to keep a costume. Sometimes you can buy bits and pieces if the costumes aren't rented. But Lily wasn't the type to part with her money. Did she steal them? Or were they gifts?

Even more curious than how, is why. Why keep so many ingenue costumes all these years? Mementos, perhaps? An unwillingness to accept the fact of her age? Beth was right: The supervain Lily would have died if she'd seen her real age listed in the obituary.

Hidden behind the costumes is a shelf of scrapbooks dating to Lily's birth. I flip through a chronology of family Christmas photos, an unsmiling mother and father in rigid pose with four unsmiling children. In one snowy photo, the clan stands before a large sign: WELCOME TO PARKERSBURG, WEST VIRGINIA. ALMOST HEAVEN.

Flowery script lists each name in red ink. Lily is not Lily. She is Beatrice. Not London, Berolzheimer. How many of us swap our birth names for more appealing inventions? That I changed my name when I started in show business isn't something I'm in a hurry to tell people. Shifting from Miriam Tiersky to Morgan Taylor seems a dated affectation in these days of Schwarzenegger and Snodgrass.

After a few pages, Lily's family disappears from the scrapbook as theater takes over her teenaged life. Unlike the glowing testimonials on her living room walls, this history of Lily's life contains negative moments. Bad notices, plays closing after one week, stubs of train tickets to Hollywood and back, a can of brittle film labeled MGM SCREEN TEST.

There are people who never toss anything, who form attachments to minutiae. I am like that, find peculiar comfort in piling great quantities of useless stuff around me. I will likely end up one of those old ladies they find dead on a bed stacked high with newspapers dating back to the Boer War.

But Lily was a fastidious housekeeper. Not at all the pack-rat type. Why keep old costumes, bad reviews? Why preserve moments of her life—the rejections, the failures—she would undoubtedly rather forget? Perhaps Lily thought her life so important that she kept the record, the good and the bad, for posterity. Like the watercolorist I once met who was obsessed with having her work survive the ages. She showed me her paintings, quoting chapter and verse on archival paper. From what I saw of her artwork, her energies would be better spent paying more attention to what she put *on* the paper. The same way Lily could have put more effort into updating her outdated acting style.

I don't find anything that might take suspicion off of Beth. And I don't like Lily London one bit more than I did before I came. I put Lily's mail into a shopping bag with a two-week supply of dog food and a few of Hamlet's toys. I'll bring Lily's mail to Beth to go through.

It isn't until I am back in my apartment and see Roblings's note, *Your Mother called,* that it hits me. What's missing from Lily's scrapbooks, from the life displayed on her walls, is contact with the rest of humanity.

Once the young Lily left home, she seemed to leave all human bonds behind. There were no mementos of men in her apartment, no love letters, photos, pressed corsages. No evidence of lifelong friends, for that matter, male or female, no vacation photos, trips with loved ones. She was totally alone, unconnected, until Hamlet and then Beth came into her life.

Roblings investigated Lily's apartment. He must have noticed the same thing. One more reason Beth is the only viable suspect in Lily's death.

THE PHONE RINGS late at night, disturbing me mid-memorizing. Hamlet's sharp little barks hit me directly between my eyes. "Shhhhh," I say, setting my script aside, letting him jump on my bed to keep him quiet while I answer.

Lyle is frantic. "Beth...attack...police station."

"Beth was attacked?"

"No, no, she had an attack." His voice cracks. "I could kill those guys. How could they—"

"How is she?"

"Stable."

"Where is she?"

"Lakeview Hospital."

"I'm on my way."

"They've given her something. She'll be out until morning."

"I'll go first thing."

"I-I-I..." He stops. Takes a deep breath. Somewhere in his childhood he stuttered, learned to overcome it. It tries to sneak back when he's agitated.

"Take your time," I say.

"Th-the cops thought she was putting on an act. I had to explain to them about the multiple sclerosis. Had to. You understand."

"Of course."

"Beth doesn't. She's furious. W-won't talk to me."

Pride goeth before the seizure. "Try to get some rest," I say. "I'll call you after I see her."

SEVENTEEN

I STEEL MYSELF against acrid hospital smells, follow a long corridor to Beth's room. Her door is open. A young woman in the bed nearest the door has slathered on full makeup and styled her hair into an elaborate sculpture. She talks on the phone, hugging it between chin and shoulder while adding a coat of red polish to already perfect nails. I nod, tiptoeing past the curtain separating their beds. Beth lies limp as a rag doll, looking small and helpless.

"This sympathy ploy won't work," I say.

She opens her eyes, smiles. "Morning."

"Thought I'd subject myself to hospital coffee. I hear it builds character."

"Toxic waste will do that." She presses a button, shifting the bed to a sitting position. "Don't you have rehearsal?"

"I'm not called today."

"Ah." She rubs her eyes. "Why are you up so early?"

"I'm doing battle at Junque and Stuffe around ten."

"My love to Harold."

I fluff a pillow, set it behind her back. "Truth is, I had to flee my house before that demented dog ripped my last pair of panty hose."

"Hamlet's at your place?"

"He destroyed yours. And the pound won't take him. I threw him out the window a couple of times but he always found his way back." She laughs. A good sound. "You know, I'm not falling for this sick routine. You're getting that mutt back the second they spring you from this place."

"You're a hard, hard woman."

A nurse comes in to do nurse-type things and I stare out the window, cringing, unable to watch. Needles, tubes, swabs. Instruments of torture. I will never become sick. I will simply grow old gracefully and, one fine day, swoon delicately onto a velvet-covered chaise. End of play. Applause, applause.

The roommate's getting on my nerves. Never stops talking. One of those Chatty Cathys who prattles on forever about nothing. I played one once. Had to find my way into the character. At first I thought she feared silence. But I came to understand that what she really feared was not getting a chance to be heard. My throat hurt after each performance. The actress part of me feels tender understanding. Beth's friend part of me wants to glue this woman's lips shut.

After a while Beth calls, "Coast is clear." I pull up a chair, pushing aside her tray of separating orange juice, clotted oatmeal, cold coffee.

"Want to talk about what happened?"

She makes a face. "This is a stupid disease. Doesn't leave you your dignity. Comes and goes as it pleases." She smooths her sheets with trembling hands. "I was with the Grand Inquisitors, trying to explain I had nothing to do with Lily's death or Diana's death or monsoons in Japan, when my body disconnected from my brain. I felt like a spastic marionette, my arms and legs jerking in all directions. Not a pretty sight, I reckon."

"Did it hurt?"

"Only my pride." She reaches for the water container. I beat her to it, pouring a glass, unwrapping a new straw. The roommate has grown quiet. At first I think she is off the phone, but I hear her whisper. Perhaps talk of death has caught her attention.

I hold the glass for Beth, bending the straw to her lips. "You were lucky Lyle was there. To explain."

"That Benedict Arnold?" She takes a couple of sips. "He told them. Betrayed my confidence."

"The cops thought you were faking, trying to get out of their interrogation. Lyle had to tell them."

"What if some cop-shop hack gets wind of this? Writes a little blurb for the columns: 'Actress stricken by MS while being questioned in friend's murder.' Talk about a double whammy. It will be the end of me." She hands me the glass, sinks into the pillows. "Who wants a damaged actress? No one, that's who."

I feel the roommate listening. "You're overreacting."

"Don't be naive. Do you honestly believe that the same people who stay up forty-eight hours straight working a telethon for MS would actually *hire* someone who has it?"

She closes her eyes, exhausted. I can't tell her she's wrong, because she's not. Our industry has the biggest heart in the world, until the pocketbook becomes involved. Money for the arts is so tight no one can risk hiring a sick star.

"Look on the bright side," I say.

"Which is?"

"I don't see any armed guards outside your door. Looks to me like the cops don't consider you public enemy number one. I'll bet they're out right now trying to find the real killer."

The phone rings. I answer it. "Lyle," I mouth. Beth shakes her head. I make excuses to Lyle, tell him to try later.

I should get going. I debate a few seconds before handing Beth the chewed envelope with Lily's will. "This came for you."

With her emotions already close to the surface, Beth doesn't make it past "The last will and testament." She sets the envelope aside and polishes off a small box of tissues. I scrounge another from the visitors' waiting room down the hall. She can't stop crying. I could kick myself for bringing the will. But how could I not? I stand like an Acting 101 student, awkward beyond belief, hands hanging useless at my sides, not a clue how to behave.

"Is everything all right?" Miss Inquiring Mind swirls around from the other bed clutching her toothbrush and paste. She wants us to think she's on her way to brush her teeth. The bathroom is in the other direction. I plant myself between her and Beth.

"Her goldfish died," I say, staring her down until she gets it that I'm not buying her show of concern.

"Well, then..." She smiles, holding up her brush and paste, flowing off to the bathroom.

A nurse the size of a Rush Street bouncer comes in to change Beth's sheets. "Take your friend for a walk to the end of the hall," she orders, handing me a metal walker. "And no short-cuts."

We head down the hall. I try to block out the sickness around me, breathe through my mouth, look straight ahead. A scene oozes up from a dark place. A person hurries down a hospital corridor. But there is no end to it. No matter how fast he (she?) runs—sides of the walls flashing by, floor tiles disappearing underfoot—he is no closer to the end. Something real? Something dreamed? A little girl's fear for her "dying" grandfather. The nightmarish scene has haunted me from childhood.

A candy striper passes, pushing a mail cart overflowing with cards and gifts. It reminds me. "I have a shopping bag full of Lily's mail at my place."

Beth shuffles the walker down the hall. "There's so much to do when someone dies. I've been paying Lily's bills, notifying everyone about her death."

"Do you want me to bring her mail tomorrow?"

"I'm not up to going through it."

"If you want, you can give me Lily's checkbook. I'll write the checks, bring them to you to sign."

"That would be a great help." We're halfway down the hall when she stops. "I can't do this."

"You can't quit. That nurse will kill us both."

"Might be less painful." After a minute she starts moving again. "It's so sad that Lily had no one to take care of her."

"She had you."

"You know what I mean. She had no family. Acting was her whole life. She never married. Her only child died years ago."

"Lily had a child?"

"She couldn't bear talking about him." We make it to a row of chairs at the end of the hall. "Just for a minute?" she asks. "Until I catch my breath?"

"Fine by me."

She eases into the chair as if she's a hundred years old, breathes in slow and deep. Takes a tissue from her pocket and dabs perspiration from her neck.

"Lily's child?" I coax.

"Lily bore a son out of wedlock."

"I don't believe it."

"I know. It's hard to imagine Lily—"

Beth's right leg begins bouncing. Little jerks. We ignore the spasm, preferring to gaze at a pastoral painting on the opposite wall.

"Her family sent Lily away to have the baby," Beth tells the painting, "then forced her to give him up."

"I saw her parents' photos in her scrapbook," I say. "American Gothic—without the humor."

She smiles. "That's them. Her baby was adopted by a Chicago couple. Somehow Lily kept track of him over the years. When he became active in his high school theater, she secretly arranged to have him hired for the summer by a small troupe she'd joined."

"She never told anyone he was her son?"

"In those years? Having a child out of wedlock was the type of scandal that destroyed careers."

Beth's leg settles down. "Poor, poor Lily."

"What happened?"

"Her son died early that summer. Asthma attack."

"How horrible."

"Lily never really recovered."

I layer this information over my memories of Lily London. It softens the edges of my dislike.

"I know you think Lily was selfish," says Beth. "But you didn't really know her. I've always thought what she did took tremendous courage."

"What she did?"

"After his funeral, she stood up and admitted to the entire theater company that he was...he was..."—Beth digs a tissue from her pocket, dabs her nose—"that he was her son."

Far down the corridor, the sheet-changing nurse steps out of Beth's room and waves. The room looks a million miles away.

"Ready?" I ask.

"No."

I help her up.

Later, as I leave her room, I promise to take care of Hamlet and not to eat him unless I am absolutely starving.

EIGHTEEN

I WOULD PERSONALLY like to draw and quarter the Wicker Park merchant who came up with the idea of May Madness Days. Mimes and clowns roam the crowds; vendors hawk food from pushcarts.

Chicagoans, cooped up too many months by a brutal winter, swarm over sidewalks, into streets, dance to conflicting rhythms of assorted live bands. It is drudgery trying to get to work, pushing through mobs of shoppers, racks of clothing, tables of wares.

I am fighting through a cotton-candy-machine crowd when I see Mr. and Mrs. Hold-Still-So-We-Can-Stab-You-in-the-Back standing guard in front of Junque and Stuffe. My little sister looks pale and thin. The handsome Adam has aged in the past months. A tightening around the mouth, a hooding of the brow.

I consider shifting course to avoid them, dart down the alley, enter the shop through the rear door. No. This is my turf. I'm not the one who needs to disappear. I make my way straight for the front door.

Sylvia sees me. Smiles. I do not smile back. Now Adam sees me. My knees feel trembly but I manage to maintain my stride.

"Miriam," Sylvia says.

I stop. "Morgan," I tell her. "My name is Morgan Taylor. Has been for ten years." She wants to return to those glorious days of yesteryear, when I loved her without reservation. I am not up to time travel this morning.

"Excuse me," I say, trying to get into the store.

Adam puts his hand on my shoulder. "Please. It's enough."

I push his hand away. "I'm not in the mood for this. I've just come from the hospital. Visiting a friend who is very ill."

Sylvia pulls him away. "This isn't a good time."

"There's never going to be a good time." He looks at me and

I see how much he's hurting for Sylvia, for the heartache I'm causing. I could end it right now. With a single word, a simple hug. I could do a lot of things I'm not going to. I don't like surprises, don't enjoy being pushed. Prefer doing things my own way, in my own time.

Adam puts a protective arm around my sister, leads her off down the street. I watch them go, aching from the soreness of the old wound. It wasn't self-inflicted, but I am the one who won't let it heal.

The shop is more chaotic than the street. Harold has dragged out every piece of goods stashed in the basement and attic, tossed them around like chum on water. Bargain hunters are in a feeding frenzy.

Harold flutters around, dapper and doting, doing his shopkeeper shtick. He is the raconteur of the ribald, the king of kitsch. There is little for me to do but write up sales and take in money. Which is, I figure, about all I can manage after this morning's emotional wringer, first Beth, then Sylvia.

By late afternoon I am selling the dregs of the dregs from a folding table out front. Harold sticks his head out the door. "It's your darling mother," he shouts, "line three."

"Tell her I was abducted by aliens."

"Kinky." He disappears into a sea of young men hell-bent on buying every cigar humidor in stock.

I take the call in the back room, collapsing into Harold's leather chair, lifting my aching feet onto the desk. "Hi, Mom," I say.

"And just who was that wonderfully sexy man who answered your phone last night? *Late* last night?"

Roblings. "No time to talk. It's a madhouse here."

"You're keeping secrets."

"I'll call you later."

"You say you will but you never do. Tell me about your new young man."

"He's not new. Not young. Not mine."

"Come to dinner. I'm cooking your favorite."

I smell a trap. "Who else is coming?"

A pause. "Not Sylvia, if that's what you mean."

"That's exactly what I mean."

"Tell her to bring a photo ID," yells my father. "It's been so long, we may not remember how she looks."

"I was just there," I say.

Mom ignores both of us. "You can bring your young man," she says.

"I'll be there," I say. "Alone."

I STAY AN EXTRA half hour after closing to help Harold straighten stock, prepare for tomorrow's onslaught. As I pack up my bag to leave, I find the photo I took from Lily's wall.

"Got a surprise for you," I say, slipping the photo in front of him.

I can't make out his expression as he stares at his young self, at the cast and crew he worked with forty years before. If I thought he'd be delighted, I was wrong.

"Why didn't you tell me you were there?" I ask. "That you knew Lily and Wexler?"

Harold hands back the photo. "Sometimes, dearheart, there are things better left forgotten. Events still too painful to talk about. Even after forty years."

He turns off the lights, herds me out, and locks up the store. We walk together in silence through the May Madness streets. It isn't like Harold to be quiet. He has the look of someone working through something. I leave him alone.

We come to my car. "Give you a lift?" I say.

"My bus will be along in a few minutes."

"Want company?"

We settle on a graffittied bench. Dusk rouses the night animals. Star light, star bright. I spot my first hooker of the night. Mid-thirties, athletic build, crotch-high skirt, plunging everything. She decorates a doorway across the street.

"May I see the photo again?" asks Harold. I dig it out, hand it to him. He shakes his head. "That was a time. We thought we had the world by the balls. In truth, we were all so innocent. Babes playing at life."

A brown sedan slows, pulls to a stop near the hooker. She

leans into the open window, negotiating. Her breasts mound over the top of her low-cut blouse.

Harold sighs. "Back then, homosexuals didn't come out the way they do now. Everything was hush-hush. Only the arts embraced us. The theater was my salvation." He runs delicate fingers over the long-ago faces. "The year of this photo, I fell in love with a young intern. I have never been so happy, before or since."

"What happened?"

"Wexler. Wexler happened. He had eyes for the same young man."

"Wexler?" I must have misheard. "The director, *my* director, Wexler?"

"The same."

I think of the newspaper clips in Lily's scrapbook. "The 'stud of the decade' Wexler?"

"Ah, the press."

"How do you explain his daughter?"

"Daughter?"

"He has a daughter. Red hair. Fortyish. She's been at rehearsals."

"I had no idea." He brushes a dust speck off the photo. "But that doesn't change a thing. You'd be amazed how many of us married and had children. It threw the rumormongers off the scent."

"I wonder if Evelyn knows about her father."

"How much do any of us know about our parents' sexuality? It is an uncomfortable topic in even the most heterosexual of families."

The driver of the brown car—someone's father, husband, grandfather?—changes his mind and drives off. The hooker sashays back to her doorway. A streetlight flickers on. The scene takes on a surreal movie-set look.

Harold dabs his nose with his kerchief. "Wexler became obsessed with my lover. I tried to hold on. Fought with all I had. But what could I, a mere wardrobe assistant, do against someone so handsome, so powerful? You can't imagine the depth of my rage."

He ages as I watch, withering. Will my anger at Sylvia last forty years? Did I ever love Adam as fervently as Harold loved his young man? Does that matter? Isn't a lover's rage about betrayal, after all?

A black four-door pulls up, honks. The hooker walks out to the curb. She bends lower this time, showing more breast by way of negotiating price.

"Do you ever see your old lover?" I ask.

"Oh, my dear," he sighs deep and long, "that's the hard thing about it. He died, you see. Shortly after he left me. An asthma attack, of all things."

I am stunned. "You're talking about Lily's son?"

Harold nods. "Of course, at the time, I didn't know. None of us did. When she told us, after...after he died, I could hardly believe it. To tell the truth, she never even seemed aware of him."

"She couldn't risk it," I say. "Lily told Beth she was terrified people would discover she had an illegitimate child."

The hooker stands, begins walking back to the doorway. Her body ripples in a most seductive way. When I go home I will put on my highest heels and practice that walk in front of my mirror. The man in the black four-door honks, calls her back.

Harold sniffs, dabs his nose, refolds the kerchief. "Weren't we some sad group? You young people think life was simpler back then. That's only because so much of our anguish was hidden." The streetlights cast weary shadows around his eyes. "I always thought Wexler gave Lily the lead in the play to help distract her from her grief."

"You think he felt sorry for her?"

"Must have. It was obvious Lily was all wrong for the part." Harold smiles. "Oh my dear, the uproar that caused. I'd quite forgotten. Wexler had all but promised the part to another actress. I caught a glimpse of her at an audition, a pixie of a gal, much more energetic and gutsy than Lily. Someone, actually, quite a bit like you."

"Now that makes more sense," I say. "I didn't understand how Wexler could cast me and Lily in the same role."

Harold's bus rounds the corner. Across the street, the hooker stands and takes a comb out of her hair. Lovely blond curls fall to her shoulders. I reckon a bargain has been struck. I see the brown sedan return, creeping up behind the black four-door. Too late, buster. You missed your chance. The lady of the night has been spoken and paid for.

Harold's bus pulls up, blocking my view. He hugs the photo to his thin chest. "May I keep this?"

He looks so small and sad. "Sure. I'll tell Beth I gave it to you. I doubt she wants much of Lily's memorabilia. She'll probably ask you to sell it off."

Normally, the promise of such a cache would perk Harold right up. Not tonight. He climbs on the bus, subdued by the ghosts of forty-year-old memories.

The bus pulls away. Across the street, the hooker and the black four-door are surrounded by plainclothes cops. The driver's face glows red under the streetlights. Sweat pours off him as he's herded away. I wonder why they don't arrest the hooker.

The brown sedan pulls up. The driver waves to the "hooker," who returns to her doorway. They all disappear into their hiding places to wait for the next victim. Won't you come into my parlor....

Things aren't always what they seem.

NINETEEN

I PULL INTO my parents' driveway. Why is this house of my birth still home? I've been away ten years, have lived in assorted apartments, lofts, basements. But my history lives in this Skokie ranch with its yellow brick and blue slate roof. The five trees my father planted when each of us was born have overgrown the backyard. Even the Sylvia sapling, planted twenty-three years ago, stands twice the height of the garage. At first, my father wasn't sure it would survive my tree's nearby shadow. He needn't have worried.

My father attacks as I climb out of my car. "This business between you and Sylvia—it's eating your mother up alive."

"If that's why you invited me over..."

He notices I haven't closed the car door. That I can jump right back in and drive off. That would leave him alone to face Mom, explain why I left. A scary prospect. He sneaks a look at the house, lowers his voice.

"Your mother warned me not to say anything."

"Smart woman."

"But how can I not? Our oldest and youngest at war. It's tearing the family apart."

"You and Uncle Morrie didn't talk for three years."

"That's different." I give him a look. He holds up his hands in surrender. "All right, all right. So I said what I said and now you know. Come in, come in. Aunt Francie's here."

The house smells of pepper steak, challah, oil paint, and turpentine. Dad retired from the shoe business and discovered painting. His newest crop lines the walls leading back to the kitchen. We pause briefly at each as he explains the initial inspiration, nuances of meaning.

I oooh and ahhh at all the appropriate places, even though my father does not afford my work the same respect. My love of theater baffles him. Such a fleeting art form. "Magician's flash paper," he calls it. "You put on a play, then—Whoosh!—you disappear. What kind of legacy is that to leave your children?"

Dad's "legacies" fill his children's walls. Landscapes, portraits, still lifes, abstracts. He consumes more canvas than the America's Cup, gifting paintings to everyone close to him, some not so close and the occasional total stranger.

The tour over, he relinquishes me to the women in the kitchen. I hug my mother, inhale her delicious blend of Chanel No. 5 and sautéed onion. She dips a ladle in the soup pot. "Taste," she says. I do. Heaven.

"Ah, the Beauty." Aunt Francie comes at me, arms outstretched. No sense ducking. She always finds me. I relax into the folds of her hug. Floral powder. Hair spray. Spice perfume. "Such a treat to see you."

She looks at me with a jeweler's eye, sees the diamond in my rough. "We were just passing by"—she picks a piece of lint from my blouse, tucks back a rogue hair—"and I said to Milton, 'Let's stop in and see my oldest and dearest friend.' "

"Milton?" I glance at my mother, who turns away, pretending not to be a party to this deception.

Aunt Francie, the family matchmaker, pulls me to the doorway, where I get a view through the dining room into the den. A forty-something man sits on the sofa, intent on a TV baseball game. "My cousin's son on Leonard's side," Francie whispers. "Recently moved to Chicago from Cleveland."

She whispers, I know, lest another single woman swoop down and steal this catch before I have a chance at him.

Introductions are made, Aunt Francie talking nonstop to help get us through this awkward patch. Finally, we all sit to dinner. By tactical error, Mom has seated Milton facing the den where the TV—sans sound—stays on. Both Milton and my father strain to watch.

Mom and Francie extol Milton's virtues, talking about him as if he weren't seated next to me. To hear them tell it, this man is the greatest catch since Onassis: brilliant conversationalist, successful businessman, never married, loves theater, music, dancing.

I look at the disinterested, uninteresting Milton and think of the old punch line: "Are you going to believe what you see or what I tell you?"

During a commercial break, I make a stab at conversation. Milton's single-syllable responses echo from a cavern deep in his sinus passages. A little nervous laugh punctuates every other sentence. He does a funny thing with his mouth that makes a soft smacking sound.

Later, I will sit Mom and Francie in front of the All Sports Channel, tell them: "I will personally force you to watch sports the rest of your matchmaking days should you ever, *ever* try to fix me up again." Sometimes, tough love's all they understand.

Milton brightens when Francie runs a quick list of some of my "famous" acting jobs.

"I've seen your floor-wax commercial," he says. "Very well done."

"Thank you."

"If I waxed my floor, I'd certainly use that product. But, heh-heh, that's why God created cleaning services. How much does something like that pay?"

Men always ask about the money. Women are curious about the work. "I dunno," I say. "Figure I average about a hundred thou a week, give or take."

His beady eyes widen.

"What a kidder." Aunt Francie jabs her elbow into his ribs by way of emphasis. "Did I tell you?"

God forbid I make more than he does. Men of a certain age don't take kindly to the idea. I've found it's the young men who are more receptive to the idea of woman as economic provider. Not that, with my particular employment history, out-earning a boyfriend has ever been an issue.

"No, really," he says. "Whaddya earn for something like that?"

"Bupkes. Fact is, I'm just another starving artist."

After dinner, Mom shoos the men into the den for coffee and dessert so she can pump me for information.

"So"—she stirs milk and sugar into my coffee—"tell me about this man in your apartment last night."

"What man?" asks Francie.

"That was no man," I say. "That was a cop. He was at my apartment on police business."

"About those terrible deaths?" asks Francie.

"You remember Lily London?" asks Mom.

"I remember." Francie clamps a sugar cube in her front teeth, loudly sucks coffee through. "Thin," she says.

"Very thin," agrees Mom.

All three of us sigh.

"Thin women are selfish," says Francie. "Thin women put themselves before their families." She breaks off a piece of coffee cake to dunk. "I never match my older men with thin women. Not that I would complain if I lost a pound or three...."

"Emaciated isn't attractive," says Mom, pushing a plate of cookies my way. "Especially after a certain age."

Energetic gossips, Mom and Aunt Francie pump me for information about Lily and Diana's deaths. I think it wise not to mention the use the killer made of Mom's kugel. I try to steer the conversation toward Mom's work at the local newspaper, Dad's new career in art, but Mom is stuck on murder.

"Poor Diana," she says. "I saw her in *Teeth*. Such a gifted actress."

"You think she was gifted?" I ask.

"She was married?" asks Francie.

"Not that I know of."

Francie nails me with a warning look. "Today's world is a dangerous place for a young girl alone," she says.

"Thirty isn't so young," I say, meaning I can take care of myself.

"Exactly," says Francie, meaning it's time I married.

No matter how I dip and dart, the topic of my singlehood follows. I spin the conversation off to the side. "Beth's in the hospital," I say, catching myself as I'm about to mention the MS.

"She must be terribly run down," Mom says. "Grief will do that. I know how close she was with Lily."

"I hope she has insurance," says Aunt Francie. "I have friends who thought they were covered but weren't."

"Actor's Equity," I say. "It's great insurance." I wonder if Beth's found out if they'll cover replacing her old fillings.

The baseball game ends and the men return to the table. To save my sanity, I allow my thoughts to float off to Detective Roblings—how easy he is to be with, how upsetting his suspicions about Beth. I must make him see that Beth is no murderer. Her fragile health, her precious independent life, depend on his believing that. And if he won't back off? Well, then I must simply—or maybe not so simply—get him out of my mind.

As the evening grinds on, Milton hogs center stage, extolling Cleveland's virtues. I find it some small comfort that even my mother's eyes—with their visions of me floating down the aisle in an antebellum gown—begin to glaze over.

TWENTY

IT IS ONE OF THOSE nights my mind won't be quiet. I toss, I turn, sip hot tea, warm milk, read, pace. I'm too hot, I'm too cold. Somewhere around one thirty, I drift off.

Lily London floats toward me, gauzy as a Monet, holding out a sweet piece of kugel. "I'm not hungry," I say. She keeps coming. Syrupy cream drips through her bony fingers, makes dull splats across the floor.

Thunder explodes. I bolt upright, tangled in sweaty sheets. My heart pumps painfully. The clock flashes 12:00 and 12:00 and 12:00. Sometime during the night the storm knocked out power. I turn on my bedside lamp, squint at my watch. It is two in the morning.

Hamlet paces, his sharp nails clicking on the hardwood floors. I flop back in my pillows, trying to recapture sleep before it escapes.

Too late.

Hamlet waits at the side of the bed, tilts his head, gazes up with those big black eyes.

"You just think you're so cute, don't you?" He pants. The thunder scared him, too. "All right," I say, patting the bed next to me.

He jumps up, circles twice, and settles next to me. I am not—repeat, *not*—bonding with this canine Lilliputian. I am simply sprinkling a few drops of the milk of human kindness. I make a nest of my comforter, tucking it around the trembling creature.

I take my script from the nightstand and go over my lines. This usually puts me to sleep. Not tonight. An hour later, I make myself another pot of tea, then curl in bed with the shopping bag filled with Lily's mail. As long as I have the time, I might as well weed out catalogs, flyers, and other junk before I bring the mail to Beth. I toss everything except for a few bills, including a returned electric bill Lily forgot to stamp. There is no personal correspondence, no postcards, letters, invitations. What a sad and solitary person.

Hamlet snores softly. "If it weren't for you, she'd have no one," I say. No wonder Lily took him everywhere. How empty her life would have been without him. Without Beth.

I open an insurance company envelope. Lily's Equity dues statement and check are stapled to a letter bearing the insurance company's letterhead.

Dear Ms. London,
Please find enclosed your Equity check mailed to us in error. We still await your completed medical form 1072A. For your convenience, we enclose another copy of the form. Please fill this out and return it in the enclosed envelope as soon as possible.

The date on the Equity check is a month old. Leave it to Lily to think so far ahead. Not like some of us who race to the office in a panic the day our membership expires. Well, Lily won't be needing Equity or health insurance anymore. I jot a note on the insurance company letter informing them of Lily's death and instruct them to address all further correspondence to Beth.

I have to dig my address book out of my audition bag to look up Beth's zip code. I used to be able to hold a tremendous amount of numbers in my head, addresses, phone numbers, birthdays, anniversaries, some remembered since childhood. But the new longer zip codes, ever-changing Chicago area codes, and people moving to new addresses every other month have done me in. I must write things down. It makes me feel old. I keep forgetting to take a memory course.

A gold Priscilla's Produce label sticks to the cover of my little phone book. Must have fallen off the banana or orange I tossed into my bag at the audition. I press the gold sticker inside my phone book cover. An old habit from my childhood sticker days. There was comfort in that collection.

I have fond memories of Priscilla's, a produce wholesaler on South Water Street. A couple of years back, I worked on a John Hughes movie being shot in the district. No matter how early my first call, the market was already open. The hustlers drove up at 1:00 a.m. bringing truckloads of produce to sell. Buyers rolled in around three. Sidewalks and streets became clogged with crate-filled dollies and trucks. The film company shot interior scenes in Priscilla's, which means I got to spend time with some great characters.

I finish writing Lily's checks and set them aside for Beth's signature. The storm has quieted to a steady rain, and I again try to sleep. My mind won't settle. I am haunted by images of Beth, pale and lethargic, wasting away in that prison of a hospital. The best medicine, of course, would be to catch the real killer so the police would leave Beth alone.

The gold Priscilla's sticker shines like a beacon from my phone book. Maybe, if I find out who sent Wexler the fruit basket with the deadly grapefruit...I flip to Priscilla's number and dial. The phone rings seven times. I'm about to hang up when Angie answers, her harried voice nearly drowned by the din of the morning market.

"Priscilla's."

"Angie, it's Morgan Taylor. I was an actress in the movie—"

"Hey, gorgeous. How're you doin'? Long time. You famous yet?"

"Working on it."

"What can I do you for?"

"Well, it's sort of an odd request. But there was a fruit basket delivered to—"

"Hold on."

The receiver clanks on the desk. Angie goes off, shouting at someone. Street-wise, gum-cracking Angie runs Priscilla's front office. "Angel Angie" we called her. She let us actors use the office phone and the office toilet, and the office heater to warm ourselves between exterior shots. She also made sure there was a steady supply of hot coffee and fresh fruit nearby.

She grabs up the phone. "This place is gangbusters," she says. Lets loose a lusty laugh. "Better call me later. Or come on down. God knows we could use some class."

Come down and do what? But I'm awake and restless and it's a whole lot of long minutes between now and dawn. I figure I've got nothing to lose. Might even stumble on something of use to Beth or Roblings.

I throw on some clothes. Hamlet's little clickity-click nails remind me I have another living creature besides myself to think about. I consider taking him along. Bad idea. Too dangerous with all the crates and trucks and galumphing giants in hob-nail boots. Still, I can't just leave him alone in the storm. I finally turn the bedside radio to a talk station. Hamlet nestles into the comforter, lulled by the sound of human voices.

I'VE MISSED the raw energy of Market Street, the pungent smell, the chaotic urgency. A movie set can do that to me. Ground me in a place so solid it seems part of my natural history. I pull behind a guy loading tomatoes into his truck, wait for his space.

It'll be fun seeing Angie again. She's pure Chicago, hard and sweet, a straight-up gal. For some reason, she thinks she owes me. John Hughes, with his sharp eye for character types, made her an extra in the office scene. I saw she was nervous, taught her a few little tricks, the kind of shtick that gets you on camera as much as possible. She thought I did something miraculous. In truth, she was a natural.

I pull into the space and run through the storm toward Priscilla's, careful not to step on rain-slicked pieces of vegetables and fruits littering the street.

Somehow, Angie survived the final cut of the film, remaining on screen for nearly a full minute. "My family thinks it's the greatest thing since cannoli," she said. Mom always says, what goes around, comes around. Angie is the kind who remembers a favor. I make my way back through the cavernous warehouse to her office.

"Hey, Movie Star." She's all smiles and hugs, a curvy blond with big hair and attitude.

"Hey, yourself. You own this place yet?"

"Who'd want this dump?"

We chitchat between phone calls, pickups, deliveries. There is a rhythm to asking and giving favors. After the right amount of time, Angie asks what I need.

"I'm trying to find out who sent a fruit basket to Martin Wexler." I give Angie the date and address of the delivery.

She sits me at a table and drops a large ledger in front of me. "I don't have time to check the book," she says. "You're welcome to go through the orders, see what you can find."

A steaming cup of fresh-brewed coffee and a carrot bran muffin appear. I settle in, flipping through piles of orders. The names read like a Who's Who of Chicago movers and shakers. Nothing for Wexler. I check other names on orders sent around the same date. Other addresses. Look for something. Anything. Nothing rings a bell.

I tell Angie. She shakes her head. "If the fruit basket came from Priscilla's, it's in that book."

I'm tired. It's possible I missed it. I try again. Nothing.

"Could the police have taken the paperwork?" I ask.

She shrugs. "I was in Cincinnati for a wedding when the cops came around. Marty, one of the owners, said they looked through the orders. They weren't supposed to take anything without saying. But, maybe…"

I go back to the beginning, check the numbers on the orders. They are in sequence. Nothing is missing.

"Every order gets written up in that book," says Angie.

"Not this one."

"Are you sure the fruit was from Priscilla's?"

I take out my phone book, show her the gold sticker.

"Well," says Angie, "unless someone's counterfeiting our sticker, the only way there wouldn't be paperwork is if the fruit was a Peter Ruby."

"What's that?"

"Gift assortment. Real special stuff. From us to whomever.

Like when the Pope came. Or when the mayor's wife had a baby. We crate up a sampler of our best, send it with a card. People like when you do things like that. They remember, tell their friends.''

"Would you have sent a Peter Ruby to Wexler?"

She laughs. "With all the theater in Chicago? We'd go broke sending gifts to every new production. No, no one sends a Peter Ruby without my okay. Wexler never got one."

I'm at the end of it. Brick walls loom in every direction. "There was fruit," I say. "I saw it. Touched it. Put it in my bag. It came from Priscilla's."

Angie glances around. We're alone. "There is one other way," she says. "But you can't say anything."

"What?"

"Sometimes the guys in back pick up a few bucks doing a cash deal. They're not supposed to, but…it's like, someone walks in with a handful of bills. Less than a retail basket would cost, but enough. One of the guys throws together an assortment. Bim bam boom, the basket's out the back door, the cash is in the pocket, and no one's the wiser. That kind of basket doesn't leave a trail."

A crack opens in the brick wall I've been banging my head against. The thinnest shaft of sunlight squeezes through. "Do you think—"

"Forget about it. If that's what happened—and I'm not saying it is—you'll never trace it. A guy does that kind of thing, he keeps quiet. Risk losing his job? No way."

She sees I'm not letting go. That this means something. She remembers she owes me and it's payback time.

"I'll ask around," she says.

"It's important. It's for a friend."

"I'll give it my best shot," she says. "But don't go getting your hopes up."

Too late. It's how we actors pass our lives. And then we die.

TWENTY-ONE

I AM SORELY tempted to drive to rehearsal but can't convince my miser gene to part with fourteen bucks for the parking lot. Unfortunately, the three-sided wind shelter at my El station is worse than useless against rain whipping in from the south. I arrive at rehearsal so sodden, chilled, and exhausted that I risk a cup of coffee from the big pot on the sideboard. People sneak glances to see if I keel over. If I do, it's more likely from lack of sleep than poisoned java.

I set my coffee on the rehearsal table and collapse in a chair. I dragged home from Priscilla's after dawn. Had to walk a terrified Hamlet in the torrential downpour. I seriously considered holding him out a window, see if he'd do his business midair.

Dogs. What a concept.

We actors are not morning people. By evening, you can't shut us up. But we wake up slow. I sip coffee, going over my lines as quietly as those around me.

"Good morning, ladies, gentlemen." Wexler breezes in and starts immediately. No postmortem. No indication that what happened, happened. No mention of the recently entombed Queen Tut. "Today we begin blocking the play."

I brace myself. A play when you're sitting is a whole different animal from a play when you're standing. Until now, I could hide behind the table, my script, cups of coffee. Blocking requires trying to read lines and move at the same time. At best, I find blocking awkward, embarrassing. An entire ensemble standing, exposed. Wexler moves us around, configures us in various combinations while we try to read lines from our scripts. We criss, we cross, we tiptoe around, casting suspicious glances, as if it's the other actors guilty of stinking up the place.

Blocking is bad enough under normal conditions. But it's terrible in this space so recently occupied by Diana's body.

"What are you doing?" Wexler snaps at me. "I told you to cross stage right."

I can't. An invisible negative force field keeps me from stepping on Diana's body. "Maybe we could move the stage to the other end of the loft," I say.

He fixes me with a glare. "It's fine where it is."

I wither. Try again. My moves are skittish, like a horse around snakes. I catch Wexler smiling. He's enjoying keeping me on edge, off balance. I teeter until noon.

A group of us decide to taxi to Rush Street for lunch. We sit over juicy hamburgers at Griller's Café, gossiping, swapping war stories. When we come back, Wexler and his daughter have laid out pages of beautiful costume renderings. We gather around to see what Wexler's New York designer has in mind for our characters.

I look at the sketch of my outfit. "We have a dress like that," I say. The words fly out too fast to catch.

"We?"

"Where I work. At Junque and Stuffe."

I shrug like it's nothing. But the others jump in, telling Wexler all about Harold's fabulous collection of period clothes and accessories, many of which would be great for the play.

"I'd like you to take Evelyn there," says Wexler.

She pulls a pencil from her frizz of red hair, checks her calendar. "I'm free after tomorrow's rehearsal," she says. "If that's good for you."

I speed-scan for a worthy lie. How can I hand-deliver this daughter of the hated enemy into Harold's shop? They stand, waiting. "Sure," I say, "tomorrow's fine."

Afternoon rehearsal goes well. I catch a glimmer of ensemble, a hint of how we might work together. Once we go "off book" and are free to move around unencumbered by scripts and notes, the play will begin to flow. Brenda has learned not only her lines, but all of ours. It makes the rest of us look like sluggards. She has also mapped each of our characters' interior landscape and manages, during moments of quiet time, to share her insights.

"Your character," she confides while Wexler blocks Mother and Son, "is dealing with unresolved anger at an uncle who abused her as a child."

"Brenda, there's no uncle in the play."

She tisks, as if she finds me hopeless. It's mutual. "It is so obvious from the stage directions," she says. "Daughter needs to overcome…"

I tune her out. It's amazing to me how people like Brenda find the time and energy to live so many other people's lives. I can barely manage my own.

We are packing up at the end of rehearsal when someone whispers, "Cop." I glance at the stairs, where Roblings has stopped to catch his breath. The last time he was here, Diana was sprawled on the floor. A few of the cast quickly flow around him down the stairs. Roblings plants himself in my path.

"A moment?" he says.

Brenda and her small clique of anal retentives watch with open interest. I grab my stuff and lead Roblings down the stairs. "Yes?"

"We can't identify some fingerprints on the piece of kugel foil we found in Diana's bag," he says. "Who, exactly, did you see handle it?"

I try to remember. "I watched my mom wrap the kugel in her kitchen."

"Was anyone else around?"

"No. It's just her and Dad, and he went to watch the news. I brought the kugel home. The next morning, I put two pieces in my audition bag. Me and Mom were the only ones I actually saw touching it."

"We have Diana's prints, and yours. I'd like your mother's."

I haven't gotten around to mentioning to Mom how someone poisoned her kugel. I explain this to Roblings as we hit the street. It is still raining.

"Need a lift?" he asks.

Of course I need a lift. I am still clammy from this morning's bout of El-platformitis. But I want to visit Beth in the hospital on my way home and I don't want Roblings tagging along. He has upset her enough.

The wind whips rain in my face. Somewhere a dog barks. Hamlet. I keep forgetting. Before I visit Beth, I need to go home to walk him. I hope he has good bladder control. Bowel control. The thought of what I might find waiting on the rug makes me queasy.

"Thanks," I say. "A ride will be lovely."

HE IS A graceful driver. Weaves in and out of rush-hour traffic with great rhythm. Smooth starts and stops, easy lane changes. A dancer, this Roblings of the big feet. He spins stories of his Los Angeles boyhood, of chasing tiger swallowtail butterflies among lantana that grew big as bushes, "not like the puny plants we get in Chicago." He confesses his recurring nightmare of falling into a La Brea tar pit, being sucked down among the woolly mammoths and other unfortunates encased in primordial tar for all eternity.

A word-weaver, this detective. Mind painter. Storyteller. I feel small pulsings in my nether regions. I am not at all sure I want to feel anything. Not for him. My future lies in the safety of a Lester, a nine-to-five professional man with great quantities of money socked into mutual funds and real estate holdings. I must have a good hard talk with myself, give up this crazy actor's life for something "normal." Normal does not include a Roblings. His type doesn't fit anywhere in that picture.

He coasts to a stop in front of my apartment, turns toward me. I would never grow tired of looking at those eyes. I jump as a car honks impatiently behind us. "Thanks," I say, opening my door, gathering my bags.

"Do you know why Diana came to that first rehearsal?" he asks.

I am so braced for him to make a move on me that I don't, at first, understand what he's talking about. The car honks again.

"Diana was at rehearsal because she was my understudy," I say.

"That's not the reason."

Several cars are honking now.

"You go on in," he says. "I'll park the car and come up."

I smile all the way up the stairs. What does Roblings know about Queen Tut that I don't? Nothing, that's what. It's just a lame excuse to stick around.

Hamlet jumps all over me, wagging his stub of a tail, yapping, racing out of the room, flying back with his leash. A part of me is thawing. Not that I'll ever like dogs, but Hamlet isn't like other dogs. He doesn't drool, smell bad, hump my legs, bark nonstop. Best of all, he peed on the newspaper I laid out, held the rest. God love him.

We're on our way out of the building when Roblings jogs up. I make room for him under my huge golf umbrella, a hopeful gift from Lester. I might have been more receptive to the sport if golf, like skiing, allowed one to swathe oneself in designer sportswear and hang around the chalet without ever having to actually *do* anything athletic. Although, my brother Arthur the Adventurer, who is currently scaling a mountain in Africa, says any activity that doesn't require a jockstrap isn't really a sport. I think he means that for women, too.

I have trouble juggling the leash and holding the umbrella high enough to cover Roblings.

"Let me," he says, taking the umbrella, slipping an arm around my waist as he covers us both. Much better.

"What did you mean about Diana?" I ask.

"When Diana died, I asked Wexler for a list of cast members. Diana was the only understudy on that list. You must have wondered why."

"I assumed Wexler was holding Diana in close reserve in case I loused up."

"Is that usual?"

"No. But just because a thing's never happened doesn't mean I don't live in fear it might. We all have our tar pits."

He laughs. Hamlet stops to sniff a tree. Roblings leans close. His scent mixes with the aroma of spring soil. Not fair. My defenses are dissolving.

"I asked Wexler," he says, "why just Diana, why not under-studies for all the major parts?"

I'm almost afraid to ask. "What did he say?"

"Diana called him after he cast you in the role. She told him you were secretly suffering from multiple sclerosis."

"I'm what?" I shout, startling us all.

"She suggested, because of the disease, you might not be up to the rigors of rehearsal and performance."

Anger rips through me. "That back-stabbing, double-dealing…"

"Easy, sport. She's also dead."

I roll that around a while. It helps put things in perspective. "So, Wexler had her come to rehearsals as insurance."

"He said it was her idea. He couldn't exactly fire you before there was a problem. But if she attended rehearsals, she'd be ready to take over when you fell apart."

"I can't believe Wexler let her move in like that without at least talking to me first."

"About?"

"I don't have MS."

That stops him cold. Obviously, the thought never occurred. "You don't?"

"No."

"What would make Diana came up with something like that?"

It wasn't hard to track. "She must have overheard me at the Equity office. I was checking insurance information for Beth. I guess Diana assumed I was asking for myself."

"So, when you beat her out of the role, she called Wexler."

"Sounds vintage Diana. Now I understand why he's been watching me so closely. He's waiting for me to foam at the mouth or something." Hamlet squats. I turn away, pretending not to notice. "Didn't you think it odd that Beth and I would both have MS?"

"It could just as easily explain the bond between you. People who share particular hardships tend to draw together. Divorce, cancer, death. There's comfort in being with people who under-stand what you're going through."

Hamlet finishes taking care of business and tugs toward home. Roblings and I turn, changing leash and umbrella hands, his other arm sliding nice and tight around my waist. That's when I notice the car.

It's been moving slowly down the street behind us. I'd seen it a couple of times when Hamlet stopped to sniff. I'd noticed it on the far outer fringes, the vague way I might notice the sound of a jet or a distant siren. But when we turn to go back, the car slows to a stop, starts backing up.

"I think that car's been following us," I say.

Roblings's body shifts. Animal on alert, energy focused on the car. The car's windows are rain-streaked. It is hard to see inside. One thing is clear: The driver is definitely staring our way. Roblings takes a couple of steps toward the car. The driver speeds off.

I don't realize I'm trembling until he puts his arm around me. "Probably just someone trying to catch an address," he says.

Oh, I like the feel of this Detective Roblings, the comfort of his large hands on my back. Stop. No more dead-end relationships. I must look toward the future.

"I'm not usually this skittish," I say, pulling away.

"With two murders so close to home, you have a right to be jumpy."

"Do you ever get used to death?"

He chews on this. "No. But I've learned how to hold death at a distance so I can do my work."

Winds gust, whip the rain hard. We run up my stairs, Roblings valiantly trying to shield us with the umbrella. There is an awkward moment in the foyer. He waits for me to ask him up. Part of me wants to. Another part must feed Hamlet, then go to the hospital. I can't mention Beth. Roblings might insist on driving me to the hospital. How can I bring Beth's tormentor to her sickbed? I turn Hamlet loose to run upstairs.

"I have to study my lines for tomorrow," I say, "do more of Lily's paperwork." It is hard for me to turn him away. I am grateful he doesn't push it. I would cave. "Take the umbrella," I say.

"Thanks." Still he doesn't go. "Look," he says. "I still haven't found a logical connection between Lily and Diana's murders. They may be random. But I don't think so. I think they have something to do with your play. Which means any one of you might be next."

"You're scaring me."

"Good."

His kiss comes and goes so quickly he is out the door and down the stairs before it registers. Soft lips, warm. I look out the window, watch my umbrella move swiftly down the block. He'll have to return it, which means we'll see each other again. Wasn't that what I wanted? I know I am sending mixed signals, "Go away—come back," but can't seem to help myself.

I TOWEL RAIN from my hair as I call Beth. At first I think the far-away voice comes from a bad connection.

"I'll call you right back," I say, hanging up, redialing. It's not the connection, it's Beth. I barely recognize her voice. She's slipped into a severe depression. I am thrown off guard. How am I supposed to act? What do I say?

"Maybe," I tell her, "it might be better if I put off my visit until tomorrow. Give you time to rest."

"Yes," she whispers. "Yes, that's good."

I hang up, much relieved. Anything to put off a trip to the hospital. Roblings! I run to the rain-streaked window. Impossible to see. I throw open the window, lean out, look up and down the street.

No sign of him. Two sides of me battle it out. Even if I could see him, would I call him back? Do I really want to start something I may not be able to finish? Maybe when all this murder business is over, when my life is back to normal—as normal as my life ever gets...

I fall into bed with my clothes on and don't move until morning.

TWENTY-TWO

THE THEATER GODS have turned a deaf ear. On the El down this morning, I specifically prayed they make Wexler forget about looking for costumes at Junque and Stuffe. Harold will flay me alive or, worse, fire me for hand-delivering the daughter of his hated rival to his door.

I am barely up the rehearsal-loft stairs when Wexler hails me. "My costumer is flying in from New York," he says. "She'll be here in time to join you and Evelyn on your costume hunt."

I force a smile. "Great."

He hovers a moment. "Feeling all right?"

A casual enough question, until I consider the reasons behind it. I flash a broad smile. "Just fine."

He ambles off and I try not to feel guilty. I briefly consider calling him back, telling him that I don't, in fact, have MS. But, he hasn't mentioned it so why should I? Serves him right. If only he'd talked to me as soon as Diana told him I was sick. I could have set him straight, avoided all those uncomfortable moments of him and his staff sneaking glances at me.

Actors arrive in dribs and drabs, gathering in the rehearsal area.

"Hello, darlings, hello, hello." Annie Andrews, a grand old Chicago actress, sweeps in, blowing kisses. She is as wide as Lily was slender, as effusive as Lily was reserved. Annie exudes the elegant presence of a Helen Hayes, the spunk of a Katharine Hepburn, and the warmth of Maureen Stapleton. It's a dynamite mix onstage and off. We've worked together in a few plays, some staged readings. I've always been a little awestruck. She makes it all look so easy.

She spots me. "There you are!" Cheerful, breezy, unaware the others consider me the prime suspect of the group. She throws open her arms. "Come hug your dearly beloved mum."

"Oh, Annie." I accept the hug. "How wonderful!" What a relief. Unlike Lily London, Annie knows her way around a part, is generous to other actors in a scene.

"I was finishing up a film in France during your auditions," she says, "thought I missed my chance. Then all this terrible business happened and, well, a friend called my agent, my agent called Wexler, Wexler called me, and the rest, as they say, means a paycheck."

"You have no idea how happy this makes me."

For the first time, rehearsal is fun. Annie injects new life into the production. Untainted by horrific memories of Diana's death, she moves across the stage like a cool breeze. My lines flow and I am amazed how rarely I need to refer to my script. God bless Wexler for hiring Annie. If this keeps up, I might just have a great time, get some good reviews, have a long run, get a Jeff nomination. Omigod—what will I wear for the awards dinner?

BY DAY'S END, I am having such a swell time I forget I am supposed to squire Wexler's daughter and costumer to Junque and Stuff. Unfortunately, Rochelle Blanc arrives on cue. She is in her early forties, funky, with an attitude.

About everything.

None of it good.

It's creepy to be introduced to someone who doesn't look at me. Her emerald-green contact-lensed eyes dart like pinballs, up and down and all around. For her, I don't exist.

I slouch in the back seat of Evelyn's car, eavesdropping as she drives us to the shop. The two women gossip about New York theater, their lives, their friends. Being invisible gives me time to formulate a plan, some deception that will allow me to sneak the women past Harold's gossip-sensitive nose. I can't afford to lose my job at Junque and Stuffe.

While Evelyn parks, I lay out the ground rules. "You can't tell Harold who you are," I say.

"Why on earth not?"

Because your father and Harold were in love with the same

man. Because your father stole Harold's lover away from him. I can hardly tell Evelyn the whole sordid story. So I lie.

"Harold's a hungry old shark," I say. "He'll shoot his prices into the stratosphere if he knows you're on budget from the Heartland Theater."

I cross my fingers and keep them crossed as we enter the shop. Harold is his best charming self, kissing hands as I introduce the two women as old theater friends. I never once claim they are *my* old friends. Let Harold draw what conclusions he might.

Evelyn and Rochelle charm Harold right back, fabricate some story about helping out a friend who's costuming a local production. The words *community theater* stick in Rochelle's Broadway-coated throat. But she manages the small lie.

Harold, God love him, is in fabulous form, asking all the right questions, getting a feel for their project. It takes about two seconds for the women to appreciate that they are in good hands. They follow him like converts, up to the attic, down to the basement. Every other sentence out of Rochelle's mouth is "Do you know how much this would cost in New York?"

"If you could find it, my dear," says Harold. "Which, of course, you can't."

Evelyn and Rochelle remain wonderfully vague about their project. The usually prying Harold, much too busy putting the wardrobe together, doesn't press for information. Three hours later, I help them load the garments into Evelyn's car and send the dynamic duo on their way.

I stop back to say good night to Harold. He is glowing.

"Those costumes will absolutely make his play," he says.

Uh-oh. "*His* play?"

"Oh, don't be coy." He replaces trays of jewelry into the display case. "It doesn't suit you."

I tense for the explosion. Nothing. "Did one of the women give it away?"

"Not at all. I thought them both quite accomplished liars."

"Then how did you know they were buying for Wexler?"

He runs a knuckle over his mustache. "I may forget some of my lovers, my dear, but never a character I've costumed." He straightens the accessory display. "They're like old friends. I'd have recognized them anywhere"—a sly smile—"even if several actors in your company hadn't called last night alerting me Wexler's costumer would be in."

"Who called?"

"No matter. Every one of them swore they personally recommended my shop to Wexler. They figured it should be worth some sort of finder's fee."

I take the glass cleaner and paper towels from behind the counter, spray fingerprints off display cases. "You don't seem upset."

"Why ever should I be?"

"You hate Wexler."

"Ah, that. Indeed I do. Though I must admit I'm feeling a tad better now that I've charged him triple my usual prices and added a little finder's fee for each of the actors who called. What better salve for an ancient wound than a little comeuppance?"

Although I am the one who blurted out Junque and Stuffe to Wexler, who hand-delivered Evelyn and Rochelle to Harold's door, I leave without laying claim to a finder's fee. The theater gods have shown mercy after all. My job will be waiting after my run is over. No sense pushing my luck.

TWENTY-THREE

SOMETIMES I BURROW so deep in my own little world that no outside light gets in. Didn't I know Beth was still recovering? Didn't I see her in the hospital so weak she could barely stand? Still, her first night home, I bring Hamlet along when I visit. Yes, I admit I fully intend to leave him.

Beth opens the door, leaning heavily on a four-toed cane. She tries a smile. It doesn't work. I follow her in, heartsick as she navigates furniture in jerks and starts.

"You sit," I say, settling her on a kitchen chair. "I'll cook."

Hamlet jumps up to her lap and she strokes his coat as I chatter nonstop about the play and rehearsals and anything I can think of to push away my fear for her. She listens without energy, an audience I can't reach. This is not my sunny Beth. This is another creature altogether.

"Voilà!" I say, setting out the spaghetti, garlic bread, salad.

She humors me, picks at her food. "This is good. Thanks."

After a while, I can't stand the sound of my own jabbering. I shut up. She flows into the quiet space.

"I lost the industrial," she says. "I told them I was in the hospital with the flu. They were real understanding but they couldn't afford to wait for me."

She stabs her fork into the spaghetti, twirls it around and around. Doesn't bother picking it up. "One way or another, word about my MS is going to leak out." She tilts her head, shifts from soft friend to ballsy hooker, squeezes her tender voice through her nasal passages. "I ain't never gonna get woik in this town again," she says. "I'm on the skids, down and out, a has-been of a never-was."

I smile, grasp this glimmer of the true Beth as a sure sign of hope. I pat her hand. It is icy cold. "Don't make any life decisions until you feel better," I say. "Give yourself time to heal. Any word from the insurance company about replacing your fillings?"

"Nope."

"If you like, I'll call Equity tomorrow. Sic Rosie on them. She'll know how to dig information out of those guys."

"Thanks. That'd be great."

She can barely sit straight. How is she going to take care of herself? "Maybe you should go back to Lyle's place until you're stronger."

"Hard to do, kiddo." Her tears come lightning fast. "We broke up."

"That coward. Did he—"

"No, no, no. I broke up with him. The police have been harassing him because of me."

"You want to blame yourself for global warming, too?" She doesn't smile. I try to rub heat back into her hands. "Beth, the police questioned all of us who were at the loft the day Diana was murdered. That includes Lyle."

"It's more than that. Some cop claims Lyle was following him." She shakes her head. "They're making up stupid things like that, leaning on him because he's my boyfriend. So I broke it off. Maybe now they'll leave him alone."

After dinner, Beth settles on the sofa with Hamlet. They have missed each other. I wish I could leave him here. The little furball seems able to soothe the part of Beth that's in so much pain. I bring her the bag with Lily's mail, hand her the checks I've written, wait as she slowly signs each one.

"It's silly to keep paying rent on Lily's apartment," I say. "You need to think about closing it."

She shakes her head. "I barely have energy to go to the bathroom."

We are quiet as we consider all that's involved in dismantling Lily's seventy-year accumulation.

"Harold," I say.

Beth brightens. "Harold."

"He'll love it. Let him take charge of the whole thing. Run an apartment sale, pay you fair market price for Lily's old costumes and theater memorabilia."

"I need to go through the apartment one last time," she says, "say good-bye. Take a few items that have special meaning."

"Let me know when. I'll drive you. Meanwhile, I'll tell Harold so he can begin setting things up."

Beth starts fading as she signs the last of Lily's checks.

"Come with me," I say. "Stay at my place a few days."

"That's sweet. But I'm better here, with my own stuff."

It's sad to watch Beth and Hamlet say their good-byes. I hope my offer didn't sound insincere. My cowardice in the face of serious illness weighs heavily as I leave.

Halfway to my car, Hamlet stops to sniff a hydrant. An approaching car slows. Little warning shivers stipple my nape, flash across my shoulders. *Act natural.* I bend down, scoop Hamlet into my arms, and casually turn into the nearest apartment entrance. Inside the foyer, I duck against the wall, peer out a side window.

The car creeps past. The driver scans the street for me. I've seen him at the Heartland, one of the set builders, a big bruiser of a man. What does he want with me? He stops, puts the car in reverse, backs up to the building where I'm hiding. I race across to the panel of apartment buttons, push them all.

"Please, please, please," I say, pushing them again, and again. No one buzzes me in. I dash back to the window. He's still there. Looking. Waiting.

My mind races in a million different directions. If he comes in, I'm cornered. If he gets out of the car, heads up the walk, I'll run out, screaming. Throw Hamlet at the thug to distract him while I escape. I am scanning my options when a car parked in front of the building pulls out. The car following me takes the space. Two little heads pop up in the back seat. Children. A hit man doesn't go out on jobs with his kids in tow. The driver gets out. Looks nothing like the set builder. The car was cruising for a parking space, wasn't following me at all.

I leave the safety of the foyer, letting a perturbed Hamlet finish his business at the hydrant. The car, I see now, is not the same car that was tailing me and Roblings the other night. Could that have been Lyle? Beth said he was accused of following some cop. But why would Lyle follow Roblings? And why hasn't Roblings said anything to me?

THERE ARE two messages waiting when I get home. Mom, her voice bubbly, excited, tells me all about having her fingerprints taken down at police headquarters. Leave it to a writer to consider the experience even mildly appealing. Then a nameless, phone-numberless client dictates a lengthy order to his nameless paper supplier. He doesn't leave a number, assumes his order is being taken care of.

This kind of stupidity irks me. Why don't people listen? I clearly state my name and number on my answering machine message. Very clearly, so even a casting director can understand. No one but a total imbecile could mistake my phone for an office-supply house. My anger is bigger than the event. It is not until I am soaking in a hot tub, scented candles burning all around, that I tap into the real source of my anger. There was no message from Roblings. He hasn't called since our walk in the rain. Since I sent him off without inviting him up. I toy with the idea of calling him. What do I want from the man?

TWENTY-FOUR

REHEARSALS SPEED BY. Our ensemble is hyped. Macabre interest in the play's dark history coupled with Lily and Diana's murders have sold out the house for the first few weeks.

Every morning I open the papers and read another of Evelyn's little publicity teasers—sly innuendoes, second-guesses, vague rumors. Wexler is all over, on TV and radio interviews, local entertainment and news shows.

The swell of energy propels us through rehearsals. We are mounted square on the back of a winner, racing hell-bent for opening night.

It can't last.

I brace for tech week syndrome, await my insipid inevitable shift from euphoria to panic. One night I go to sleep confident that I *own* the play, and the next morning I bolt awake, terrified I'll forget every bit of dialogue and stage business.

Tech week rehearsals are a nightmare. I make the same dumb mistakes over and over and over. Demon voices taunt:

You're no good.

You're going to get fired.

You can't do it.

If my days are dismal, nights are hell. I can't sleep.

The script stinks.

The producer stinks.

The director stinks.

The other actors are obnoxious human beings.

I am angry at everyone and everything.

Roblings. Why doesn't he call? I've begun falling asleep fantasizing how the scene would have played had I invited him up that night. Several times I start to dial his number, hang up. Again. And again. Then I dial, wait until it rings, and hang up.

My phone rings. I practically rip it off its cradle.

Not Roblings. Not nearly. A monotoned tenor introduces himself. Another of Mom's poker club's fix-ups. I tolerate him for ten minutes, painting dark red polish on my toes as he crawls through a detailed account of how he reconditions fifty-five-gallon steel drums for resale to the secondary market.

The Lord works in mysterious ways.

I hit my boredom limit, cut him off, have no trouble at all dialing Roblings. I am, of late, attracted to fewer and fewer men. I must learn to strike when there is even faint interest. Besides, it's not as if I am without real, concrete, defendable reasons for calling. I have several. His need to return my umbrella. My need to inquire about Mom's fingerprints. And to ask if it was, in fact, Lyle in the car following us that night.

I feel warm fuzzies when he answers.

"Morgan?" he says. Sounds of the police station echo in the phone. "Morgan Taylor. Name sounds vaguely familiar."

"*Time* magazine's Woman of the Year," I say, "cover of the *Sports Illustrated* swimsuit issue, lead article in *Variety*."

"Ah, that Morgan."

We fall into easy conversation and I wonder why I waited even one day to call. He puts me on hold. When he picks up again he has moved to a quiet room.

"You think that was Lyle following us?" I ask.

"I know it was. I caught the license plate numbers, ran a trace. He claims he just happened to be driving in the neighborhood."

Neither of us believes that. But I let it drop.

"Your mom's a nice lady," says Roblings. "Made me give her a tour."

"She had a good time. Were her fingerprints a help?"

"I'm left with one unidentified print on the kugel foil. A fourth person handled it."

I shiver. "The killer."

Someone calls his name. "I've got to go."

I don't want him to. "Next Thursday," I say. "Our preview. I'd like you to come."

"What time?"

"Eight o'clock."

"I'll be there."

"I'll leave your name with the box office."

He hangs up and I immediately want to call back, tell him to forget it. If he's in the audience, I'll be doubly nervous. The preview, coming at the end of tech week, is the first time we perform in costume. Its function is to get us used to an audience. Wigs fall off. Dress trains get caught in piano benches. Props fall or fail. Previews are always awful. Always.

What if *I'm* awful? What if he hates the play? What if he's like Lester, who once said my actor friends remind him of tall children? What if…

"If, if, if," Grandma Belle likes to say. "You worry too much, tatalah. If, if, if. If my grandmother had balls she'd be my grandfather. You've got to be like the old Eskimo put out to sea. Just go with the floe."

I've lost count of Grandma Belle's husbands. Four, for sure. A couple more she hints at from time to time. She loves her little secrets. I never could understand her need to be married. She can't understand my reluctance.

I slide between the cool sheets, hoping sleep finds me quickly. Hamlet paces. Waits until I pat the bed. He's up in a flash, curled at my feet.

Adam wanted to get married, start a family, but I wasn't ready. For some reason, I thought he'd hang around until I was. Grandma Belle was the only one who came right out and told me it served me right when Adam left me for Sylvia. "Maybe next time," she said, "you will be quicker to say yes."

"But what if it doesn't work out?" I asked.

"You want guarantees?"

"I don't like surprises."

She has a deep, throaty laugh. "Surprises are the best reason to keep living. If you know how the movie ends, why bother going? One man is only one man. There will always be plenty of other bees buzzing around your honey."

Except I don't want to settle for drones. Life's too short for mediocrity.

I begin to drift. Maybe that's what intrigues me about Roblings, my inability to define the man. He seems to shift each time I see him. It's true, I don't like surprises. But it's even more true that I bore easily, lose patience with people who are always the same. I am attracted to the ones who are continually unfolding. Roblings is the unfolding type.

Why didn't I invite him to come the following week, to see the real play at a real performance? I fall into a troubled sleep, knowing the answer, wishing I didn't. I don't want to wait that long to see him again.

TWENTY-FIVE

I FIDGET ON the stoop outside Lily's apartment.

Beth called early this morning. "I am going stir crazy," she said. "I'd like to go over to Lily's, pick out a few keepsakes before we close the apartment. Do you still have her key?"

"I do, indeed."

"I know your previews start tomorrow. I wouldn't bother you if I weren't absolutely climbing the walls."

"Not a problem. I can meet you there right after rehearsal."

I am so relieved Beth feels strong enough to venture out that I push aside my own need to have a quiet, meditative night before tomorrow's opening.

Lyle's car pulls up, catches me off guard. Looks like their breakup was all smoke and mirrors. A split meant to throw cops off his trail but keep him in her life. I am not emotionally prepared for a face-to-face with Lyle. I have some tough questions he might not want to answer.

It takes a while for Beth to climb the stairs to the apartment. She wrinkles her nose at the stuffy air. Lyle and I jump to open windows. "I'd like to go through Lily's things alone," Beth says, abandoning me and Lyle to the living room.

I break a nail prying open a reluctant window. "Why were you following us the other night?" I say.

He tries to look surprised. "I wasn't following you. I—"

"Lyle, I saw you. Saw your car."

"Let me finish?"

I fold my arms across my chest.

"I'd just come from the hospital. Beth was in such a bad way, so depressed, I...I didn't know what to do. I thought talking to you, someone who loves Beth as much as I do, might help. I was pulling up to your apartment when you came out with some guy.

It was hard to tell in the rain, but he looked like that detective. I couldn't believe you would be so lovey-dovey with the cop who's hounding Beth.''

"So you followed?"

Lyle looks sheepish. "The second he turned my way, I knew it was him. There can't be another mug that ugly on this earth."

Of all the ways I think about Roblings, ugly isn't one of them. I've always preferred weathered faces to pretty boys.

"Not that it's any of your business," I say, "but he gave me a lift home from rehearsal. We didn't even talk about Beth. It was the way you were shadowing us that made him wonder."

Lyle's eyes narrow. His voice turns low, threatening. "You'd better watch out for that guy. He's too suspicious of everything and everyone. You can't trust someone like that."

"Well, right this moment, I'm not so thrilled with you, either." I head back to check on Beth.

I find her crying softly over a pile of Lily's clothes. With all that's been going on in her life, Beth hasn't had time to mourn her old friend's death.

"I'll go out to the cemetery this weekend," she says, "lay flowers on her grave."

I soothe a hand over her back. "Anything I can do?"

She looks around the room, takes in the sheer volume of Lily's possessions. "It's overwhelming. I thought I had a lot of paperwork with being sick. Medical record keeping, files. But death, death is an avalanche. There's no end to what needs to be done."

"I asked Lester if he'd help you with the legal stuff."

"He called last week," she says. "Came to see me in the hospital. What a sweetheart." She runs a hand absently over one of Lily's puffy-sleeved sweaters. "He's been fabulous, putting in way too many hours getting my life organized. And he absolutely refuses to send any sort of bill. Every time I ask he says, 'A friend of Morgan's is a friend of mine.'"

That makes me feel nice and guilty. Lester's helping Beth, hoping he and I will get back together. We won't. He has to know that. I'll try to break it to him gently. Again.

Beth sets the sweater on a pile of sweaters just like it. "I've sent him some of my special homemade brownies by way of thanks," she says. "I'll pay him a real fee as soon as we settle Lily's will."

She finishes culling the items she wants, a few photos, Lily's fishing-tackle makeup box, a Spanish shawl with long silken fringe. She stops a moment on the way out of the apartment, takes one last slow look around.

"Call Harold," she says softly, "tell him to go ahead, sell what he can, donate the rest."

The bright sun is a shock after the dark apartment.

"We'll drive you home," says Beth. "Now that I'm out in the real world, I hate to go back inside. Is that ice cream place still on your corner?"

We stop for double-dip cones. Beth wants to try to walk a little way, so we stroll down the block to my building. A florist's truck pulls up. The driver juggles a large white box while scanning the mailbox names.

"Help you?" I ask.

"Lookin' for Morgan Taylor."

"That's me."

"These are for you."

I tangle with the box while Beth and Lyle hover. The "Break a Leg" card is signed *J.R.*

"Keeping secrets?" teases Beth. "A new man in your life?"

"This is nothing like that," I say, my face on fire.

She laughs. "Have you checked the price of roses lately?"

"Roblings," says Lyle.

I could kick him.

"Auto-da-fé Roblings?" Beth shivers. "You have very strange taste in men."

"I like who's talking," I say. If Lyle takes offense, he doesn't show it.

Beth and I kiss good-bye and I promise to give her a detailed account of tomorrow night's performance.

ROBLINGS IS OUT OF his office. I don't leave a message. I'll thank him in person tomorrow night.

I stand at the sink, going over my lines as I clip rose stems on a slant under running water, a trick learned from Grandma Belle. A oft-married woman receives many flowers along the way, learns many useful tricks. "The running water keeps oxygen from entering the fresh cut," she told me, "makes the flowers last longer." At least I take her advice about some things.

I am carefully setting each magnificent salmon-colored rose into a glass vase when Hamlet starts whimpering. He's standing at his empty food bowl, which sits next to his empty water bowl. It's amazing I haven't killed him yet. Although, it's still early in our relationship.

I abandon the flowers to take care of him. Spoon food from the tin, cut it into little pieces, wash and fill the water bowl. I finish putting the flowers into water, then sit cross-legged on the floor next to Hamlet, scratch his head as he chows down. Giving sustenance to another living creature creates a peculiar satisfaction.

He stops a moment. Looks up into my eyes. Blinks. Waits. Tilts his head. Does that floppy-ear trick. Makes a small whimpering sound.

"Yeah, okay," I say, "okay. I like you, too."

He smiles. I swear. Then goes back to his meal.

Now that Beth's better, she'll probably be wanting Hamlet back. Why doesn't this delight me? If I didn't know me better, I'd think I was hoping to have him around a little while longer.

TWENTY-SIX

I PREPARE the canvas, cleansing my face with astringent-soaked cotton pads, studying myself in the dressing-room mirror. Over the next twenty minutes, I metamorphize from me to Her. Daughter is much paler. Hard lines pull down the corners of her mouth. Dark circles ring her eyes. Her life has been hard and cruel and she wears it like a badge.

The interior landscape shifts as well. Every line of makeup helps me make the emotional shift from Morgan to Daughter. I ache with her despair, am weighed by her depression, suffer the pain of her heavy heart. I think of Beth, unfair target of a murder investigation, trapped in a body that has betrayed her. She grieves for a dead friend. Suffers guilt for involving her boyfriend. The depth of her anguish overwhelms me. I draw on it to build Daughter. By the time I finish making up, the world has gone bleak; I see no point in going on.

Time is called and, as I move toward the stage, I catch my heel, tearing the hem of my dress. Wanda from Wardrobe stitches me up. "Hold still," she says, but Daughter fidgets, edgy about yet another fight with Mother. Murray Banks, aka Brother, hands me my missing earring. "Found it in a shoe in the men's costume area," he says. Theater elves, no doubt, sneaking around, leaving objects in all the wrong places. The earring, its mate back in the dressing room, will have to wait until I make up for act 2.

I take my place onstage. Theater dust settles in my nostrils, coats my throat, dries my lips. The undercurrent of audience hums through me. My heart has grown to three times its normal size, thuds painfully against my ribs.

House lights down. Cue music. Curtain up. Applause, applause.

I am off like a shot, words and movements racing before thought. Much too fast. I bring down the pace. The night moves on. Lights mis-cue, lines go unanswered, doors stick, music fades in and out. Preview night is everything I feared it would be. But we are a troupe of professionals. Remain cool under fire. So cool we are unfazed by the assortment of disasters making the audience laugh in all the wrong places.

By the middle of act 2, we find our rhythm. Since intermission, Daughter's outlook has taken a huge turn for the better. In this act, she falls in love and defeats Mommy Dearest. My between-acts trip to the makeup box put a rosy blush on her cheeks, removed the circles from under her eyes, and turned up the frown lines around her mouth. Daughter has become less Timid Beth, more Flamboyant Grandma Belle. I pick up the tempo, play the part broad, for laughs.

Five, ten, fifteen minutes fly by with nary a glitch. During my brief moments offstage, I sneak glimpses at the audience from the wings. Roblings is not in the seat I reserved for him. But my sister Sylvia is here. Last row, far right. She sits unsmiling among laughing strangers. She's come alone—no Adam, no Mom and Dad—to watch her big sister. The same way she has come to every preview week of all my plays. My cue snaps me back into the play and I leave her behind.

Near the end, waiting in the wings for my final cue, I peek out from behind the curtain and spot Roblings in the back of the theater. Pacing. Nervous energy? A little attention deficit disorder, perchance? Sylvia's seat is empty. She left so I wouldn't know she'd come. It's like Sylvia not to want to upset me. I feel a twinge of tenderness, a pale shadow of sisterly love. This time anger is slower to wash it away.

As I move closer to the stage, focusing on Annie, who is delivering my cue, I feel my earring pop out. I whirl, snatch it midair. Something whizzes past my head—where my head would have, could have, should have been, *was*, in fact, mere milliseconds ago—and crashes at my feet.

Glass and metal explode. I stifle a scream, cannot move. The floor is covered with the twisted remains of an overhead light can. Onstage, I see Annie mouth her lines, but I cannot hear. Characters around her begin ad-libbing, their movements jerky, off tempo, stalling. I cannot move. Annie does an elaborate bit of stage business with a piece of candy, which gives someone backstage enough time to figure out what needs to be done. I am pushed onstage. Cannot think of my line.

Annie touches my arm. Repeats her last line and tucks in a few words of what I need to say. Thank God *responsible* actors learn all the lines. I hear my voice, feel my mouth working on automatic. My movements feel stiff as a fifties hairdo. I manage to make it to the end.

Two actors lock their arms in mine, hold me up for the curtain call. I can't stop shaking. Death came to visit, its foul breath a whisper away. I force a smile, watch as the audience disappears behind the closing curtain.

The cast surrounds me.

"What happened?"

"Are you all right?"

"It sounded like a bomb."

I am numb. The specter of death looms a whole lot larger when it's aiming at me.

Roblings is in the wings as we come offstage. He and the stage crew huddle over the wreckage. The rest of the cast files slowly past, pausing to take a look, like mourners at a wake. I bring up the end, grateful it's not my body on view.

"You okay?" asks Roblings.

I hug myself, still shaking. "What happened?"

He points to the connecting end of the light can. "It looks as if the threads are stripped."

"On purpose?"

"That leko's older than God," says one of the stage crew.

I'm not convinced. "Someone could have rigged it," I whisper to Roblings. "Someone who wanted me—"

"It looks like an accident."

"But—"

"You were great in the play."

"Are you trying to distract me?"

"Yup." He leads me away. "But that doesn't mean I don't think you were great."

I wasn't. But I'm relieved he thinks so. We follow the cast toward the dressing room. Family and friends crowd the corridor. Roblings stops outside the door.

"You're sure you're all right?"

"Shaky."

"You have every right. That was a nasty scare."

"You really think it was an accident?"

"I'm going back, take a closer look."

"Good."

"Can I buy you dinner?"

"Tonight?"

He laughs. "Yes, tonight."

Wexler's sure to hit me with notes I'll need to absorb before the next performance. But, hey, you gotta eat. "Give me ten minutes to change and scrape off an inch of makeup."

"I'll be here."

I find that incredibly comforting.

Everyone in the dressing room is laughing, chattering. The men lob sweaty socks over the partition dividing our dressing areas. I usually like to take my time after a performance, languish in the warm womb of giddy gossip. Tonight, I'm a wreck from the double hit of performance and near-death experience. I cream off makeup, tear off my costume, dress in my civvies, and toss my gear in my bag. I am half out the door when Annie stands and claps her hands for attention. "You are all invited back to my apartment for wine and pizza," she says. "My treat."

A chorus of insincere protests goes up.

"I insist," she says. "It's something I want to do in Lily's memory. I know in my heart, she should be standing in my place onstage. Please, feel free to bring your friends."

She passes out little slips of paper with her address. I take one, tell her I'll try to get there. It's an empty promise. There's no way I'll bring Roblings. He'd be too out of place. Also, I'm feeling the need for some quiet, settle down my innards.

Wexler comes in. "If I might have your attention a few minutes," he says. "I have notes."

The ten-minute wait I promised Roblings stretches into a half

hour. I edge toward the door, desperate to leave but not daring
to. The second Wexler finishes, I bolt for the lobby.

Roblings is gone. I check inside the theater, backstage. I finally
find him outside, leaning against the building, enjoying the warm
night air.

"Sorry," I say. "Wexler kept us after school."

"Hungry?"

"Ravenous."

"Come on. I'll buy you the best meal in town."

TWENTY-SEVEN

MY DIGESTIVE SYSTEM is on full battle alert—stomach growling, tongue swimming in expectant juices, head lighter than usual—as we walk east from the theater toward Monroe Harbor. The only class-act food spot in this direction is the yacht club. Veddy tony. I sure didn't peg Roblings as the yachting type. Then again, I'm a chronically lousy judge of character. Just ask my mother's poker club.

I glance down, checking whether one might see the hidden row of tiny gold safety pins holding up my torn hem, if one should care to look. Seems all right. Over the years I've become adept at invisible pinning. Learning to wield a needle and thread is way down my *long* list of "Things I Really Should Learn to Do." With luck, the yacht club will have the kind of subdued lighting designed to mute the lines of aging faces. My clothes, with their interesting collection of tears, stains, and wrinkles, don't stand up well to bright lights.

We reach Monroe Street and the Drive just in time to miss the world's shortest green light. Twelve lanes of high-speed traffic whiz past. Roblings offers his arm as we wait. I take it. It'll help slow my fall if I pass out from hunger.

It bothers me that Roblings has not mentioned the play. Oh, sure, he threw out some obligatory compliment following the performance. But I crave more. Like most actors, I long to talk about Me after a performance. And I so rarely get the chance. The trick, here, is to introduce the subject without seeming to. Casually bring his thoughts back to the theater.

"I still can't believe that light nearly killed me," I say. "You're positive it fell by accident?"

"Someone would have to have been standing on a very tall ladder in order to drop it on you."

I'd been alone in the cramped wings. "I probably would have noticed a ladder."

He smiles. "Figured you might."

A thought niggles. "Could the can have been rigged? Released by some kind of remote control? I mean, anyone who's seen rehearsals knows I'm the only one in that spot at that time of the performance."

"I checked everything. The threads were stripped from years of use. It was a freak accident."

I believe the man, allow myself the luxury of relief. He still doesn't mention anything about tonight's performance. Oh, sure, it's possible for me to say "Did you enjoy the play?" but that feels like begging. I prefer to formulate a clever line, idea, introductory thought—arrange a few bon mots about my fellow actors, the evening's more amusing moments, titillating inside gossip.

I am working on the exact phrasing when the light changes and we head out across the drive. We nearly make the other side when a blonde in a snazzy red car, anticipating the green light, jumps into the intersection, slamming on her brakes inches from Roblings's legs. She lays on her horn.

I feel Roblings's firm hand on my back gently push me onto the safety of the curb. Instead of moving, he plants himself in front of her car, staring at her. Never mind that she now has the light, that cars behind her honk. She leans out her window, yelling something lost in the roar of traffic. I know her type, played her enemy in a couple of movies. She is a movie-line cutter, a sneaky lane-changer, considers societal laws and rules for ordinary, less beautiful people. She steps on people so often she doesn't notice the bodies anymore. Until she comes up against someone like Roblings.

She is still screaming, an ugly mouth on such a beautiful face. Roblings slowly lifts his arms, his massive hands spreading up and out. I think: Lon Chaney, sitting at the piano in *Phantom of the Opera*, about to strike the first chord. Suddenly, Roblings slams his hands on the hood. The car rocks violently. The sound carries like a shot across night traffic. The driver jerks her head inside, frantically rolls up her window. She stops honking, has the good sense not to make rude gestures.

She looks around. Her wide eyes say "This man is obviously mad." No one seems interested in becoming involved. Cars behind her pull away.

Roblings holds up a hand and waggles a finger at her. Naughty girl. He takes his own sweet time ambling toward me. As soon as he clears the bumper of her car, she peels away. A calm man, this Roblings. Grounded. But that is not to say he is a man without passion. I can't remember ever meeting anyone quite like him. I'll have to study him more closely.

"Still hungry?" he says.

"Can't wait."

We walk along the joggers' path skirting Lake Michigan. I have *steak* seared so deep in my thoughts that I don't immediately understand why Roblings is leading me into line behind a stream of fishermen, tourists, Rollerbladers. I'm thinking Caesar salad, double-baked potato. I am not thinking Tony's Pump Room, the name stenciled in neon colors on the side of the metal hot-dog cart. A toothless old man wearing a Cubs hat and White Sox T-shirt serves up hot dogs and Polish to a line of late-night diners.

No! I need real food. Sustenance. Something requiring a china plate and metal utensils. The words are almost out when it occurs to me this may be all the good detective can afford. What if Roblings supports three ex-wives and fifteen rug rats, as well as aging parents and assorted siblings? What do I know of his situation?

I am sorely tempted to offer to treat us to a grand meal except: (1) I don't have that kind of money, and (2) I don't have that kind of money.

A twentysomething couple in line ahead of us can't keep their hands off each other. I realize I am staring when Roblings gently directs my attention toward the boats bobbing in the harbor. For the first time, I notice what a beautiful evening this is. Full moon on still water. Balmy air. Seductive smells of hot dogs and pretzels. The line moves up. The couple in front of us progresses from playful kissing to an open-mouth-probing-tongue sort of thing. Roblings, facing me, misses the show.

"I've got some good news and some bad news," he says.

I brace myself. He hated the play. Hated my performance. "Give me the bad news first."

"I'm having trouble identifying the fourth set of prints."

"Prints?"

"Fingerprints. On your lunch. The kugel foil?"

"Ah." I force my mind from Play to Murder, affect a nasal Mae West. "So, you still don't know who done it."

"Right."

"And the good news?"

"The prints don't match any of the cast members."

"Thank goodness. You wouldn't believe how we've been watching each other."

The amorous couple has become entangled, arms and legs twisted like a monkey puzzle tree. Roblings catches something in my look. Turns to see. Stares with open interest. Takes his own sweet time turning back to me.

"Can you think of anyone else who might have had access to your lunch? Anyplace besides the rehearsal loft where you might have—"

I shake my head. "I've gone over it a hundred times. It went from Mom's kitchen to my kitchen to rehearsal."

"No one was in your kitchen?"

"No one." I speak slow and clear. "Not Beth. Not Lyle."

Chef Tony barks a command and the lovers break apart long enough to order. We move up. My stomach rumbles, a five on the Richter scale. Roblings is polite enough not to notice.

"That means," he says, "someone snuck into rehearsal, rummaged through your bag, poisoned one piece of kugel, left without being seen."

"That's not as impossible as it sounds. The first day of rehearsal is a total zoo."

"But it's risky. Very risky. What if you caught them, or someone else had seen them?"

I shrug. "Sounds like the murderer is either dumb or lucky."

"I don't think dumb."

"That's not very comforting."

"Murder usually isn't."

"Know what's really scary? If Diana didn't steal my food, I'm the one who'd be six feet under. You'd be standing here all alone."

It's our turn. Tony takes one look at Roblings and starts assembling his order.

"Hey," Tony directs his rasp my way, "what's a classy lady like you doing with this bum?"

"You know," Roblings tells him, "you're not the only hot-dog stand in the city."

"The only good one." Tony loads Roblings's dogs into a cardboard box, adds Orange Crush and chips, then winks at me. "What'll you have, gorgeous?"

I look at the two hot dogs smothered with fresh tomatoes, chopped onions, peppers, relish, mustard, sprinkled with celery salt. I am so hungry I can barely talk. "That looks perfect."

"Beautiful *and* smart," says Tony. He fixes the dogs and hands them to me with a slight bow. "This should take the edge off."

Roblings takes out his wallet. "Get outta here," Tony growls, "you're blocking my paying customers. Next!"

WE SIT ON the jetty, dangle our feet over the lake. The beam of the full moon reaches toward us across still waters. I practically inhale the first hot dog, washing it down with an icy cream soda. Roblings paces himself, a neat eater. He catches me watching.

"The best," he says.

"The best."

Roblings tosses fragments of hot-dog bun into the water. There is sudden movement beneath the surface, thrashing, like water coming to a boil. A nearby fisherman casts a line our way. Off to our left, Navy Pier's giant Ferris wheel circles lazily. Faint voices float down. Happy voices.

"A Chicago hot dog," says Roblings. "Moonlight on the lake."

"A brilliant and breathtakingly beautiful companion."

He smiles. "I was going to say that next."

He bends toward me, slowly, his breath all celery salt and mustard and Vienna Kosher. I swear, this man has the softest lips in the world. I worry briefly about tongue, my mouth still working on bits of hot dog and chips, but his kiss is a pristine foray, short and sweet.

After, we stroll along the shore toward Navy Pier. Moths to light. The narrow mile-long building, formerly ship dock, university, Indian powwow site, convention hall, is enjoying its newest incarnation as a major city attraction. Bright, bold, and lively, it sparkles with Las Vegas wattage. We weave through the sculpture garden, local artists' works sprouting like exotic plants along the lake. Vendors hawk souvenirs and food from pushcarts. A crowd leaving the Imax Theatre pushes past us. The moan of a tenor sax from a live blues band floats in the air, invites people to come and dance.

It must be Roblings's protective arm around my shoulder that makes me think it's all right to get on the Ferris wheel. It isn't until the gondola door slides shut and the ride begins that air presses in around me. It's hard to breathe.

Inhale.

Exhale.

Slow and easy. Calm. Stay calm. Stupid. How could I be so stupid? I panic on any balcony higher than the first floor, can't breathe in glass elevators sliding up and down the outsides of buildings. What am I doing heading five stories up in a Ferris wheel?

Our gondola rocks slightly in the night air. I gasp. Roblings squeezes my shoulder reassuringly. Slow, now, easy. The wheel will not tip over. The gondola will not disengage and plunge us to certain death. The ride will be over in ten minutes. I can last ten minutes. I can last—

"I've been digging through theater archives," says Roblings. "Found some information on the original production of the play. Came across your boss's name."

"Of course. Wexler was the original director."

"No, I mean your other boss."

It takes me a moment. "Harold? How do you know—?"

"The morning Diana was murdered, you said you stopped by Junque and Stuffe to pick up your pay."

"I did."

"I know."

"You checked me out?"

"Don't sound so hurt. It's my job."

"Why would I lie about something like that?"

"You wouldn't believe the things people lie about."

Tension creeps into my shoulders, welds my neck in place. I crick my neck side to side, roll it around a bit. Roblings rubs his thumb in circles between my shoulder and neck. Heaven. I don't mean to moan. It just slips out.

"Tell me about Harold," he says.

Dilemma. Yes, I want Roblings digging for a murderer someplace other than in Beth's backyard. But I sure don't want him bothering Harold. "Aren't there other suspicious people around," I say, "people I don't know, don't care about?"

"I don't create suspects," he says. "I work with what I've got. I'm not much of a believer in coincidence, which is why it interests me that Harold was involved in this play, knew Lily, forty years ago."

"You are way off base on this one. Harold's a sweetheart. A *harmless* sweetheart. Hires actors so we don't starve between roles. Pays us on time. He also happens to be one of the best sources of theater gossip in the city."

"What's he like?"

"He's a fabulous friend. If Harold likes you, there's nothing he won't do for you."

"And if he doesn't like you?"

Aye, there's the rub. Harold can be a bitch on wheels. Destroy you with one scathing look, one well-aimed word. I've seen him in action in the store. He does not suffer fools gladly. Roblings waits. A gust of wind hits the gondola broadside, sets us swinging. This is not fun.

"And if he doesn't like you?" Roblings says again.

"You are *so* on the wrong track," I say.

Roblings sees I'm not going to bad-mouth Harold. He regroups. "Did Harold like Lily? Diana?"

This man doesn't let go. Only one thing for it. I slip into my Liza Doolittle cockney. " 'E 'ated them," I say. "Loathed and detested, is wot. Thought they overacted something fearful. Hacked 'em into wee small pieces with an antique silver butter knife and served 'em to the 'ogs."

Roblings is not amused. That's tough. He started it. This is the slowest Ferris wheel in the world. I look down. Big mistake. Dizzy. I am not going to make it out alive. Far down the pier, a big band strikes up. "Stella by Starlight" floats on the night air.

"Look," he says, "two women are dead."

"Well, Harold didn't kill them."

"Then let me find that out. Stop protecting him."

"I'm not—"

"Did he know Diana?"

"No. I don't think. At least, not personally."

"But he'd know who she was."

"Harold lives for the theater. Sees everything in town, no matter how awful."

"That's a yes?"

"Yes."

"And we know he and Lily go back at least as far as the first production of your play. Could there have been anything between them?"

"You mean romantically?"

"Anything. Love, hate, friendship."

"She was hardly his type, for any of that." How much do I tell without betraying a confidence? Since Harold makes no secret of his sexual orientation, I give that up to Roblings. He asks a few easy questions, probes so gently that before we're back on the ground, he's somehow gotten me to spill the forty-year-old tragedy of how Wexler stole Harold's young lover.

"The boy turned out to be Lily's son," I say. Roblings's left eyebrow goes up. "Then he died. Asthma attack." His other eyebrow lifts. The light is dim but I think I make out a smile. The big band music swells dramatically, underscoring my story. The effect is comical, melodramatic. "He died," I say, "without ever knowing Lily was his mother."

Roblings has the good grace not to laugh. "Some soap opera," he says.

"You can't make up a story like that."

"Who would want to?"

"Exactly."

Maybe it's the music, but the whole thing suddenly sounds silly. All that intrigue, unrequited love, secrets, death, a mother's loss. Yet it seemed so believable when Harold told me. I suspect the problem is Roblings. He lacks the actor's willingness to suspend disbelief, our insatiable craving for drama. A trip to the grocery, a visit to traffic court, a walk through the Laundromat; we create theater everywhere in our lives.

My legs wobble when I step out of the gondola. Roblings slips a hand under my elbow and we join the stream of people strolling along Navy Pier. Grandma Belle has a variety of photos of her and three of her husbands walking like this along the old Edgewater Beach Hotel boardwalk. It always looked so romantic, my grandmother beautifully dressed with matching gloves and shoes, gazing lovingly into her husbands' eyes as they strolled along the lake. I used to stare at the photos, fall into them, fantasize walking the boardwalk with my husband one day. I was a teen before I learned the city had torn down the boardwalk years ago, hauled in a zillion tons of landfill, created acres of public park and a six-lane expressway where Lake Michigan used to be.

I assume Roblings has been quiet because he, too, is enjoying the walk. I am wrong.

"None of my research," he says, "turned up any hint of Wexler's homosexuality."

Great. The whole time I'm gearing up to feel all warm and sexy, he's been chewing on what I told him about Harold. Tenacious, this Roblings. Not much comfort on a cold night, I wager.

I repeat what Harold told me. "Those were repressive times. Wexler was the bright young darling of the theater world, couldn't risk the wrong kind of exposure."

"Isn't that pretty redhead his daughter?"

"You think she's pretty?"

"I think she's proof Wexler had at least some sexual interest in women."

"He may have dated to hide his homosexuality."

Roblings whistles a soft tune between his teeth. My father also whistles while he thinks. It used to annoy me until I moved into my own apartment. Now I find it kind of endearing. Roblings stops midwhistle. "So, you don't think Wexler and the late great Lily London might have had one of those director-actress affairs?"

I laugh. "You never met Lily."

"I'll take that as a no. And you also don't think Harold and Lily…"

"Not a chance."

His beeper sounds. We find a phone and I wait while he makes a call. "I have to go," he says.

He can move fast when he wants, this plodding detective. We hail a cab and are back at his car in five minutes. He offers to drive me home but I am too wound up from the evening. I ask him to drop me at Annie's place. I've had enough of civilians for one evening. What I crave is the family of theater people.

TWENTY-EIGHT

ANNIE'S DUPLEX, joined at the hip to its twin next door, is nestled in the bosom of a blue-collar neighborhood. The street of two-story buildings sits dark, quiet, all the God-fearing hardworking neighbors snug in their beds. Only Annie's place is ablaze with lights.

A crowd of people smoke on the front porch or sit on the tiny lawn. More people have spread out onto the neighbor's porch, lounging in wicker chaises and chairs. I hope they don't make trouble for Annie. She probably didn't know what she was letting herself in for when she invited us all over.

Theater people track free food and good company like heat-seeking missiles. We tend to turn out in great numbers for funerals and parties. I squeeze past the bodies sprawled on the stoop, side-step pizza boxes and beer cans, wade through the pungent haze of cigarettes, cigars, and pot.

I recognize stage crew, friends of cast members, theater friends. Annie has also invited staffers from SAG, Equity, a few of the other theaters. This is probably her one big party for the year. Maybe the decade. If I had the money I'd do this, take care of all my entertaining in one evening. I owe everyone. Not that actors keep score. Whoever is flush shares. Except, of course, for people like Lily who sock their money away in stocks and bonds while living like parasites off the rest of us.

A shout goes up as I enter the house. I follow the noise to the living room, where the ensemble is playing a raucous game of charades.

"Morgan, Morgan." Annie waves. "Over here." She is radiant, beaming, twenty years younger without her Mother makeup. "We claim Morgan," she says. The other team boos as she hands me a hat filled with folded pieces of paper. "They've been trouncing us," she says. "Now we'll show them." I close my eyes and pull out a slip of paper. I read the phrase. Once. Twice.

"Got it," I say.

The other team snatches the paper from me, makes all manner of rude noises over my selection. My mind races a thousand different directions. How to act out... How to—

"Go!" says the timer. I make the sign for "song."

"Song!" yells my team.

I turn my back on them, bend forward, flash my pants down and up.

"Moon over Miami!" they scream.

"Yes!"

"Five seconds!" yells the timekeeper. Our team pulls ahead and we immediately launch into the next phrase. This is what I needed. To be with my people. Like battle-weary soldiers, we are most ourselves in the company of comrades. We have, all of us, been through the war. Understand its horrors and heroisms. The night's tensions fall away—the rough-edged performance, the light falling, Wexler's complaints about the production, the enigma that is Roblings. Gone. I feel light. Almost weightless.

I meet a few old cronies of Annie's who, it turns out, also live in the neighborhood. Evidently, this area houses an enclave of theater people who bought in the fifties. It is after midnight before the hordes begin moving out. I join a cleanup detail, picking up pizza boxes, empty cans. "Please don't fuss," says Annie. "Leave it for tomorrow."

We ignore her. She's a tidy woman, hardly the type to go to sleep with the place in such a mess. I grab a garbage bag and tackle the rooms off the long hall, picking up dead soldiers, paper plates, straightening chairs, wiping wet rings off antique wood tables. This apartment is everything Lily's wasn't. Bright, alive, it's filled with positive energy. Pictures of family and friends cover the walls, are grouped in antique frames on dressers and nightstands. Annie's life is all about family, children, grandchildren. And dogs. A wide assortment of breeds and sizes are threaded through Annie's life. What is it with actors and dogs?

More family photos line the hall. I stop in front of a huge

portrait showing Annie in a formal pose with a pleasant-looking man. He has a thick head of white hair and the longest earlobes I've ever seen. Every inch as wide as Annie, the two of them look like a geriatric Tweedledee and Tweedledum. His certified public accountant's license is beautifully framed, as are several magnificent photos with labels stating that he had won various photography competitions.

"That's my Walter." Annie has come up next to me, her arms brimming with stained tablecloths. "The photo was taken at our fortieth wedding anniversary party."

"Was he here tonight?"

"I lost him last September."

"I'm sorry," I say. "He looks like a nice person."

"He was. Very kind. Truly, a gentle man." She wipes a speck of dust off the photo. "We're not easy, you know, we actors."

"So I've heard."

"Walter was my biggest fan, helped keep me grounded." She sighs. "I don't understand how people like Lily London manage without someone in their lives. All those years... What did she do when she didn't get a part, when rehearsals or performances didn't go well?"

"She had Beth to lean on."

"It's not the same. My Walter would tell me how wonderful I was, even when I was horrible. He gave me the strength to try try again." She straightens the corner of his CPA license. "I still talk to him, you know. Friends are all well and good, but nobody listens like Walter."

She looks at me. I know that look from my mother. Brace myself for the inevitable. "Is there someone special in your life, dear?"

"Not at the moment," I say.

"Well, don't wait too long." She continues down the hall to the laundry room.

I study the photos lining the hall back to the kitchen. Time travels backward, Walter's white hair grows darker, Annie grows thinner. I wonder if I, too, will widen with age. Lily didn't. She stayed thin her whole life. Perhaps it's a happy marriage that spreads you out as time goes by, like those of my mother and her poker buddies.

The last photos are of Annie when she was around my age. She reminds me of a healthy Beth. Clear skin, slight peachy tint, bright eyes, well-toned body. The contrast makes the ravages of Beth's illness all the more heartbreaking. Will Beth ever have a wall filled with photos of husband, children, grandchildren? Will I?

We finish cleaning around one, and Annie sends us all off with bags of homemade cookies. "Since Walter died, I've had no one to take care of," she says. "It's nice to bake for someone again."

I can't imagine how it would feel to lose a man I loved after forty years of marriage. I can't imagine marriage.

Wanda from Wardrobe offers me a ride. We're leaving Annie's when we spot beer cans and pizza left on the neighbor's porch.

"Slobs," says Wanda.

We climb over the low railing connecting the two porches and quickly collect the garbage. "I'm glad we saw this stuff before the neighbor," I say as we take it back to the alley.

"She wouldn't have cared," says Wanda. "Nice old lady. She stopped by the party early in the evening. I had the feeling she really wanted to stay, but she had to get back. Annie says her husband's pretty sick. It's hell getting old."

Wanda flips the lid off a full trash can. We jump as a small possum scuttles out from behind, backs away, staring at us with ugly pink eyes.

"A baby," says Wanda. "How cute."

"You crazy? It looks like a bald rat with thyroid trouble." I keep my eyes on the varmint as I toss in the garbage and help push down the lid.

We follow the possum as it waddles down the alley toward the street. It ducks under a parked car but I feel its eyes follow us down the block. Wanda takes a parking ticket off her windshield and tosses it in back with a bunch of others. I scrunch into the front next to a stack of heavy-wool Confederate Army coats.

"Thank goodness for war," she says. "Half the television and film work I do is about one war or other."

We drive past Annie's as she's turning out the lights. It's not good, an old woman alone like that. What if someone breaks in? What if the murderer—

I shudder. Shake it off. Force the bad thoughts out, let the good thoughts in. Annie has many wonderful friends on the block to watch out for her, call for help if help is called for. All right, so it's not the same as coming home to Walter, but at least there are people around ready with a friendly word and a cup of coffee. Old people know how to be neighbors. I can't name one person in my apartment building. Well, maybe the Potters across the hall. And Rooster Man. But everyone in Chicago knows Rooster Man.

I AM OUTSIDE my door, fishing for my keys, listening to Hamlet claw the other side of the door, when it occurs to me that I should bring him to visit Annie. I bet she'd love the company. Better, if the two of them get along, Hamlet could move in with her. He certainly deserves a home with someone who will fuss over him the way Lily had.

"Hold on, hold on," I say. The second I crack the door, he jumps all over me, darting away, running back. "Will you calm down?" I try to sound firm but he's not buying it. Maybe that's because the more he acts up, the more I'm smiling and laughing. It's a great big warm fuzzy coming home to someone happy to see me.

Later, snuggled in my bed, yielding to the weight of sleep, I experience one of those moments when I feel the desire to share my life with someone. It doesn't happen often. Especially not after some of the dates I've had. But tonight is rough. It was fun eating a hot dog at the Lake with Roblings, riding the Ferris wheel. I enjoyed his company, in a mildly adversarial sort of way.

And Annie's love for her dead husband reminds me that, Grandma Belle aside, lasting love is possible. I drift off, thinking how nice it might be to have someone besides Hamlet waiting at the door to greet me.

TWENTY-NINE

Opening night.

Two of the most exciting and terrifying words in an actor's life.

Opening night.

Yes, thank you, I would love surgery without anesthetic.

Yes, please push me out of the plane without a parachute.

Yes, total tooth extraction would be just peachy.

Titanic-sized disasters happen on opening nights. Of course, there can be an upside. Sometimes. But that's something you never know until after.

Opening night.

It can go a million different ways. All of which I try not to think about as I put on makeup, costume, wrap myself inside a bubble of calm. Good-bye real world, catch you later. Hello Mother, Brother, Sister, Boyfriend.

"Five minutes. Five minutes, everyone." The disembodied voice comes and goes down the hall. "Five minutes." The air crackles with energy as we fall into line.

Whose idea was this? I've changed my mind. I need to go home, wash my hair, do my nails. We cluster in the wings, listening as the producing director makes a pitch for coming performances, subscriptions, inviting one and all to enjoy wine and goodies in the lobby after the play. Then the theater goes still.

Music up.

Lights.

Curtain.

Mother goes onstage. Then Brother.

Something wicked knots my innards. I feel the new leko dangling overhead like a loose tooth. It will fall again. This time it will find its target. Cleave my poor head in two. I dare to look up. The lights sit tight in their nice neat rows. Not a waggler among them. My nervousness is not about death-by-light-can; it is about life-by-acting.

Cue Daughter.

I step onstage. Every scrap of nervousness, misgiving, and fear that crippled me during the weeks of rehearsal disappears. Poof! I enter the "zone."

Lights blind me, but I sense the audience the way a snake senses prey—part movement, part scent, part sound. This group is lively and responsive. They energize and inspire our ensemble. Rhythms click as we hit all our emotional and physical marks exactly right. What are the odds of that, me bucko? Nil to none. I get high on the rarefied air. Oh yes. It is one of those magical nights that make sense out of this insane way of life.

Excuse me, but why does a relatively sane, moderately intelligent young woman subject herself to the humiliation and degradation of cattle calls, low pay, arrogant directors, inept technicians, ego conflicts, and other slings and arrows aimed directly at her heart?

Because of moments like this. Exactly like this. When the world and my muse dance in perfect step. Mystical moments erupt, unexpected. Magic happens. And then we are done. Just like that. After weeks of rehearsal, it is over in an eye-blink.

Daughter speaks the last line of the play. A moment's pause. Then thunderous applause reaches past Daughter back to Me. My heart pumps dangerously fast as I free-fall into the sound.

Annie squeezes my hand as we take our third curtain call. I squeeze back, profoundly grateful to play my Daughter to her Mother. Lily London, may she rest in peace, had no clue how to bring such heart and warmth to a part. I close my eyes, thanking the theater gods for gifts received. Maybe, if I'm grateful enough, they'll do it again.

Brenda Moore strolls ahead of me from stage to dressing room. Each of her anemic white arms is linked with those of two well-tailored financial-looking types. Her laugh runs up and down the scale. How witty the men are, how much fun she is having with them. Brenda might only have forty-eight cards in her deck, but that's all she needs to play this particular game. I could get work, too, if I flirted with the right people. "If, if, if," Grandma Belle likes to chide, "if Paris were a cork, you could put it in your pocket."

I sit at the makeup table, slather cold cream over my face. What do I want most right now? Now that the play is over and the audience is leaving and the theater lights go down? What do I really want? I want to climb into my grungy clothes, join the rest of the cast for greasy burgers and cheap wine, and relive every delicious moment of the enchanted evening.

I tissue off the cream. What I must do, what we all must do, is dress like civilians, affect our best manners, and mingle with members of the board, the backers, the press—all the mucky-mucks who make theater possible. Lord bless them one and all.

I wash my sweaty self as best I can in the women's room sink, dab on lighter makeup, and slip into something less comfortable. This gearing up to go from one performance to another takes nearly superhuman effort.

Beth comes into the dressing room, beaming, a thinner version of her old self. "You were fabulous," she says.

"You made it!" I jump up, hug her, feel the jutting back-bones she's hidden under her oversized sweater.

"Twisted my ankle," she says, loud enough for the others to hear. She's wrapped an ace bandage around one leg to explain why she's using a cane. She sinks into a chair.

"I have to go out front and make nice," I say. "Come with me. It will do you good to see everyone."

She begs off. "I'll wait here. Revel in the roar of the grease-paint, the smell of the crowd."

I laugh. "You're sure?"

She nods. "I'm still a little shaky around crowds."

"Can you stick around, go out with us later?"

"I'll try. I slept a lot during the day. I might have enough stamina to make it a couple more hours."

THE THEATER LOBBY is one large party. A phalanx of waiters circulates with food and wine. I enter the fray, inhaling a few small hors d'oeuvres from a passing tray. They don't begin to take the edge off.

Evelyn brushes past me, working the crowd. Lively, gracious, Wexler's daughter has a way of making each VIP feel as if the play couldn't have happened without him or her. It's obvious she's done this before, many times. Wexler, cemented in place, waits for people to come to him. Evelyn brings a steady stream to pay homage. She is his best promoter. I wonder how much of his comeback is due to her energetic efforts.

"Morgan?"

I turn to a man I don't know. Fifty-ish, good-looking in a slick soap-opera sort of way, he shows a smile of even white teeth.

"Hello," I say, smiling, holding out a hand. He could be any-one. I play my Most Charming Self. He takes my hand in a firm grip. I catch a whiff of expensive aftershave. Nice.

"I'm Stan Parker," he says.

No clue. "Oh, yes," I say. If he's someone important—theater critic, play producer, casting director—the last thing I want to do is ask, "Who the hell is Stan Parker?"

"You don't know me. I'm a friend of your Aunt Stella's."

"Ah." Aunt Stella is the only one of my mom's poker buddies who never fixes me up. Until now. The entire world is conspiring against me. Paranoid? Moi?

"When I told her I was coming here tonight, she said I must say hi. So, hi." The crowd pushes against us as new food is passed. "I know you're busy. I don't want to keep you."

"I hope you enjoyed the play."

"You were perfect. The way you captured the Daughter's con-flicted emotions. A difficult role. You really nailed it."

I warm to this perceptive man. "Are you in theater?"

"I wish." His smile crinkles fine lines around hazel eyes. "I'm at the Board of Trade. But theater is my passion. I see every play in Chicago and try to get to New York every other month or so." He releases my hand, "It was nice meeting you," and then he is gone. Interesting.

"Morgan." Evelyn waves me over. "These charming people would love to meet you."

I float to the middle of an expensively dressed group, graciously allow them to shower me with kind words.

All right. I lied.

Not only do I want to be out here schmoozing the muckymucks and the money people, I thrive on it. It's been so long since I've done live theater that I'd forgotten how much I love the attention. People touch my arm, my shoulder, wanting to be near the star. I accept it as humbly as possible. "Yes, thank you, how very kind of you to say so. But remember *(slight lowering of eyes)*, I am but one part of an ensemble. Everyone helped make the play a success." Pish-tosh. I am too, too modest.

It is nearly an hour later when I realize that most of the others have left. I've been deep in conversation with two producers interested in having me read for a musical they're putting together. "Of course I can sing. And dance. And play the piano." If I get the role, I'll learn to do it all. "Always say yes," Grandma Belle told me. "It creates options." They give me their cards and we agree to have our people call each other.

I head back into the theater, cutting across the stage to get to the dressing room. Brenda, still in full costume and stage makeup, gives a behind-the-scenes tour to her crowd of admirers. They block my way. I reroute, squeezing behind the backstage scrims, ducking through a dark passageway. Nearby, a stagehand's radio blares a basketball game. There is barely any light in this area. I must feel more than see my way through.

"De-fense! De-fense!" scream the basketball fans.

Wha—? I nearly bump into two dark forms entangled in an embrace. What stops me from ramming right into them is catching the scent of expensive aftershave. If my nose is as good as I think, the fragrance belongs to Stan Parker. Aunt Stella's friend is in an unmistakably intimate hug with another man. A faint light glints off Wexler's silver hair.

"De-fense! De-fense!"

The hors d'oeuvres and champagne claw their way up my throat. I swallow them back. Hot sweat erupts from every pore. I grab a nearby cable to steady myself. The men don't turn.

Haven't heard or seen me…yet. The deafening screams from the basketball game mask my footsteps.

"De-fense! De-fense!"

My legs feel numb as I back up. Please don't let the men turn around. Please let the radio keep blaring. Please don't let me bang into anything. I back out of the darkness into the light, remember to breathe.

"Just what are you doing?" The urgent voice behind me is low, threatening. Warning shivers bolt up my spine. I turn and face a glowering Evelyn. She stands, legs apart, arms crossed.

"I'm not doing anything," I say.

"You're spying."

"I am not. I'm on my way to the dressing room."

Her eyes narrow. "I know exactly what you're up to."

"I have no idea what you're talking about."

Her upper lip curls. A dog about to attack. "If I hear one word, one innuendo, the slightest hint of a rumor, I'll know where it came from." She hesitates an instant to be sure her message is understood, then turns and storms off. How hard this must be for her. How much she must love him to protect him like this.

I am trembling as I go to collect Beth. One thing is certain: Lily lied to Beth. Lily claimed Wexler was attracted to her when they worked together all those years ago. It's obvious Lily said that to build herself up in Beth's eyes. How sad, when there wasn't any need. Beth's love for Lily was unconditional.

THIRTY

WE SQUEEZE AROUND Act Four's pushed-together tables passing bottles of rotgut red, ordering burgers, pasta, anything cheap and filling—in that order. Conversation is stuck on theater critics spotted in the audience.

"I definitely saw Martinson wink a few times," says Brenda. "I'm sure it's a good sign."

Murray affects a comic twitch. "Nervous tic, luv," he says. Twitch. Twitch. "Occupational hazard for critics. Comes from wincing. Anyone see the *Times* critic?"

"I watched her nibs from the wings," says Annie. "Her head drooped a bit at the end of the first act. Couldn't tell if she was concentrating or napping."

"When will the reviews come out?" Brenda asks.

Annie sighs. "They didn't review the last play I was in until after it closed."

We share a round of horror stories, actors' names misspelled, titles of plays gotten wrong, theater names mixed up, addresses and times sheer fantasy.

"To the good old days," says Murray. We hoist our glasses. "To waiting up together for the morning editions, bracing for opening-night reviews. We'll not see those days again."

"Here, here." We drink a melancholy toast.

"Could she really have been sleeping?" asks Brenda, two beats late as usual.

"Very possible," says Annie. "Although when Murray dropped trou, she did seem to perk up a bit."

"Wish it had that effect on my girlfriends," he says. "Oops, don't turn 'round. The heavy hitters have arrived."

We all turn. As waiters bang in and out of the kitchen doors behind us, Wexler, Evelyn, the producing director, artistic director, and a few members of the board flow across the restaurant to reserved tables near the windows.

"I would love, just once," Murray says, "to sit above the salt."

"Quitcherbellyachin'," I say. "Travelin' steerage ain't all that bad. Look at all the fine upstandin' people you have to commiserate with."

Murray gives us a doleful look. "My point, exactly."

"Here." Beth puts a saltshaker under Murray's chair.

He wiggles his rear like a bird settling on the nest. Sighs contentedly. "Much better," he says.

An hour passes as we devour everything not bolted to the table. Beth pushes food around her plate, trying to make it appear that she's eating. A noble performance for my benefit. Although, her color does seem less pasty, more its old healthful glow. I look harder. Nothing has changed.

We are awaiting dessert and coffee, passing time by hanging spoons from various areas of our faces, when Wexler comes over.

"There is a dead spot at the beginning of the second act," he says, "that bit when Mother and Son move around Daughter as if she's invisible? You need to pick up the pace. It didn't get the laughs it should."

I glance over at Wexler's table. Catch Evelyn's eye. She shoots daggers my way. Direct hit. Don't worry, little lady, I'm not squealing on your dad. A gifted actress such as myself, one with a spoon hanging from her nose, has more interesting things to discuss than her director's sex life. Like...like...

"So," says Wexler, "I'll have these suggestions typed up and leave copies in the dressing room for tomorrow's performance. Any questions?"

We couldn't think of a one.

"All right then, tomorrow." He abandons us for the more refined group at the grown-ups' table.

"It wouldn't have killed Mr. Warmth to say 'Nice job,' " says Murray.

We remove the spoons from our faces, use them to stir cream into our coffees.

"I think," says Beth, "that what this evening needs is a toast to Lily's memory."

We all hoist glasses. Annie arranges her face in a brave smile, but I know she's uneasy about the way she got the role, as if she's dancing on Lily's grave. Beth's eulogy only freshens the guilt. I keep quiet, weighing Annie's discomfort with Beth's need to commemorate Lily in this particular surround, with the cast of this particular play on this opening night.

"Toast Diana, too, of course," says Beth. "But most especially Lily. What a great loss her death has been. Such a dear, dear friend. Not a day passes that some small thing doesn't trigger memories of my time with her. And so, to Lily, who first had the joy of appearing in the play forty years ago. And whose spirit guides us all."

We drink. A lot. Quickly. Beth's eulogy invites the specter of death to our celebration, throws the wettest of towels on the evening. The party fizzles as, one by one, people remember the late hour, how tired they are, places they need to be.

She gives me a wan smile. "I really know how to clear a room."

"Don't worry about it. Everyone's tired. It's been a long day." I dig my keys out of my purse. "Come on, I'll drive you home."

"Murray already offered," she says. "My place is on his way home." We hug and I watch her make her unsteady way out.

That's it, then. The night is over. Except I'm wired. I rarely sleep right after a performance, need a few hours' winding-down time. I have no desire to go home and stare at the walls until four in the morning. I need to be out. Need late-night buddies to hang with. Trouble is, most of the people I see out after midnight are kids searching for loud music and cheap booze.

There are a few adults who work late shifts.

Such as?

Oh, firemen, nurses, certain police detectives.

The house phone next to the coat check beckons.

I find Roblings's card in my wallet—a sign if ever there was one—and drop in the coins. Slowly punching in his phone number, I try to think what I will say. He is probably knee-deep in blood and gore. Spent the night poking the decaying underbelly of man's inhumanity. And here I come, all bright-eyed and cute, fresh from a lovely evening in the theater.

My finger hovers over the last number.

And just what are we doing?

Asking a friend if he'd like to join me for a late-night...a late-night...

A late-night what?

I'm not sure.

What do you want it to be?

I don't know.

Where is a script when you really need one? I have no idea what to say. Which comes, as my acting teachers drilled into me, from not having a clear idea of what my character wants. Motivation. What is my motivation?

Grandma Belle's advice floats up. "You're like the belly dancer working at the same old grind. Get out a little. Live life. Take a chance every now and then." Easy for her. She keeps a divorce attorney on retainer.

I push the last number, then immediately hang up. I'll have to think of another way to amuse myself these next few hours.

I find Annie outside, trying to hail a cab. "Come on," I say, "I'll give you a lift home."

She's feeling talkative, which is fine with me. "This is one of those hard times," Annie is saying. "No one waiting at home to share the big moments. I'm usually pretty good, try not to feel sorry for myself. But I do so wish Walter were alive to see this. He likes this kind of play. Old-fashioned. Predictable." She smiles wistfully. "He never did understand my love of experimental theater. Liked his world simple, recognizable. A meat-and-potatoes kind of guy." We pull up to her duplex. A dim light glows on the front porch. The house is dark. She hesitates a moment, as if bracing to go inside. "Well, thank you again. See you tomorrow."

Curtains shift in the next-door neighbor's window as Annie shuts the car door. A vague form peers out. Must be Annie's friend with the sick husband. My parents live in this kind of neighborhood where people look out for each other. Last year, their eighty-year-old neighbor noticed four men in jogging suits leaning against a van, smoking. She called the police. "I just don't think joggers smoke," she said. Four squad cars arrived immediately. Turns out the "joggers" were part of some radical foreign political group bent on kidnapping a local politico. "Old people are the best," the cop told my folks. "They know how to watch and they're not afraid to call us."

Annie looks fragile as she climbs the front steps. I picture her walking through empty rooms haunted by photos of loved ones dead and gone. I live alone too, but I've always lived alone. More or less. It must be more brutal when you're used to forty years of coming home to someone you love.

The idea hits. "Annie. Annie, wait." I run after her. "Look, I have to visit my parents tomorrow after the matinee. Sunday dinner sort of thing. Anyhow, I was thinking, if you'd like, I can bring Hamlet over for a visit. Let him stay with you a couple of hours. My dad's allergic to dogs, so Hamlet would just be sitting home alone. This way you can spoil him a little. He's really a cute dog. If you like dogs." Which I know she does from all the dog photos in her house.

"I…you're sure it's not out of your way?"

"I pass right by. After the matinee, I'll run home, pick him up, bring him over."

She's beaming like a kid at Christmas. "That will be lovely," she says. "Yes, that will be very lovely. Thank you, dear."

I leave feeling fabulous. Hamlet is just the tonic Annie needs. I'll bet a small dog can restore joy to an aching heart. And if things go well, who knows? Hamlet may have a new home. My mother's poker buddies aren't the only matchmakers in town.

THIRTY-ONE

OLD BOTTLES of nail polish—Blimey Limey Green, Halloween Black, Vampire Red—help me amuse myself into the wee hours of the morning. Accompanied by old English war movies and cups of Sleepytime tea, I paint intricate designs on my toenails. I strive for artistic. What I get is Kandinsky on speed. Hamlet holds reasonably still while I paint his toes black with green and red polka dots. Around four, I finally unwind enough to climb under the covers.

Tappity-tappity-tappity. Hamlet's fashion-forward nails click back and forth on the floor, waking me around the crack of noon. He tilts his head at me, leash in mouth.

"Go ahead without me," I say, pulling blankets over my head. When I was out of work I spent leisurely Sundays in bed, reading the *Times* cover to cover, occasionally not getting dressed at all. Careful. The theater gods are everywhere, hear everything. They may consider this a wish and grant it.

Hamlet jumps up on the bed, prancing over my body, rattling the leash. I peek out. "All right, all right. Go brush your teeth and comb your fur. I'll be there in a sec." He refuses to be distracted. Maybe, if I roll out slow, I can walk him and feed him without waking up.

Outside, he darts down the steps and heads left, our usual route. This time I pull him right, down two blocks to the newsstand. Luckily it's a beautiful Sunday. Crowds of walkers keep the surly vendor busy while I sneak peeks at the *Sun-Times* and *Tribune* theater sections. No reviews. Not one word. I knew there wouldn't be any; didn't we talk about it last night? Still, there's always the off chance I was wrong. The critics never seem to come when I've turned in a great performance. Some kind of perverse critic-radar lets them hone in on off nights.

Depressed, I lead Hamlet home. He has the compassion to do his business quickly. Back upstairs, I fall into a pot of coffee and the Sunday *New York Times*. I barely make a dent in the arts section before it's time to leave for the matinee performance. I set out Hamlet's food and gather my bags.

Glancing in the mirror on my way out, I see where last night's wine, food, and lack of sleep have ballooned the bags under my eyes. I lean in for a closer look. The overhead light plays mean tricks. Grandma Ruth's face stares back at me. My luck. The rest of my siblings take after Grandma Belle's side of the family, the side that doesn't age, that eats what it wants and still stays slim. Next incarnation, I'm going to pick my dominant genes more carefully. I slip on a pair of dark glasses. Don't want to terrify small children and dogs on my way to the theater.

ROBLINGS LEANS AGAINST his car in the theater parking lot. He straightens as I pull in, ambles over.

"Morning, Detective," I say. My voice sounds like wet mud.

"Rough night?"

I try clearing my throat. Air through sludge. "What brings you out in daylight?"

"Want to check a few things."

He waits as I gather my many bags—what *are* all these things I drag around?—walks me to the theater. Twin sisters, on the far side of eighty, strain to open the theater door. Bent like a couple of Vaudeville hooks, they are identically dressed: floral silk dresses belted at the waist, large bows clipped like gardenias above their left ears. Both women carry ebony canes with gold swan-shaped handles. Roblings reaches over their heads, holds the door.

"Thank you," they say together. Same voice. Same tonal quality. Like Sylvia and me. I wonder if these two also sang duets when they were young. Sylvia and I would work on harmony for hours and hours. I miss Sylvia. The thought catches me off guard. I am stunned by the powerful truth of it.

Roblings and I follow the sisters in. I spot Frick and Frack, two of the funnier characters on staff, working the ticket booth.

Their real names, something like Laura and David, are hardly ever used. They look up when we enter, eyes widening in mock terror. Shtick. I assume they're reacting to the presence of Roblings the cop. Frick reaches in his pocket, pulls out a half-dollar, flips it in the air, slaps it onto the back of his hand.

"Heads," calls Frack. Frick peeks at the coin, winces as if he's just been stabbed. He jams the coin in his pocket and lurches like Igor to the ticket window. "Yesssssss?" he hisses at the twins. This bit of improv, I realize, has nothing to do with Roblings.

Roblings's voice pulls me away. "You once told me," he says, "that any food found backstage is fair game for actors."

"That's right."

"Lily died because she ate something intended for Wexler."

"Yes."

"The question is, would a nice old lady like Lily London have stolen the fruit from the basket?"

"I don't think she was all that nice."

"Is that a yes? She would steal?"

"In a heartbeat."

My answer doesn't please him. "Then the next question is, when, where, and how did she get it?"

"That's three questions."

He gives me a look. Sighs. Takes out his notebook and flips through in search of something.

Over at the box office, two ancient voices rise in protest. "This won't do. Not a bit."

"Ladies, please," says Frick. He turns the ticket-office computer screen toward them. "Look." The theater's seating plan displays available seats in green. Sold seats in red. The screen is mostly red. Frick points to two green seats in the balcony, several rows and sections apart. "This is the best I can do for you today."

One sister points third row center. "You will put us *here*."

Roblings, sensing that I am easily distracted, slides his hand under my arm, guides me off to one side. "I need you to help me understand what happened here," he says. "If all of you steal food—"

I bridle. "It's hardly stealing. It's more by way of a time-honored theater tradition."

He lets it slide. "All right. But you see my problem?"

"Not really." I try to stay with him, but my mind is already shifting into my role.

"I'll keep this simple. My problem goes to motive. Did Lily and Diana happen by chance upon poisoned food? Or did someone purposefully hand them the food."

"Different scenarios. Different motives."

"Exactly."

"She can't hear," shout the sisters, pointing at one other. A line has formed behind them, people wanting to buy or exchange tickets.

"We have audio aids," says Frick.

"Can't abide those things." They jab the computer screen with gnarled fingers. "You put us *here*."

"Those seats are taken."

"Here!" they insist. Third row center.

Roblings ignores the side show, seems focused on the space around us. "I'd love to know what happened here the morning Lily died," he says. He checks his notes. "Beth drops Lily off around eight-fifteen and watches her walk through these doors. Lily is never seen alive again." He flips a page. "The custodian opened these doors at seven thirty. The fruit basket was already on the Equity monitor's desk when she arrived at eight forty. Somewhere in that hour, the fruit arrived and, by theft or design, Lily got hold of a grapefruit."

Crew begins arriving. Cast. More people join the box office line. "Well," I say, "I'd better be going—"

"How did the fruit basket get here? Who delivered it?" Roblings folds his arms, rocks back and forth on barge-sized feet.

Murray and Brenda walk in, spot me with the good detective. Guilt by association. Their disapproving expressions speak volumes, none good. They pass without a word. I check my reflection in the glass door to see if "Guilty" is branded on my forehead.

"I really need to get ready," I say.

Roblings nods, distracted. I sense him moving into the world

of the murder the way I move into the world of a play. I pause
a moment, try to feel Lily's presence. She floats regally through
this space. What happened to you, Lily? She doesn't answer. I
strain for an image, an idea. Nothing. Out of the darkness comes
the stare of her eyes, lifeless on the bathroom floor. Guilt niggles.

"If only I had gone to the bathroom...*that* bathroom, before
my audition," I say. "Maybe I could have frightened off whoever
killed her."

"Let it go," he says. "You'll drive yourself crazy."

"That's what we actors do. We thrive on angst. If I were well
adjusted I'd be a lawyer, a real estate agent, sell perfume at
Field's."

Evelyn walks in with Wanda. They are in heated discussion. I
try to distance myself from Roblings before they see me. No such
luck. Evelyn gives me the evil eye. She probably thinks I'm sic-
cing the cops on dear old Dad. I'm usually better at reading people. I liked her so much the first time we met, was grateful to
audition my Daughter with her Mother. How can she be such a
delight onstage and such a dragon lady off? Will the real Evelyn
Wexler please stand up? I am much relieved as they weave
through the box office line and head downstairs.

Poor Frick slumps at the ticket window. The elderly twins are
wearing him down. "Ladies, we've had this discussion before.
Many, many times before. If you want good seats, I am *delighted*
to give you good seats. I *live* to give you good seats. It is my
raison d'être. But you must make reservations *in advance*."

"In advance!" says one. "At our age, we don't buy green
bananas."

"And they're a whole heap cheaper than your tickets," says
the other.

More cast members arrive. See me with Roblings. "I really
need to go," I say, hurrying off before Roblings can stop me. As
I pass the box office, I hear the twins say "Senior Discount."
Frick screams.

IN THE DRESSING ROOM, sitting alone in front of the long wall of
mirrors, I feel decidedly leperlike. Everyone keeps a healthy dis-

tance. The makeup areas to my right and left remain open. Easy banter passes over and around and through me. I am invisible. Cast members who didn't actually see me with Roblings have obviously been told I was with him, drew some of their own where-there's-smoke-there's-fire conclusions.

I pretend I don't notice I've been sent to Coventry, busy myself studying photocopied sheets of Wexler's notes. But the more I'm ignored, the more agitated I feel. This has to end. By rights, I should be milking enjoyment from every second of this run. Instead, my Shining Moment is being tarnished by some joker bent on killing people. This is becoming highly personal.

Annie, bless her heart, comes in and moves her makeup box right next to mine. I could kiss her.

A rumpled Wexler shuffles into our dressing room. Deep folds of skin bag under his eyes as if he hasn't slept for days. "Gentlemen," he calls over the partition, "if you will. I need a moment." The men, in various stages of dress, join us.

Wexler's speech slurs as he takes us through his notes. Directors usually disappear once a play opens, move on to the next job. It's clear that Wexler doesn't have a next job. Which is why he needs this play to be a critical and financial success. This could mean endless tinkering with our lines, staging, and blocking. Doesn't Equity say we get paid extra for stuff like this? I'll check my contract. Better, I'll ask Murray to call Equity. He is deputy, after all. It will give him something to do besides turn up his nose at me.

It is hard to figure out exactly what it is Wexler wants. His focus jumps from one scene to another, one actor to another. We try to follow but only seem to upset him with our questions. Has he been drinking? Taking drugs? Is the pressure wearing him down?

Evelyn passes the doorway, pauses a moment as her father harangues us for lackluster performances. I try to read her. Sad, I think. Weary. She moves on before Wexler sees her. We are greatly relieved when he finally storms out.

"Well, wasn't *that* special?" says Murray. "I hear ticket sales are a disaster."

This surprises me. "I thought we were sold out."

"Those were early sales. The advance was terrific because of the curiosity generated by the murders. Old news, old news. Unfortunately, word-of-mouth after the previews hasn't been all that great. People are waiting to buy tickets until the reviews come out."

"I've always felt this play a bit of an old chestnut," says Annie.

"If you ask me"—Brenda looks directly at me—"what this play needs is another murder."

Is it my imagination or do several of the others glance my way? I become extremely busy with my makeup, have no desire to attract unwanted attention. "Pretend you're the mother of the groom," Grandma Belle's voice cautions, "sit down, shut up, and wear beige."

The matinee goes surprisingly well, considering all the new directions we have to remember. We adjust our timing, our movements, our intonations à la Herr Wexler's suggestions. Even our mis-cues and stumblings work—one person remembering a change that another person forgets. The audience loves it. Laughs frequently and loud, if often for the wrong reasons. Not what Wexler intended, I reckon, but if it works, it works. If only we can duplicate our mistakes next performance.

A huge deli tray is waiting in the dressing room after the performance. The accompanying note, from Wexler, apologizes if he seemed harsh earlier. "We all want this play to be the best it can be and sometimes that means sacrifices of time and energy."

This is Evelyn's work. I recognize her tone of writing from publicity releases. How exhausting it must be to spend her life smoothing the waves her father creates.

Call me crazy, but the gorgeous tray heaped with expensive meats and cheeses holds absolutely no appeal. None of us who witnessed Diana's death go anywhere near the food. Her contorted face, Saint Vitus' dance, the sound of her nose crashing against the floor, are impressions burned deep into memory. No corned beef in the world is worth that risk.

Outside the theater, I pause to take a deep breath of cool, clean air. I half expect to see Roblings in the lot, leaning against his car. He's not. At first I feel disappointed. But after the way the cast ostracized me for being seen with him, I also feel relieved.

I don't remember the ride home. My mind is on the play, the troublesome way I'm being treated by the other actors. Am I going to be "the suspect" the rest of the run? Will this cloud of suspicion follow me to new auditions, other plays, my entire career? "Ah, yes, Ms. Taylor. Weren't you involved in all those murders over at the Heartland?" Once half-truths, innuendos, and lies rise from the muck, they tend to grab hold, take on a rotten life of their own.

"Oh, the unfairity of it all," as Grandma Belle would say. Feelings of being the Victim take hold and I am on the verge of some serious breast-beating when, for some reason, the character of Blanche DuBois from *Streetcar* comes to haunt, "I have always relied on the kindness of strangers."

Well, not me! I'm no victim. I don't need to rely on anyone. Where is it written that I have to be a spectator? As soon as I get home, I'm calling my buddy Angie at Priscilla's. I never followed up to see if she was able to find out who sent Wexler's gift basket. I've been putting it off, afraid she came up empty. As long as I don't call, I can cling to a thin thread of hope.

Just deciding to make the call clears my sinus passages and sets my spinal column straight. Angie's my ace in the hole. If there's anything to find, she'll dig it up. She has to. Was Angie right? Did some guy working in the warehouse make a few quick bucks selling produce out the back door? And, if she gets him to admit it, will he remember what the buyer looked like?

Priscilla's answering machine comes on. They're closed. I leave a message for Angie. "Call as soon as you get this message," I say, "anytime, day or night."

I know Roblings has drawn a blank at Priscilla's. No record of an order. No record of a delivery. That doesn't mean there's nothing there. Just because he's good at what he does doesn't mean he's infallible. Roblings has his methods, I have mine.

I feel better than I have in a long time. Positive. Hopeful. Something is going to break soon. I sing snippets from "Cockeyed Optimist" as I ballet-leap around the apartment, packing a few of Hamlet's favorite toys for his visit with Annie.

THIRTY-TWO

HAMLET CHASES his tail in the car. Over, under, around. "How am I supposed to drive?" I ask.

He climbs on my lap, licks my face before sticking his head out the window. Dogs.

"I'm sure this isn't safe. Aren't there laws against this sort of thing? Sit down and put on your seat belt." Nothing works. He smiles all the way to Annie's.

She's waiting on her porch as we pull up. Hamlet starts barking, going crazy until I open my door. Annie whistles and Hamlet races straight for her. I'm left holding the bag with his leash, water bowl, favorite toys. I thought it would take at least a *few* minutes for them to become best friends.

"I'll be back in a couple of hours," I say. "Here's my parents' number in case you need me."

"You go, have a good time." She cradles Hamlet in the crook of her arm. "I have a backyard in need of a little dog." She nuzzles his nose. "You'll be good and tired when Morgan comes back, won't you? Yes you will, you cute thing."

THE EXPRESSWAY, isn't. Traffic crawls along at ten miles an hour. Even if I get off at the next exit, the ride's going to take a good forty minutes. I'll call Annie from my folks', tell her it'll be more like three hours before I pick up Hamlet. I'll have to remember to let Beth in on my matchmaking plan. Even though she's not able to care for him, Hamlet's more her dog than mine. And if Beth gets back together with Lyle-the-allergic, it's a sure thing Hamlet is history.

The three expressway lanes narrow to one. Roadwork. Except no one works on Sunday. So why not remove the orange cones until tomorrow? Let weekend traffic flow. That would be too logical.

Breathe in, breathe out. Breathe in, breathe out. It's a pain to make this drive every week. Do I need this? It would make my life infinitely easier if my parents moved into the city. What do they need a big old house for anymore? Every month something else needs fixing: hot-water heater, roof. They're paying taxes for a small mansion when all they use are the kitchen, bedroom, bathroom, and den. Maybe I'll mention it to them for the hundredth time—if I ever get off the expressway.

By the time I get there, my parents are already preparing dinner. Dad's assembling the salad. That's usually my job. "Sorry I'm late," I say, taking over tearing the lettuce. "Traffic was a bear."

The usual bombardment of questions about my day, my life, my everything, doesn't happen. Nothing happens. An eerie quiet fills the kitchen.

"We're moving," says Mom, without preamble. Something in her tone sends a warning buzz up my neck.

"Say that again."

"Moving," says my father.

"You're kidding."

"Don't I wish."

Quiet again. Mom doesn't look at me, is extremely busy surgically separating a chicken's wing from its breast. I'm missing something here. "This is so weird," I say, testing the waters. "The whole ride here, I was wishing you'd move into an apartment downtown. And, now…where are you moving?"

"Naples," says my father.

"What about Naples?"

"That's where we're moving."

"Italy?"

"Naples, Florida," says Mom.

The solid bottom of my world shifts underfoot. "You're moving out of state?"

"I thought you'd be happy," she says. "You're the one always after us to sell this place."

"Yes, but I want you closer, not farther away."

"Well"—her voice is crisp, snippy—"we can't always have what we want. Can we?"

DINNER IS DREARY. This dinner, the one following an opening night, is when my parents traditionally pump me for every last delectable detail. I should be regaling them with bon mots of lines missed, cues blown, costume changes gone awry. Tonight the conversation revolves around their move.

"I've been offered a job as the science and social reporter for the *Naples Express*," Mom says. Her voice is level, no joy, no excitement. "With your father retired, there is nothing to keep us in Chicago."

Dad turns to me. "What am I going to do in that cultural wasteland?"

"Same thing you do here," Mom tells him.

He ignores her, pleads his case to me. "They have palmetto beetles the size of Volkswagens. People saddle them up, race through town. Do you have any idea how hot it is in summer?"

"Chicago has miserable summers too," says Mom. "And, as far as cultural events go, the last time you went to a museum was to chaperone Morgan's eighth-grade class. Besides, Florida beetles are tamer than Chicago rats…both the two-and four-legged kind."

I listen in silence. Why now? Why are my parents suddenly upending their comfortable lives?

After dinner, we go to the attic. The high-beamed, unfinished area runs the length and width of the house. Freezing in winter, sweltering in summer, it has been used only for storage. We can barely squeeze through the years of accumulation, our family history crated and boxed. My section has the most stuff, dating back to grade school.

"We're not moving any of this," Mom says. "Take what you want. Anything left after June twenty-fourth, gets tossed in the alley."

"You know I don't have room."

She shrugs, unconcerned. "Rent a storage space. Give it away. Donate it. Do what you like. We are not schlepping this to Florida."

I stare after her as she goes back downstairs. This is not my real mother. My Real Mother would *never* talk to me that way. She would have started the evening asking how my performance went. This impostor didn't ask once. And my real mother wouldn't ask me to part with my possessions.

"You know, this is all because of you and Sylvia," Dad says.

"What is because of me and Sylvia?"

"Your mother never once talked about moving. Leave her children, her grandchildren? Never. Now, she can't stand being in the same state with you two."

"You *can't* be blaming this on me."

"I can and I am. I'm telling you what is. Your mother is not the same woman. She doesn't laugh, she's short-tempered. Your sisters say it's change of life. But I say it's a broken heart."

He leaves me to attic ghosts and dust motes. I sit in the old rocking chair, comforted by the rhythm of wood chair creaking on wood floor. Mom is the heart of our family, solid, grounded, the reason the rest of us felt free enough to go off in our quirky directions. She has never, ever been anything but excited for me, for my career.

I rock faster, staring at my hoard of stuff. When am I supposed to sort through it all? How can I afford a storage locker? Maybe one of my siblings has space I can use. Maybe—a violent shiver runs through me—maybe I could move forward in my life if I cut anchor, stopped dragging around dead weight.

Let go.

Just let go.

It's too much to think about now.

ON THE RIDE BACK to Annie's, I feel frightened for my parents, for their future together. Why have they, at this late date, uprooted their lives, thrown themselves into the chaos of the cosmos? It's upsetting seeing fresh sparks rising out of sedentary lives.

Annie doesn't answer her doorbell. I go around to the rear yard. Hamlet's toys are everywhere. I knock on the back door. No answer. Try it. Locked. Knock again. Listen for Hamlet's bark. Silence. "Annie?" I walk along the side of the house, calling up to a variety of windows. "Hamlet?" This is when one of those cute little cellular phones would come in real handy. The problem is, they come with a not-so-cute monthly bill.

I find a pay phone at the grocery on the corner. Annie's line is busy. I walk back, ring the doorbell again. Still no answer. Still no Hamlet.

Now I'm getting nervous. It's dark outside. A seventy-year-old street-smart Chicago native doesn't walk these streets this late at night. Even if Annie took Hamlet visiting, she would have left a note. I go back to the grocery, try calling again. Busy. I call the operator. "This is an emergency. I need to reach my mother but she's on the phone. Please break through...."

"One moment please." She comes right back. "There is no one talking on the line. Perhaps the phone is off the hook."

This time I run back. Annie's neighbor must have a key. I bang on the door. Yes it's late, and they're old, and the husband is ill. But this is an emergency. No answer. A loud fan whirs in an upstairs window. They must be sleeping. Can't hear.

Everything about this feels wrong. All the front windows are locked. Around back, one of the kitchen windows is open a crack. I pull over a shaky wrought-iron table, stack three lawn chairs on top so I can reach the window ledge. I'm out of shape. Running up and down my front stairs may keep me trim, but it does nothing to strengthen my upper body. Which is what I need now. My arms ache with the tremendous effort of hauling my body up and through the window. Rough wood scrapes my arms, a loose nail rips through my slacks, scratches my thigh. When was my last tetanus shot?

The window is over the kitchen sink and I wiggle through onto the counter. The house is dark. I recoil at the briny smell of corned beef and dill pickle. My stomach lurches at a sickening backsmell. Light from the other room casts dim shadows in the kitchen. A small form lies just inside the kitchen door. "Hamlet?" I say, moving down from the counter, tiptoeing to the matted pile of fur. "Hamlet?"

My eyes are adjusting now. Hamlet lies still in a pool of urine and vomit. I kneel beside him, rest my hand on his small stomach. "Hamlet?"

A sound from the other room. Fear prickles my back as I look through the doorway. Annie lies sprawled on the living room floor, unconscious, her fingers clutching the phone.

I grab Hamlet, rush to Annie. Her skin is so white it glows. "Annie, Annie," I shake her, "Annie. Please. Annie," frantically push down the phone button for a dial tone, call 911. "Help. Something's happened. Send an ambulance." I give the address. The woman tries to ask questions but I drop the phone, see if I can't do something.

Why don't I know first aid? I kneel over Annie's body, stick my finger in her mouth, be sure she hasn't swallowed her tongue. No, that's for drowning, or is it seizures? Should I induce vomiting or give mouth-to-mouth? What if I make things worse? I bend my ear to her mouth. Hear her breathing. Feel good warm breath.

Hamlet is the one not doing so well. I push against his stomach. "Don't be dead," I tell him. "Don't be dead." His body is warm. Good sign, right? Is that a heartbeat I feel? I spend a millennium rubbing Hamlet with one hand, patting Annie's cheeks with the other before the ambulance finally arrives.

"You can't bring the dog," the driver says.

"I can't leave him."

"Against rules. Health department."

"He's very sick."

The guy looks at me like I'm nuts. "Then an ambulance is the last place I'd put him."

They are taking Annie's vital signs, putting her on a gurney, moving out of the house to the ambulance. I tag along, carrying Hamlet.

"Where are you taking her?" I ask.

"Weiss Memorial."

The oxygen helps bring Annie around, but she's still more out than in. When she does try to say something it's muffled by the oxygen mask. I smile encouragement, make soothing sounds as they load her gurney into the back. Then the doors close and the ambulance peels off, sirens wailing.

I run back to the house. I've got to get Hamlet help. Fast. Don't know a vet. Can't find a phone book. I run around in circles holding his limp body, frantic because he's dying and I'm not doing anything to save him. He's shivering now. I wrap him in blankets. Need help. Immediately, or Hamlet will die. I call Roblings, manage a couple of coherent sentences.

"Don't move," he says. "Stay calm." I hear him dial another phone, talk to someone. "All right," he says to me, "the cavalry's on its way. Tell me what happened." I'm telling him what little I know when the wail of a siren pulls up and stops outside. "That'll be Frank," says Roblings. "Go with him. I'll talk to you later."

I fly out of the house, jump in Frank's car, which happens to be a canine unit complete with dog in wire cage in back. "I called ahead," he says. "The doc will be there by the time we arrive." Frank does not stop, works his siren and horn until we pull up in front of the Chicago Veterinary Hospital. He stays with me while Thelma, a beautiful young vet who looks about twelve, works on Hamlet.

"It is definitely something he ate," she says. "Maybe food poisoning."

I tell Frank about Annie. He calls Weiss Memorial, tells them to check Annie for food poisoning. A little while later his beeper goes off. "I have to leave," he says. He strokes Hamlet's matted coat. "Poor little guy. You hang tough," he tells me. "This one's a fighter."

Hamlet is a fighter. A survivor. He'll make it through this. Whatever *this* is.

"He's small," says Dr. Thelma. "Even a tiny bit of bad food could have a devastating affect on his system."

She is, I realize, preparing me for the possibility that Hamlet won't make it. Frenetic air molecules dart before my eyes. The world grows wavy as my knees give way. I am on the floor, dizzy, sick to my stomach.

The vet's cool hands press against the back of my neck, my forehead. "Did you eat whatever your dog ate?" she asks.

"No."

She helps me sit, gently pushes my head forward until the dizziness passes. "Go to the waiting room," she says. "I'll come in as soon as there's a change."

An eerie place, this waiting room. I keep the ceiling lights off, opting for the quiet light of a table lamp. The place is deathly still. I sit on the edge of a chair, my body bent in half, head hanging down. It helps ease the nausea. For someone who hates sickness, I seem to be wallowing in it lately. I take bigger and bigger breaths until I'm able to sit up.

Minutes tick past. Fifteen. Thirty. I get up once to check on Hamlet but barely make it to the door before dizziness sets back in. I'll wait here.

I call the hospital. "I'm Annie Andrews's daughter," I say, so they'll give me news, "calling from Florida," to explain why I'm not at "Mom's" side.

"She's doing well," says the floor nurse. "We pumped her stomach and now she's asleep. We'll keep her overnight for observation. Most likely, they'll release her in the morning."

"Do they know what caused it?"

"Not yet. They suspect food poisoning of some sort. Your best bet is to talk to the doctor in the morning."

Someone pounds on the outside door. "Will you get that?" Thelma calls from the operating room.

I brace myself, expecting a grieving owner holding the bloody body of the family cat. Or dog. Or parrot. Through the peephole, I see Roblings's face looking back at me. I let him in.

"You look lousy," he says.

"Nice to see you, too."

"How's Hamlet?"

"He's in with the vet. I...I'm not good in there. Maybe you could go check for me?"

He does. I pace the waiting room. I've never felt so helpless. Roblings comes back. "She's still working on him," he says. "Tell me what happened."

For the second time, I tell him what little I know. He makes a call. Sends a couple of cops to Annie's house, see what they can find. Fifteen minutes later they call back. Roblings listens, turns to me. "Do you know anything about some corned beef?"

I don't believe this. "Not again."

"Is that a yes?"

"Wexler sent a deli tray."

"To you and Annie?"

"To the whole cast. It was in the dressing room after today's performance."

"You didn't eat anything from it?"

"You kidding?"

"Good girl. But Annie did?"

"I didn't see anyone touch it. We're all still a little skittish about theater food."

"But she could have? Maybe took some home."

"It's possible."

He's back on the phone, urgent this time, telling his people to go down the cast list, call everyone. See if they're sick. If they are, tell them to get to a hospital. If not, warn them away from eating the food.

I try to sit still but wind up pacing again. Roblings goes back to check on things in surgery. Hamlet doesn't deserve this. I should have returned him to Beth days ago, given him a more stable home with a more responsible person. Ha. Annie is a "more responsible person." A lot of good it did Hamlet.

It is after midnight before Roblings's footsteps echo down the corridor. I brace myself for the news.

"He's going to make it," says Roblings.

I am so prepared to hear "death" that his words don't immediately register. Relief overwhelms me and I start sobbing. I never cry. Am embarrassed by this outburst. Roblings doesn't turn away, seems comfortable with my emotions. Wish I were.

Dr. Thelma comes in, peeling off latex gloves, wearily pushing a lock of hair off her forehead with the back of her hand. "I'll keep Hamlet overnight," she says. "He should be his own sweet self by morning. Lucky for him you came along when you did."

ROBLINGS MAKES CALLS as he drives me back to Annie's to pick up my car. "A few other people at the theater ate those cold cuts," he says. "The custodian says he wrapped everything the cast left and took it home. Says he made himself 'a couple of real Dagwood sandwiches.' He's feeling just fine, thank you."

"None of the others are sick?"

"Just Annie. And Hamlet."

"Prophetic," I say.

"What?"

"In the dressing room before the performance, Brenda said what we needed was another murder."

"Brenda's the cute blonde?"

"You think she's cute?"

"And why would she say something like that?"

"Ticket sales are off. Another murder would stoke the public's interest."

He waits while I climb into my car and start the engine. I roll down the window. "You don't—you *can't* believe Beth is responsible for this, too."

"She and her boyfriend are up in Door County," he says. "It's a six-hour drive from here."

A nonanswer. But I don't press it. I thank him for his help, then drive off into the night. The fact that he knows where Beth and Lyle are means the police are keeping tabs on them. Beth is still a suspect. Does Roblings think she paid someone to poison the food while she's out of town, to throw suspicion off her? That's how the good detective's mind works.

The voice on my answering machine is Angie's assistant at Priscilla's. She got my phone message. Angie is on vacation until tomorrow. Will I please call back then?

I will. But I know in my heart if Angie found out anything she'd have called. Why did I get my hopes up? It's a great big world out there. How do you begin to find one small killer?

THIRTY-THREE

THE THEATER IS DARK Monday and Tuesday, which gives me time to nurse Hamlet back to health. I cuddle him almost nonstop. He whimpers if I leave his sight for a second. Annie, also back home, has turned off her phone. The recorded greeting assures everyone she's just fine. Please leave a message. She'll call when she has time.

On Tuesday, I wrap Hamlet in a blanket, keep him on the seat next to me as I pick up Beth.

"You're sure acting strange for someone who hates dogs and sickness," she says. I shoot her a look, which she cheerfully ignores.

Lily's apartment looks as if a tornado touched down; dishes and pieces of furniture strewn about, the carpet filthy with scraps of papers, threads, rubber bands, price tags. I hold Hamlet close. He lifts his head, looks around, closes his eyes again. If he recognizes his old home, he is too weak to show it. Beth is quiet. This is hard for her. But it has to be done. We need to close the apartment, suture this part of the wound so she can get on with her healing.

Harold greets us with a Cheshire cat smile. "You wouldn't *believe* the traffic," he says. "All those eager-beaver buyers, money just burning holes in their very deep pockets. They were lined up an hour and a half before we opened. All in the advertising. The phrase 'Estate of the famous actress Lily London' created monumental interest."

His house-sale workers scurry around, packing the leftovers. "I found these in the pocket of an old costume," he says, pulling out two fabulous antique pins. He pins a silver tragedy/comedy mask pin on Beth, an Art Deco woman's head on me. "They are much too beautiful to sell."

"I never saw these," says Beth.

"Oh, our Miss Lily had all sorts of goodies tucked away. A real pack rat. Lucky for us."

One of his workers calls and he leaves us to the wreckage. "It's eerie," says Beth as we wander the rooms. "Like moving through the skeleton of someone you knew."

"You all right?"

"Sad. Losing a person you love leaves a huge hole in your gut."

Later, Harold sits Beth down at a folding table and hands her a bag brimming with receipts to go through. I take Hamlet outside and sit on the stoop. Gently, I unwrap the blanket from his tiny body, let the sun's healing rays warm him.

"This will keep you busy," says Harold, handing me a glass of iced tea and a large cardboard box. "Theater stuff," he says. "Thought you'd enjoy a look-see while Beth finishes up." He gets that gossipy look I know and love, kneels on the stoop beside me. "I heard about the latest episode in Wexler's little melodrama. Poisoned cold cuts. *Quelle surprise.* It's a miracle no one died."

"Hamlet nearly did. And Annie was terribly sick."

"Wexler orchestrated the whole thing. I have no doubt, whatever." He pats the side of the box. "Have fun. I'll see how Beth's doing."

I rummage through the box of theater mementos, many from the time Lily starred in my play. Fascinated, I become lost in the old programs, reviews, director's notes. My nostalgia for a longago time in theater comes bittersweet as I scan scripts typed on manual typewriters, read fountain-penned letters. It's not fair to love my work so much and have so little opportunity to do it. If only I had Brenda's hustle, could clone Murray's schmoozing factor. Lily London knew how to self-promote, keep working despite mediocre talent and out-of-date style. This is not sour grapes talking. This is the sound of Truth. Every theater school should make Sucking Up 101 a mandatory course.

Hamlet suddenly crawls from my lap, hobbles down the steps, yapping at an old bag lady.

"Hamlet! Come!"

He ignores me, tugging at items overflowing from her shopping cart. Terrified, she backs away from him.

"Hamlet! No!" I run down, scoop him up, shake a finger. "Naughty! No!" The woman cowers on the far side of her cart.

"I am so sorry," I say. "Are you all right?"

"Damn dog," she says. "Should be on a leash. We got laws, y'know."

"You're right. You're absolutely right." We stuff the scraps Hamlet dislodged back into the pile. I dig a few bills out of my pocket, fold them into an old boot lying on top of her bags. "This should cover any damage."

She snorts, pushes her cart down the street, its squeaky wheels accompanied by the soft clop of unlaced gym shoes. Hamlet growls softly in my arms. "Hush," I say. "Hush."

Poor old woman, all alone, no place to go. Something about her—tiny body, wispy white hair—reminds me of the murderess at the police station. I have to ask Roblings if they ever found out what drove the old woman to bop her husband of sixty years over the head with a skillet.

Harold escorts Beth down the steps. I hand him the box of Lily's mementos. "It's a hoot seeing photos of people who played our roles forty years ago," I say. "I'd love to show these to the cast."

"Anytime," says Harold. "They'll be in the closet at the shop. I'll use them for window display. Maybe during the Theater Festival."

BETH SEEMS preoccupied on the ride home. Hamlet, wrapped in his blanket, sleeps on her lap. She strokes his head slowly.

"A penny," I say.

"Lyle is pressuring me to marry him."

"The man's head over heels."

"I've noticed."

"Do you love him?"

She pauses before answering. "That's not the issue."

"What's the issue?" She doesn't say. "Leaves the toilet seat up? Tosses socks on the floor?'' A small smile. ''What, then?''

''I do love him. But I'm afraid I'd be marrying him for all the wrong reasons.''

''Like?''

''Like I'm vulnerable right now. My future's this huge question mark. I have no idea how far the MS might progress. I might have the mild type that never gets any worse. Or I could wind up...wind up''—she presses her lips together, mustering courage—''wind up in a wheelchair unable to do the most simple functions.''

''But Lyle knows all this. And, for some perverse reason, he isn't daunted.''

''Which is another reason not to marry him.'' Her slight smile is mischievous. ''He's obviously not too bright.''

We round the corner. Two men lean against a black car stationed outside her apartment.

''Here we go again,'' she says.

''Cops?''

''Yep. They were waiting yesterday when I came back from Door County. I guess I'm somehow supposed to have poisoned Annie while Lyle and I were hundreds of miles away.'' She gently lifts Hamlet off her lap and onto the seat between us. ''If only Lily had been as poor as I thought. If only she didn't leave me a small fortune in her will. Then the police would *have* to look someplace else for her murderer.''

''What possible motive could you have for poisoning Diana and Annie?''

She shrugs. ''Throw the hounds off the scent.''

Two young women walk down the block. The cops watch appreciatively. They haven't noticed us yet. ''Don't go home just now,'' I say. ''Come with me to visit Annie. Let these lugs wait.''

''Wish I could. But I'm at the end of my energy.'' She gathers enough strength to open the car door. ''Need a good long nap. I'll talk to you later.''

The cops snap to attention as she approaches. They say something to her, then escort her into her apartment building.

I cry as I drive to Annie's. Been doing that a lot lately. Not at all like me. But the frustration is just so great. Knowing Beth is

innocent and not being able to help. How do the families of innocent people who are put in jail survive the anger? I can't begin
to imagine how I would play that role.

ANNIE IS DELIGHTED to see Hamlet alive and recovering. I feel
the same about her.

"How've you been?" I ask.

"Exhausted. Friends, reporters…it's been nonstop. Such fuss
over nothing. I saw my doctor this morning. She gave me a clean
bill of health. I'll be back onstage tomorrow night."

"I called—"

"Yes, sorry I didn't call back. So many people left messages.
I was going to tackle the list tonight."

We settle in the little screened sunroom off the front porch,
look out over the quiet street. Hamlet curls on Annie's lap. She
rubs noses with him. "I'm glad you don't blame me for the other
night," she tells him. "Poor little baby. Yes, so sweet." He licks
her face then settles in to have his ears scratched.

"What happened?" I ask.

"It's so silly, really. There was that beautiful tray of food in
the dressing room after the performance. I don't eat cold cuts,
myself. Too much salt and fat. But no one else was eating it and
it seemed such a waste. I thought it would make a nice treat for
Hamlet's visit. I didn't think anyone would mind. So I wrapped
up a few little things and brought them home and put them in
the fridge."

Hamlet rolls over, begging for a tummy scratch. Annie obliges.
"After you dropped him off, Hamlet had a good long romp out
in the backyard. A real ham this one"—she nuzzles him—"aren't
you, sweet thing? Yessss, you are. I gave him a nice little bath
in the kitchen sink. Then I took out the meats and set them on
the table, meaning to tear them into little pieces and put them in
his dish.

"That's when the phone rang. I left him for just a bit. By the
time I came back, he was writhing on the floor. Evidently, he
pulled the package of meat onto the floor and ate a good part of
it. That's when I began to feel ill."

"Why would you be sick? You said you don't eat cold cuts."

"I don't. But as I was setting them on the table, I took a tidbit of the turkey. A taste, was all. It was nothing I even remembered doing until the police pressed me on the matter. I barely managed to get to the phone before I passed out. The next thing I remember is paramedics putting an oxygen mask on my face."

"Was anyone else here?"

"Just me and Hamlet."

"What about earlier, when you were still at the theater? Is it possible you might have left the package of cold cuts where someone could get to it?"

"I left it on top of my makeup case while I returned my costume to Wardrobe. Anyone could have tampered with it."

"Who was around?"

"Everyone. Actors, board members, the managing director, Wardrobe, Evelyn. It's probably easier to think who *wasn't* there." She strokes Hamlet absently. "What I find most troubling is that someone in our troupe might be responsible for this. I haven't harmed anyone. And Hamlet certainly hasn't."

As I'm leaving, Annie compliments me on the beautiful pin Harold gave me. I tell her about the house sale at Lily's place. "I should do that," she says. "I don't have a square inch of extra space around here, and I don't have use for ninety percent of the stuff."

"This is nothing. Lily had closets full." I tell her about the box of mementos Harold put together from the original performance of the play.

She claps her hands. "What fun. I would love to see that."

I promise to bring it to the theater.

A LETTER HAS BEEN slipped under my apartment door. My name is scrawled in bold letters across the front. A threat? A warning?

I lift the flap, ease out the note. Adam's writing slants across the page.

You have every right to be angry with me, but what you're doing to your sister isn't fair. Sylvia has idolized you her whole life. It's not her fault you weren't ready for marriage when I was. Did it ever occur to you our breakup might be a blessing in disguise for us both? Now that I've experienced real love, I know that what you and I had was great friendship and mutual admiration. But it was not love. If you are ever lucky enough to find the right person, you will know what I mean.

Sylvia and I are going to be married September 21. She wants you to be her maid of honor but won't ask for fear you will refuse. She couldn't stand that. Please, for all our sakes…"

I read and reread the letter. Toss it away. Rescue it. Toss it again. My hand trembles as I pour a shot of the cognac I use to numb menstrual cramps. I down three quick shots. It isn't until the fourth that the pain starts to dull.

THIRTY-FOUR

THE PHONE SHATTERS my liquored sleep. I fumble for the phone. Radio-clock numbers glow bright red in the black room. 2:05.

"'Lo?"

"Hey, Garbo. It's Angie." Her Chicago-Italian twang cuts through the fog. "Back from a week in Vegas."

"Hey, Angie."

"Got word you called."

"Right."

"You sleeping? Cripes, I'm sorry. The message said call right away. Anytime."

"Yes. No. This is fine." My tongue weighs three pounds. "I was wondering if you found out who sent that fruit basket to Wexler."

"Yeah. Sure. I called you on this."

I snap awake. "Did you say yes?"

"I left a note the size of Texas for my temp to call you. Ah, hell, I thought you got it."

"Who? Who sent it?"

"Would you believe, the old gal herself?"

"Priscilla?"

"Bingo."

"I thought you told me she's a hundred-fifty-year-old cigar-smoking, poker-playing, stud-chasing golfer retired to Sun Valley, Arizona."

Angie laughs. "True. But some of the old-timers still call her for favors. It's like they think paying retail's a mortal sin."

"You're saying one of her old friends sent Wexler the fruit."

"The way I get it is, this old geezer calls Priscilla for a favor, she calls the warehouse and tells the guys to put a Peter Ruby together, heavy on the citrus. Then she tells them to run it over to Wexler at the theater. Which is why I never had paperwork.''

My mouth goes dry. I am one number away from winning the jackpot. "Were you," I ask, "able to get the friend's name?"

"Yeah, sure. Hold on a sec." She clanks the phone on her desk and I listen to the sounds of the warehouse coming alive in the wee small hours. *Please let her find the name. Please don't let it be on the scrap of paper the temp lost.*

Angie picks up. "Harold Shaw."

It kicks the wind out of me. "Harold…"

"Shaw. Some old-time theater character. Ever hear of him?"

"Yeah. Yeah, I've heard of him."

"The information here lists a business. Junque and Stuffe?"

"Thanks."

"Hope this helps. Keep in touch."

HAROLD! WHY HAROLD? I go around and around trying to come up with one innocent reason Harold would send a gift to Wexler, a man he hates, has hated for forty years. There is no innocent reason. Only dangerous, deadly ones. Harold sent the fruit, that's a fact. What is not a fact but is disturbingly possible is he somehow poisoned the fruit before it arrived at the theater.

Ridiculous. Harold would never hurt anyone. Besides, why would he take action now, forty years after the fact? Isn't time supposed to heal all wounds? Didn't Harold cheerfully overcharge Wexler's daughter for costumes for the play? I was there. I saw him with Evelyn and the costumer. He didn't seem a man seething with hatred. But what other explanation?

Maybe time doesn't always heal. Maybe, sometimes, it also magnifies ancient hurts. Like the old woman who whacked her hubby. All right. So let's assume this is possible. He tries to poison Wexler, kills Lily by mistake. But then, why keep going and kill Queen Tut? Why poison Annie and Hamlet? No matter how I push the pieces around, they don't fit the puzzle.

Night crawls toward dawn. I waver between calling Roblings and calling Harold. I'll have to tell Roblings. But first I'll confront Harold. He's been too good a friend for too long. I won't sic the dogs on him without warning. And I'm not going to do it over any damned phone. This has to be face-to-face.

Once I decide, I fall into exhausted sleep, not waking until the alarm goes off at ten.

IN A DIFFERENT lifetime, the one in which my mother still loved me, it might not have occurred to me to volunteer to help my parents pack thirty-five years of marital accumulation. But since my unsettling visit on Sunday, I've tried to think of ways to build Brownie points. Yesterday I called my parents and volunteered to come over this morning to help. That was before I found out about Harold. I need to go see him.

I dial my folks. This is a hard call to make. No matter what I say, I'm going to look bad. As if my offer of help was insincere. I feel like a fraud. "Something important has come up," I tell Dad. "Not that packing isn't important"—dig myself in good and deep—"but this can't wait. I'll come help you tomorrow."

I listen as he relays the information to Mom. My real mom would have said, "That's fine, dear. Don't worry about it." This impostor manages a bored "Whatever." Her indifference drives a spike in my heart. There is a jostling of the phone as she takes it from Dad. "I should warn you. Since you offered to help today, Sylvia said she'd come tomorrow. She's trying to be considerate of your feelings." A hugely pregnant pause. "Do you think you can handle being with your little sister in the same place at the same time?"

It's a rhetorical question, since she hands me back to Dad. "You'll never guess who I ran into at Max's Deli," he says. "Remember Lester? The attorney?"

"She remembers," I hear my mother say. She never told Dad that Lester parked his toothbrush at my place for a couple of months. Dad doesn't deal well with stuff like that. Mom usually metes out that kind of information on a need-to-know basis. I wonder if this new mother will be as considerate of his feelings. I worry for him. For her. For me.

"Shame you let him get away," Dad says. "Nice guy. You two would have made beautiful children together."

"With my luck, Great-grandpa Ben's recessive genes would kick in and our kids would look like Yoda."

He laughs. "Well, any-hoo, it's a moot point. He's getting hitched."

"Hitched?"

"She's a real cutie. Tax attorney specializing in real estate. Articulate, good sense of humor. Not as good-looking as you, though. Well, see you tomorrow. I'll have fresh bagels."

I stare at the phone after he hangs up. Lester getting married? It doesn't compute. Lester still yearns for me. Is hoping we'll get back together. Why else did he run right down to the police station and hold my hand so I wouldn't have to face Roblings alone? And why else has he been doing pro bono for Beth?

I run a quick ego check and find that mine has become an overgrown, brambly thicket. Time to hack it down to manageable size. Lester wasn't on the make at all. Lester was being Lester, a genuine solid-gold nice person. I never trusted that. Never thought he'd give as much as he did without wanting anything in return. Which seems to say a whole lot more about me than about him. None of it nice.

THIRTY-FIVE

I LET MYSELF into Junque and Stuffe and lock the door behind me. Harold won't be in for another hour. I have plenty of time. I search his rolltop desk for charges or checks to Priscilla's Produce. Nothing. Most likely Priscilla doesn't charge old friends for favors. Still, I'll feel a whole lot better if I have proof in hand before confronting Harold.

I riffle the tidy slots of mail, looking for any clue as to why Harold would have sent a gift to Wexler. One cubicle is crammed full of medical forms, reports, bills. I thumb through them. Harold has been undergoing a series of tests and treatments. He's never said anything. And he certainly doesn't look ill.

Could he have a bad heart? Might he be taking the heart medication injected into the grapefruit? The medical forms contain a maze of incomprehensible terminology. As near as I can tell, none of the tests is for cardio or cardiac or anything heart related. But there are tons of blood tests. Maybe AIDS? Could he be dying? Is that the reason he's exacting revenge after all these years? If Harold's dying, he has nothing to lose by killing Wexler. Except he didn't kill Wexler. He sent fruit, which could have been eaten by anyone. That doesn't jibe with Harold's precise nature. He's not one to leave important matters to chance.

I unlock the small closet where Harold stores special items. The boxes stacked floor to ceiling are clearly marked: EIGHTEENTH-CENTURY SNUFF BOTTLES, PRE-WWII CIGARETTE CASES. Mixed in with the stock are a few personal boxes. I find the box of LILY LONDON—THEATRE mementos and remove the lid. Perhaps there is something in here I missed.

The closet light is too dim to read the faded print on yellowed pages. I turn to go into the next room.

"What—!"

"What are you doing?" An agitated Harold blocks the doorway.

Blood rush. Heart explosion. Easy. Don't confront him while he has me cornered. There isn't enough air in this claustrophobic closet. I need to get out or I'll suffocate.

"These," I say, holding out the box like a cross before a vampire. "Remember? You said I could show the cast? I thought I'd take them to tonight's performance. I didn't think you'd mind."

What is that look? Anger? Disappointment? Relief? After a moment, he relaxes, backs away. "Sorry," he says. "I've been terribly on edge of late. Such a great deal on my mind. I was just on my way to a doctor's appointment when I saw the store lights on. I was positive I'd turned them off last night. When I peeked in and saw the closet door open, I was certain I'd caught a thief."

Then why didn't he call the police? Because he's guilty of something? I follow him into the shop, clutching the box to keep my hands from trembling. If I don't confront him now, I never will. Just bite the bullet, my dear, and plunge.

"Harold, I know you sent the basket of fruit to Wexler."

His back goes rigid. I brace as he turns around. Will he deny? Run? Attack? In one graceful movement, Harold drops into a wicker chair and buries his face in his hands. He begins crying. Crying? Not a reaction I'd considered.

"Harold?" I reach out a tentative hand, rest it on his shoulder, feel the frail body under the hand-tailored suit. He cries a long time before he's able to speak.

"I…I never intended to harm anyone. Oh, dear God. You must believe that. The whole thing was intended as a joke."

"Poisoning the fruit was a joke?"

"No. Of course not. Not that. How could you think I'd do something like that?"

"What else could I think?"

"I don't know what went wrong. I had Priscilla put together a gorgeous basket, mostly citrus. The thing of it is, Wexler adores citrus but is highly allergic. Breaks out in the most hideous hives."

"That explains why he gave away such scrumptious fruit to mere actors."

"Sending the basket was, perhaps, a bit mean-spirited of me, taunting Wexler with something he loves but can't have. The same way he flaunted his relationship with my young lover. Mean-spirited, yes, but it did make me feel ever so wonderful." He pats my hand, squeezes it gently. His skin is cold. "It was a small joke, don't you see? Easily arranged over the phone."

"You never saw the basket?"

"Never. I called. Priscilla sent. Oh, my dear, you would love Priscilla. A real Damon Runyon character." He shakes his head. "How or why someone tampered with my little gift is a mystery to me, too. When I found out how Lily died, I was devastated. If I hadn't sent the fruit, might Lily be alive today? I've thought of nothing else for weeks." He pulls a handkerchief from his breast pocket, dabs his eyes. "I'm relieved you've found me out. I am sick to death of carrying the guilt."

"Detective Roblings will have to know about this."

"I understand perfectly. Don't fret, my dear. Do what you must." He pushes up out of the chair. I help him. "Now, I must get to the doctor."

"Is it anything serious?"

"Of course." He tries to sound flippant. "Isn't it always serious when it's you?"

I watch him return to a waiting taxi. He's moving slowly, with difficulty. How long has this been going on? Why haven't I noticed? For someone who prides herself on being such a keen observer of the human condition, I seem to be oblivious to flashing neon signposts.

Harold drives off and I go back inside to call Roblings. I probably should have insisted that Harold wait for the good detective. What if Harold lied to me? What if he is guilty? What if he's making his getaway right now?

THIRTY-SIX

DETECTIVE ROBLINGS has stepped away from his desk. Would you care to leave a message?"

Yes. Tell him Ms. Morgan lower-than-pond-scum Taylor is calling to rat on her dear friend Harold. "Yes, please," I say, giving her Junque and Stuffe's number. "Have him call as soon as he gets this message."

While I wait, I thumb through the desk slot with Harold's medical papers. Have I been so wrapped up in my own life that I never noticed the burdens he's been dragging around? Either that, or Harold is one hell of a good actor. The medical papers date back months. Sad that a person can look so healthy and be so sick.

Or the reverse. Lily was always complaining about her health. So, so sick. Oh, her poor heart. Ah, her delicate condition. What a conniver. A few of Harold's letters bear the rising phoenix, the same logo as the one on the letter I opened from Lily's insurance company. The letter telling her she sent them her Equity dues in error.

An old thought shifts, catches new light. If both the medical examiner and Lily's doctor say she was disgustingly healthy when she was killed, why was she contacting her insurance company? What was on that insurance form she mailed to Equity by mistake? Did they ever send it back? I call Beth.

"No," she says. "I haven't received anything like that. Maybe the people at Equity realized Lily's error and mailed the forms directly to the insurance company."

"You're probably right." That's it, then. No insurance company is going to tell me what's on a client's form.

"Speaking of insurance," says Beth, "I've arranged to have my fillings taken out."

"Your insurance will cover it?"

"Dream on. They say it's an unproved procedure."

"Expensive?"

"I've bought cars for less. But I talked to two women with MS who had fillings replaced. They both say they feel much better."

"Could be a placebo effect."

"You sound like my brother the doctor. But if it were you, wouldn't you try?"

"I'd pull out my own teeth if I thought it would help."

She laughs. "My brother says this whole issue—whether I can get mercury poisoning from dental amalgam—smacks of quackery. But hey, I've got nothing to lose. Besides, this is the perfect time. I've tidied up the last of Lily's business as best I can. Closed the apartment. I'm feeling stronger but still not up to auditioning."

"What does Lyle say?"

"Whatever I decide to do is fine with him. I might as well go for it."

She sounds up, for a change. I debate whether to tell her about Harold sending the fruit to Wexler. The fruit that killed her beloved Lily. Beth is sure to find out, sooner or later. And when she does, she'll wonder why I kept this secret. "There is one other thing…" I say, laying out the news as gently as possible.

For a long time she doesn't speak. It's too much for her to take. I never should have…

"After what I've been through these past few weeks," she says, her voice tired, "I will never, ever, accuse someone of something unless I know, firsthand, they are guilty. People are much too ready to believe the worst. I loved Lily."

"I know."

"And the police have turned that all around. They think I befriended her for her inheritance. For money I never knew she had. It's been a nightmare."

"I'm sure this will all be over soon. They'll find who did it."

"I pray for that. And I don't for one second believe Harold had anything to do with Lily's death."

Relief. "That's exactly how I feel."

"Tell him I send my love and wish him strength. He'll need it."

I wait at Harold's desk for Roblings's call, fan out the medical papers on the desk, stare at the rising phoenix. What could Lily possibly have wanted from her insurance company? I turn that around a while. What if, like Harold, she was hiding a serious illness?

All right, so let's say she's dying, finds out she's at the beginnings of a slow, dreadful death. And maybe she wants to spare Beth the pain of watching her disintegrate. She decides to commit a quiet suicide, go out nestled in the bosom of the theater she loved. She'd exit with a flourish and everyone would assume it was a natural death.

Yeah. Sure.

First of all, Lady Lily would never, *ever* stage her final bow backstage, let alone on the floor of a bathroom. Second, both the medical examiner and Lily's doctor reported that she was disgustingly healthy for a seventy-year-old woman. One doctor might miss something, but it isn't likely both would mess up. What, then?

I would dearly love a peek at that insurance letter. Beth says it wasn't mailed back to Lily, which means it may still be at the Equity office languishing on someone's desk. Can't hurt to ask.

I call Equity. "Rosie's out all week," I'm told. "Taking personal time." Figures. She's the only efficient person in the office. I'll have to wait a week. Unless... The phone person sounds young, eager to please. I ease into my question.

"I'm the one who found Lily's body," I begin, establishing celebrity status.

"Uh-huh."

"I'm working with her family, trying to clear up her estate, tie up loose ends, that sort of thing."

"Uh-huh."

"There was a mix-up. A letter she intended to send to the insurance company might have been mailed to Equity instead."

"Uh-huh."

"And we're hoping you might be able to find it for us."

"I could take a look around."

Bless you, my child. "Well, that would be super. Do you think you could do it now? We're in a bit of a hurry."

"Sure. Want to hold on or should I call back?"

I give him the number at Junque and Stuff. Tell him I'll be there another ten minutes. Give him a deadline to shoot for.

I try Roblings again. This time I get through. "I found out who sent the fruit to Wexler," I say, fast, before I chicken out. I tell him about Harold and his old friend Priscilla.

"Does Harold know that you know?" Roblings asks.

"Of course. I talked to him."

"Not smart."

"He's my friend. I owed him a chance to explain."

"You put yourself in jeopardy."

"I can take care of myself. Besides, Harold didn't hurt anyone."

"You should have called me as soon as you found out.

"He's a friend."

"Your friend just became number one on my hit parade. Where is he now?"

"Doctor's appointment."

"Where?"

I scan Harold's medical papers with their roster of doctors' names. Harold has a right to his privacy. "He'll be in to open the store at noon, like always. Harold's not guilty of anything, except a desire to get even in some small way."

"What do you think murder is usually about? Friends fighting, an argument between husband and wife, one driver cutting off another."

I hang up, sorry I called, knowing I had no choice. Yes, Harold did a small, petty, stupid thing. He's human, after all. But that hardly makes him public enemy numero uno. I hope Roblings will be gentle.

Rosie's assistant calls back. He found the letter on the bottom of one of the many piles waiting to be filed. "I'll be right there," I say.

I clean Harold's desk, replacing papers where I found them. No need for him to know I've been nosing around his personal stuff. Lily's box of mementos is on the desk. Might as well take them to the theater tonight.

A SICKENING SWEETNESS permeates the Equity office. I breathe through my mouth. "Eau de Rotting Tropical Garden?" I ask.

"Frangipani." Rosie's assistant nods at the giant floral arrangement. It dominates the table set aside for out-of-town members' mail and packages. "A gift for the star of the new *South Pacific* production. She's two days late getting into Chicago."

"Probably because she knows this thing's waiting for her."

"Thank goodness her rehearsals start tomorrow. I'll messenger the damned thing to the theater first thing in the morning."

"If it hasn't asphyxiated you by then."

He gives me Lily's insurance letter and I race out to fresh air, waiting until I'm in my car to open it. There is a medical form from Equity's new HMO, which Lily filled out. A doctor's report—it looks like information from a routine physical—is stapled to it. An accompanying letter explains that Lily's preexisting condition—Turner's syndrome—has existed since birth and is neither life-threatening nor, for a seventy-year-old woman, a condition of any import and should not impact on her insurance eligibility.

What is Turner's syndrome? I head home to walk Hamlet and prepare for tonight's performance. I call my HMO and am shuffled through a deck of receptionists. None has ever heard of Turner's syndrome, but they all promise to leave word with the doctors who will try to get back to me sometime this century. I call the reference desk at the library, leave my information request on their answering machine.

I do have one other option. Grandma Ruth. Not only is she always home, but her house is wall-to-wall bookcases laden with the thousands of books she's read over her years of voluntary confinement. A large number of those books are of the medical persuasion. Every pill, disease, treatment, alternative treatment, folk remedy, charlatan's recipe, popular quackery, and medical theory is represented in thick texts full of unpronounceable Latin names and elaborate chemical compounds. She also subscribes to a variety of health newsletters: Harvard, Mayo Clinic, *New England Journal of Medicine,* and scores of others put out, it seems, by every hospital on the planet. These she indexes and cross-references, keeping impeccable records should a symptom or condition arise.

I need to ease into this. It's been weeks since I called. Months, if I'm absolutely honest. The guilt of not visiting stops me from making contact. Once I call, I'll have to promise to go see her. The trick is not to promise. Which means not calling.

"Hi, Grandma. It's Morgan."

Beat. "Morgan?"

Oops. She knew me when. "Miriam," I say.

"Oh, sweetie, how good to hear your voice." The smell of fresh-baked cookies wafts over the phone lines. "Isn't this dreadful news about your parents moving? Whatever can they be thinking? You must be terribly upset."

The conversation takes off in altogether the wrong direction. Whoa! I don't want to discuss my parents' move. Don't want to think about it. If I ignore it, maybe it will go away. But I can't ignore the quiet terror in Grandma Ruth's voice. Her only son is moving clear across the nation. When will she see him? At least I can hop on a plane and go visit. She can't even make it off her front porch. I assume, from the way she's pouring her heart out to me, that my father hasn't told her it's my fault they're moving. Mine and Sylvia's. Well, mostly mine.

It takes half an hour before I work my way back around to the real reason I called. "Turner's syndrome," I say. She lays down the phone to look it up. It takes a while. A long, long while. I consider hanging up, letting her call back, but she wouldn't understand. All she has is time.

She returns, breathing heavily with the effort of moving. "It's a disease of some sort.... Female trouble... Difficult to understand. Here. Ah, well, the gist of it is, it makes the bearing of children impossible. Oh"—a small gasp—"Miriam. You don't...it's not..."

"Me? No, Grandma, it's not me. A friend of mine..."

"What a relief. I would hate to think you won't have a house full of beautiful children one day." Another five minutes pass discussing my lack of current daddy prospects. "When are you coming to see me?"

Before we hang up I promise to visit her next week and bring stills from my new production.

An hour wasted. I'm no closer to an answer than I was before I called. Turner's syndrome, whatever it is, isn't what Grandma Ruth said. Makes the bearing of children impossible? Ha! Tell that to Lily's dead son.

THIRTY-SEVEN

"HALF HOUR," calls the stage manager.

"Half hour, thanks," we say.

The entire company circles the round table in the women's dressing room, picking through the ancient theater treasures in Lily's box. Even Evelyn, who normally keeps her distance, has been lured by the quaint old programs and yellowed publicity clippings.

Our dresser, Mitzi, kneels on the floor next to Annie. She's been trying to mend a fresh tear in Annie's costume. The old fabric is proving no match for Annie's girth. "I can't work like thith!" she says, straight pins quilling from her mouth. She needs Annie to take off the costume, tries to shoo the men away. They refuse to leave. The old photos draw us all like magnets.

"Just one more minute," pleads Annie. "Oh! Look! The woman who played Mother looks like a lumberjack in drag."

Murray squints at the photo. "Less feminine."

"Hold thtill!" says Mitzi.

"You look nothing like Daughter. See?" Brenda passes me the photo of Lily, swathed in chiffon, lithe as a *Midsummer Night* fairy. It makes me feel Godzilla-esque. "Lily was so delicate. Fragile." Brenda sighs. "Like Diana. She would have been perfect as Daughter."

Pity she's dead, I have the good sense not to say.

"Morgan is perfect," says Annie. "Exactly right." I shoot her a thank-you smile.

Brenda the Oblivious hammers the sore spot. "As petite as Diana was," she tells Annie, "the contrast between you and her would have made a much funnier visual onstage. Sort of a Mutt and Jeff, Abbott and Costello thing."

Annie doesn't flinch at the rude reference to her girth. She has the wisdom to consider the source. I, however, don't feel as generous. How I long for a rapier-sharp retort. Where is Neil Simon when I need him?

Murray scrutinizes a forty-year-old photo of Brother. "Weird-looking duck," he says, checking the name on the back. "Never heard of the guy. Never heard of any of these...except Lily, of course. Wouldn't you love to know how they played our roles?"

"Absolutely not," says Brenda. "It might color my performance."

One can hope.

She squeals. "Look at this! Can you *believe* how gorgeous Wexler was?"

"He's no slouch now," says Murray.

"What have you got there?" booms a voice.

Wexler! We jump like children caught playing with matches. He comes to the table, smiling. When was the last time we saw him happy?

"I...I thought," I say, "the cast might like to see..."

If he hears he doesn't show it. His smile fades as the mementos on the table register. Delicately, as if afraid they'll disintegrate, Wexler lifts a photo, a program, Lily's head shots, reviews. He picks up a photo of the cast and crew, his fingers trembling. "Where did you get these?"

"They were Lily's," I say. "I thought it might be fun—"

He brings the photo closer, squinting at the faces. Years have turned the once sharp black-and-white photo yellow as old bone.

Brenda muscles her way through, leans all over Wexler, points to the handsome young man in the center of the photo. "Is that you?"

Wexler nods, half hearing.

"Could you *possibly* mean," Murray deadpans, "the person sitting in the chair labeled 'Director'?"

Brenda the brown-nose doesn't let up. She moves past "sincerely interested," goes directly to "gushing."

"Lily was *such* a beauty," she says. Wexler, lost in the photo, doesn't respond. Brenda reaches an arm across, giving him full benefit of her perfume as she drops a manicured finger on the photo. "And who is this *adorable* boy next to you?"

Wexler jerks the photo away. Too late. Brenda's finger smears an oily print directly on Wexler's lover's face. He tosses the photo on the table, leaves the room without a word. Evelyn watches sadly but doesn't follow. It is a wise daughter who knows her parents' moods.

"Nice going." says Murray.

"What?" says Brenda. "What did I do? I was just asking. Like, I'm supposed to know who any of these people are?"

Annie picks up the photo, gently blots the print with a tissue. "This young man," she says, "the one you anointed, was Lily's son."

"You know?" I say, startled.

"Know?"

"She had a son?"

"Why, yes."

"How?"

Annie shrugs. "I imagine Lily told me."

"I can't mend this," says Mitzi. "Not with you in it." She stands, her knees cracking from kneeling so long. "We'll have to finish in the bathroom. Come, come, come." She bustles Annie down the hall.

So it seems Lily's son wasn't the great big secret Beth thought. Doesn't surprise me. Lily was the type who swears you to secrecy, as if entrusting you with some great confidence, then turns around and tells the person next to you the same secret. Strictly grade-school best-friend shtick. Not particularly becoming in a seventy-year-old.

"Fifteen minutes," calls the stage manager.

"Fifteen minutes, thanks," we say.

"We'd better get ready," says Murray, leading the men's exodus to their dressing room.

Brenda and the others return to the mirrors to check their makeup, costumes. Evelyn stays, helps me repack Lily's things. She's been downright friendly since she realized I'm not running around spreading gossip about her father. She studies the photo of the gauzed Lily. "I owe her a great debt," she says quietly.

"You knew her?"

"Knew of her. I was looking forward to meeting her but she died the day I arrived in Chicago."

"What do you mean, you owe her?"

She sets the photo tenderly in the box. "You must wonder about me," she says softly. "I mean, you know my father isn't attracted to women. But there was a moment, back then, when he wondered if the psychology of the day could possibly be right. That homosexuality was a reversible condition.

"My mother was a determined young actress with more drive than talent. She managed to get him into bed."

"Lucky for you."

She smiles. "I'm not sure what she expected from the pregnancy. Marriage, I suppose, to the famous new director. Unfortunately, Dad considered me an accident, his dirty little secret. He had no interest in me. None. He gave Mom monthly checks to keep quiet. Had his friends supply enough roles on the stage and TV soaps to keep Mom happy.

"Then Lily's son died." She smooths a hand over Lily's photo. "Dad says her anguish was heart wrenching. He watched her suffer the agonies of hell for never having acknowledged her son. She was, he said, inconsolable.

"My father saw himself in her. He called my mother the next day and arranged to become an active part of my life. I was two that first time I saw him. I thought he was bigger than life. I still do. We've been inseparable since. I can't imagine my life without him. And all because of Lily London."

The stage manager passes by. "Ladies and gentlemen, places for act one."

Showtime! Everyone rushes out. I toss Lily's box next to my makeup and head for the door.

Grandma Belle stands in the doorway.

Blond hair piled high. Eyeliner Cleopatraed to brow's edge. Lips painted into a bright red heart. Leather skirt and jacket, silk blouse, high heels. Who wears high heels anymore? Sexy lady. Her perfume, something floral and expensive, invades the room.

"Grandma!" I say, delighted, reaching out for a hug. She doesn't smile back. Keeps her arms crossed. "What's wrong?"

"Time, please," the stage manager's voice drifts down the hall.

"I have to go," I say. "You okay?" She doesn't move. Trouble with her newest beau? I like when she confides in me. "I'll get you a seat out front. We can talk at intermission."

"Do you remember the sandbox your father built when you were a little girl?" she asks.

Sandbox? Is this the onset of dementia, a mental cataract clouding her once sharp mind? The timing is lousy. "Grandma. I have to—"

"DO YOU REMEMBER?"

The verbal slap stops me cold. I do a quick mental shift, out of Daughter, out of Morgan, back past Miriam to when I was Mimi. A willful little girl who desperately wanted a sandbox. Which my father built. Four wood sides, triangular corner seats covered in yellow Naugahyde. "Yes," I say.

"Good. And do you remember that no one was allowed to use that sandbox without your permission?"

"Yes."

"Even when you were not using it."

"Grandma, I really—"

"And when you were older, too old for the sandbox. When the only ones using it were neighborhood cats. Do you remember then?"

The stage manager comes up behind Grandma Belle. "Time, please." His voice urgent.

Grandma Belle lifts a bejeweled hand, waves him away. He looks pleadingly at me. "Morgan..."

"Grandma..."

She lifts a well-plucked brow. "You don't like to be kept waiting? Now, isn't that too, too bad. You'll wait until I'm through with you, young lady. The way you've kept the rest of the family waiting."

"Me?"

The manager slinks away.

"Now," she says, "about the sandbox. Your mother, who has always been much too sweet for her own good, wanted to plant flowers where *your* sandbox was. That disintegrating, splintery eyesore. You were in high school by then, hadn't used it for years, and still wouldn't let them get rid of it."

"I don't remember that."

"I'll bet you don't." Her tone—Arctic ice over rusted nails—makes me wither. She could teach Annie a few things about playing Mother. "I make it a point not to interfere in my children's lives. Lord knows I don't want them meddling in mine. However, when you went off to college, I couldn't stand it anymore. Late one night I came over with Theodore, or was it Alex? No matter. And I had him destroy that piece of filth, cart it away. Your parents were aghast that I did such a thing without first consulting them, or you, or—I expect—the United States Congress. Do you know what I told them?"

I assume it's rhetorical so I don't answer. She waits me out.

"No," I say.

"I told them you wouldn't even notice it was gone. And you didn't. I wager you haven't given it a second's thought until right now."

True. All of it.

Footsteps in the hall. Wexler appears behind her. His eyes are red as if he's been crying. My fault for bringing the photos. "What's the problem here?" he asks.

"I'm nearly through," says Grandma Belle.

"Madam, we have a play to put on."

Grandma Belle doesn't turn, keeps her eyes fixed on me. "And I, sir, have a family to run."

"I am the director, and—"

She whirls around. "And I am the matriarch. Surely you can spare five minutes."

He hesitates. I feel the weight of tonight's performance square on my shoulders. Audiences do not like to be kept waiting. Actors hate it even more, grow tense in the wings. Sweat streams down my underarms. My heart chugs loud and irregular. Cotton grows in the corners of my mouth. Something in Grandma Belle's tone, stance, body, convinces Wexler to back off. He leaves but I have a feeling he stays close enough to listen.

"You need to learn to let go." Grandma Belle's stare immobilizes me. "Just because something once belonged to you doesn't mean you have the right to hang on to it forever. Especially those things you don't need or want or use. Like Adam."

"You don't know what he and Sylvia did."

"I don't care. I know what *you* did. What you're doing. And you're going to stop it. Now."

"But—"

Evelyn passes down the hallway behind Grandma Belle. Is about to say something when she suddenly leaves. Her father, no doubt, has signaled her not to interfere. They are probably pressed to the wall within hearing distance. A humiliating death, this tongue lashing by grandmother. Can't think of any way to stop it.

"You don't love Adam." says Grandma.

"That's not the—"

"Your sister does. And Adam loves her. They're really quite nauseating about it. I expect theirs is one of those relationships which is doomed to succeed. Boring. But that's their problem.

"They should be married by now, raising runny-nosed children, getting on with their lives. It is an absolute mystery to me why Adam and Sylvia care one whit what you think, why everyone in this family is so concerned about your feelings. Because, it seems to me, you don't give a good goddamn about theirs. I love you but you are a selfish child. Spoiled from the get-go."

That hurts. I adore Grandma Belle. Her love has always been important to me. It would kill me to lose it.

"You abandoned Adam," she says, "but don't want anyone else to have him." She grabs my arms. Squeezes hard. "Adam is not a sandbox. It is time to stop the cats from shitting, to let the flowers grow. Am I making myself clear?"

"Yes." Flaming arrows of pain shoot up my arms.

"You will call Sylvia."

"Yes."

"Tomorrow."

"Yes."

"And tell her…?"

"I am happy for her and Adam. I wish them a long life and great happiness together."

She releases my arms. Blood races from shoulders to hands. The pain is excruciating. "Good girl," she says. She cups my chin in her hand. A loving gesture. "Good girl." Her anger leaves as quickly as it came. "It's best not to mention this little visit to your mother. She wouldn't understand."

"I won't."

"Good girl." She pats my cheek, leaves me to my play.

THIRTY-EIGHT

THE NIGHT IS a black hole. The emotional focus I need to do my work has been torn and trampled and shredded. I remember little from the time Grandma Belle leaves until I unlock my apartment door. Snippets.

Annie's costume rips in a new place.

Brenda upstages me nonstop.

Murray, who suffered most from my emotional absence, follows me offstage muttering. "You could have phoned it in, you know."

I'm entitled. One bad night.

Brenda leans against the dressing room door, flirts prettily with an admiring stable of starstruck studs. It's more than I can take. I turn and leave without changing. Escape. Flee.

It's not until Hamlet jumps on me, licking the stage makeup off my face, that I begin coming out of the dark. And with the coming-out comes pain. And with the pain comes crying that hits like a squall and won't let up.

I hug Hamlet close, cry loud and long into his fur. Wail at the past months' madness. Ache from the hurt I've caused people I love—Sylvia, Mom, Dad, Adam—all because I want what's mine, even when it's not. Grandma Belle is right about my not letting go. But she's wrong about why. It's not about being selfish. It's about fear of loss. Not wanting to let go of one thing before I have something to replace it.

Wiped out, weary, I head for my room to crawl into bed and never come out. Hamlet has other ideas, brings his leash, drops it at my feet. I want to wallow in depression. He wants to potty. Who has priority here?

The cool night air clears my head. Hamlet tugs me along, excited to be out in the world. Lily took him everywhere, doted on him, spoiled him. It isn't fair for me to lock him inside all day. He deserves a home with children, a yard, all that normal human stuff I don't have. Beth and Lyle aren't an option. Annie's still my best bet. I'm sure Hamlet has forgiven the poisoned cold cuts. He's not the type to hold a grudge. I'll run the idea past her, see how it flies.

Hamlet waggles up to a teen couple strolling hand-in-hand. They stop to oooh and ahhhh. The angular boy looks like a young Lester. Was it just this morning that Dad told me Lester is getting married? It seems a million years ago. Adam's out of my life, now Lester. It's better that way. Neither was right for me.

Grandma Belle thinks I'm waiting for the perfect man. I'm just waiting to fall in love. Roblings comes to mind. His quiet energy. Contained force. No easy man, this homicide detective. Forget it. He's too complex. Exhausting. I need a no-brainer. But then I'll be bored. How do people ever wind up together? Am I the only one who finds this coupling business hopelessly complicated?

I didn't intend a long walk but, once we get started, we just keep going. In truth, now that I've promised Grandma Belle to give Sylvia and Adam my blessing, I feel relieved. This tawdry little drama I created is over. We can all get on with our lives. It's too late to call Sylvia tonight. Tomorrow, while we help pack up the folks' house, we'll talk things out. I will try to act humble. Not my best side.

The walk energizes me, defuses then dissipates my depression. The woman who walked out of my apartment an hour ago is a whole different animal from the one walking back in. I give Hamlet a couple of doggie treats and pour myself a tall glass of water as I play my phone messages.

Harold: "Hello, dearheart. Not to worry. Bulldog Roblings's third degree wasn't nearly as difficult as I thought. He did say sending that fruit basket was very naughty. [laugh] Of course it was. Otherwise, what's the point? Did you know your detective friend is something of a Shakespeare expert? Can quote chapter and verse. Correctly. Wouldn't think it to look at him. Ah, well. The book's cover and all that sort of thing. I've decided to dress the front window tomorrow. Theater motif. I'll want the stuff in that box you took. Drop it off tomorrow? That's a love. Call me. I'm usually somewhere.''

Roblings: ''Thought you'd like to know *[car phone static]* friend Harold is alive and well. The whip marks should heal in time. [static]...to make it to the theater tonight. If not, call me.''

Roblings was at the theater tonight? I didn't see him. But then I didn't see anyone. Took the final curtain and pulled a Houdini. It's better he didn't see me in my fugue state. It would have scared him away for good. This way I have a chance of seeing him again. Maybe tomorrow night. I'll call.

Dad: ''Hi. I broke a crown. Need to see Doc Rosenstein tomorrow. As long as I'm going, Mom wants to have her teeth cleaned and checked before we move. Come help pack Friday, instead. Come early. Come hungry. I'm making matzo brei. I've been doing it a new way with egg whites and margarine. Healthier.''

Research librarian: ''This message is for Morgan Taylor. You called for information on Turner's syndrome. It is a genetic condition that makes it impossible for a woman to bear children. I have several books and articles I can refer you to if you like. I will keep the information at my desk for one week.''

I replay the message once, twice, listening in disbelief as she repeats the same information Grandma Ruth gave me. An old logic course kicks in, sorts things out.

FACT: A woman with Turner's syndrome cannot bear a child.

FACT: Lily London bore a son. (Supporting evidence of his existence: (1) I saw his photo. (2) Both Harold and Wexler knew him and loved him.)

THEREFORE: Lily London couldn't have had Turner's syndrome.

Maybe I misread Lily's doctor's letter. I check it again. No, here it is, ''Turner's syndrome.'' What a quack. I've heard HMO-doctor horror stories—wrong limbs amputated, botched lab reports, fatal misdiagnosis—but this is my first experience up close and personal. Wonder which Island Paradise University awarded this joker his medical degree.

It occurs to me that if Lily's new doctor was way off base with this diagnosis, maybe he also got it wrong about Lily's heart condition. Maybe she *was* sick, took medicine prescribed by a previous doctor, the medicine they found in her system. Maybe there was no murder, just an old woman whose heart failed.

I start to get excited about this new theory when I realize it doesn't explain a dead Queen Tut and a poisoned Hamlet. Darn. Hate those loose ends.

I shove Lily's insurance and medical papers in a drawer. Thank goodness I short-stopped this before Beth saw it. There's no need to subject her to this trash.

I'm still standing at the desk when the phone rings. Roblings. "Can you come downstairs?"

I look out the window. In the dim outer reaches of a streetlight, Roblings leans against his car, phone pressed to his ear. He lifts a hand when he sees me, waves. Something constricts in my heart. A violent squeezing. Breathing becomes impossible. I fly down the stairs in thirty seconds flat. Now we both lean against his car. Very close.

"You called?" I ask. Coquettish. I am not the coquettish type. He has a strange effect on me.

"Looked for you at the theater," he says.

"I left early."

"They told me." He presses his hand against my cheek. A warm hand, strong.

"You should have let me know you were coming. I could have left a ticket."

He runs a thumb over my cheekbone. "I wasn't sure I could make it. My schedule isn't always easy."

I reach up, wrap my hand around his wrist, bring his hand to my lips and kiss his palm. "You're here now," I say. This voice is not mine. This voice has no control.

He bends down, kisses me with warm, soft lips. I kiss back. Please, let me lose myself in this man tonight, wait until tomorrow to worry about all the ways he's wrong for me.

"Come up," I whisper.

He nuzzles my ear. Wild currents run through my body, out

my fingertips. "Can't," his voice husky. "I'm on my way to a call. I just needed to see you."

The next kiss is slower, deeper. It is painful to pull apart, to watch him leave. I stand, staring, long after his car is out of sight. So this is how women feel watching their men go off to war, fearing something terrible will happen before they return. Do the theater gods cover nontheatrical situations? Can't hurt to ask. "Keep him safe," I say.

The phone is ringing as I float back into my apartment. "Are you all right, dear?" asks Annie.

I laugh. "Actually, I'm fabulous. Why?"

"You left the theater so abruptly."

That was a million years ago. I have since crawled up from primordial slime and shot into outer space. "I was having an off night," I say. "Thought it better to disappear. Didn't want to hang around and depress everyone."

"I know exactly how you feel. It happens to us all."

"Not to you."

"You're sweet. I've had my share. We must swap war stories some time." Her doorbell chimes. "Hold on a sec." She puts down the phone. I hear the door open. Voices.

She picks up. "Sorry. My neighbor and I enjoy a cup of tea and a bit of gossip each night. Look, why don't you come over tomorrow? We can have a bite of lunch and talk shop. And you can pick up that box of Lily's things you left in the dressing room."

"You have it?"

"That's all right, isn't it? I wasn't sure it would be safe there overnight so I've brought it home with me. Don't let me forget to give it to you. See you tomorrow. Noonish? And do bring Hamlet. He can dig up my yard while we chat."

THIRTY-NINE

ANNIE DOESN'T ANSWER. I ring twice. Three times. Déjà vu. This isn't funny. I press my forehead against the front window. No bodies on the floor. All quiet on the western front.

I try the back door. Nothing. Return to the front. Ring. Knock. Hamlet wriggles in my arms. The door of the other duplex opens. A square-built woman in a tired housedress and stretched-out slippers emerges, wiping her hands on an apron.

"Hello, Morgan."

"Rosie?" I almost don't recognize her. Partly because she's out of place here, should be standing behind the Equity counter. But, even more, she's lost her steamroller energy.

"Sorry, I didn't hear you. I was busy with Ralph." She blows a wisp of curl from her forehead. "Have you been waiting long?"

"I didn't know this was your place."

"Oh, for years and years. I'm the one who told Annie and Walter—may he rest in peace—they should buy next door. She's a lovely neighbor. A dear friend."

"Your assistant at Equity said you're taking a week off?"

She nods. A look—wistful, sorrowful—flits across her face. "Come on over."

"Thanks, but I'm having lunch with Annie."

"She didn't leave you a note?"

"I knocked but—"

"She meant to leave a note. Said she'd tack it on her door. We old ladies can be so forgetful." A tired smile. "Her hairdresser called. He had a cancellation. Annie's been trying to get a haircut for two weeks. You know how it is. Anyhow, she dropped off a beautiful assortment of takeout from the Siam Cafe, said I should feed you and keep you happy until she gets back."

Somewhere in the distance, a kettle shrills. "Tea's on," says Rosie. "Come."

"What about—" I hold up Hamlet.

She hesitates a moment. "Yes, all right. Him, too." I gather from her tone she is not a dog person either.

She disappears into the house. I climb over the low railing separating the two porches and follow her inside.

The house stinks of sickness. Medicinal, stuffy, the air is overhumidified and oppressively warm. Something more. There's a dank back-smell, slightly acrid and thick as a wall. Hamlet's body vibrates with a low growl. My eyes strain to adapt to the dark. All the shades are down, curtains drawn, the dimmest of bulbs in the lamps. I would never picture Rosie living in a place like this. She shouldn't have to. A woman like her, who plays fairy godmother to all us angst-ridden, neurotic, demanding thespians, belongs in sunny gardens with fresh flowers and cool breezes.

I hear faint sounds from the kitchen, try to follow them through the dark house. The maple dining room table is set with three bamboo place mats, chopsticks, delicate teacups. Is the third place for Annie or will Rosie's husband—Rosie's *sick* husband—be joining us? Please let it be Annie.

A huge Spanish shawl drapes an old upright piano, its fringe hanging lifeless in the muggy air. A beautifully framed collage of our play sits propped up amidst photos of Rosie and her husband. On a background of burgundy brocade, Rosie has artistically arranged publicity photos, pages from *Stagebill,* a ticket stub.

I bring it into the kitchen. "This is great," I say.

"You like it?" Her smile shows some of the old spark. "I'm making it for Annie as a surprise. That brocade is a swatch of curtain from the old Chicago Theater. They used to present the most marvelous live stage shows before each movie. That was way before your time. But Annie will remember."

A timer bell rings. She glances at the clock, sighs. "Would you excuse me a moment, dear? It's time for Ralph's medicine."

"Can I do anything?" meaning with the tea.

"I'd be so grateful," she says, "if you'll help me turn him.

I've done something dreadful to my back and I'm having a terrible time managing.''

Hamlet barks. "Behave," I tell him, setting him on the floor. He flashes his offended "and just what kind of dog do you think I am?" expression and trots away.

The powerful back-smell grows stronger as we approach the bedroom. Even breathing through my mouth doesn't help. The smell is thick enough to touch, to knead, to mold into something horrible.

The gather of gray bones in the bed looks nothing like the man in the piano-top pictures. I have seen death masks with more life.

Rosie transforms as she approaches her husband, chirrups girl-ishly as she moves around the bed. "It's time, sweetie," she says, her voice light, carefree. She opens a vial of pills and shakes a few into her hand. Ralph has not moved. Does not seem to hear. She pours water into a glass, adds a bent straw.

"If you would," she says.

I am staring at Ralph, not paying attention.

"Morgan?"

"Yes?"

"If you could prop him up a bit."

I can do this.

I can do this.

Here I am, a nurse at the front. World War I. This desperately ill, brave brave soldier needs my superb care. Without me, he will die. But with my help, my love, my belief in his recovery, he will live to return to his loving wife and children. Thus empowered, I glide around to the other side of the bed and slide my arm under Ralph.

"Uhhhhh."

I jump back as he moans.

"It's all right," says Rosie. "He's really quite drugged. I need to get this dose into him before the last one wears off. His pain has become unbearable."

If he can take it, I can. I slide my arm behind him again. He cries out, draws parched lips over yellowed teeth, but this time I ease him up enough for Rosie to put the pills in his mouth, force in the straw.

"Drink up, Ralphie. That's my honey. Come on."

It takes forever. My arm aches with supporting the weight of his body. The smell permeates my pores, crawls up inside of me. It is, I realize with dread, the smell of Death.

"Good, that's good." She wakes him enough to understand he needs to drink the water. Talks him through each tiny sip.

His eyelids flutter open briefly. He smiles at Rosie. "You caught the fish," he says.

"I sure did."

"Not even a hook."

She gives him a huge smile. "The biggest fish ever."

"Atta girl." His eyes close.

"It's the drugs," she tells me. "Takes him in and out, sometimes to a better place. Fly fishing was his great joy."

There is such love here. It's not fair. These two deserve better than this. How she manages is a small miracle. Her transformation from tired caregiver to girlish lover is an award-winning performance. Where does she find the strength?

My arm is soaked with his sweat. I help Rosie turn him on his side, wait as she pats a cool cloth over his face and neck, props a pillow behind his back to keep him from rolling over. "Sleep, now," she says. "Sleep."

We opt for fresh air while we sip our tea, settle into side-by-side chaises on the front porch. Hamlet finds a cool place in a far corner.

"It's near the end," she says softly.

"I am so sorry."

"Yes."

For a long time we are silent, leaning back, enjoying the warm sun. It is pleasant to sit quietly with someone, not feel compelled to entertain. Roblings is easy that way. Doesn't need me to be a cheerleader. Warm tingles buzz through. I fall into a dozy place. Wake as Rosie pours fresh tea.

"You may laugh," she says, "but I was once a starstruck girl."

"You were an actress?"

"Oh, not really. I dreamed, like any girl. But my father was terribly straightlaced. Somehow, Mother convinced him to give me one year after high school to try acting. One year to sink or swim." She drops two cubes of sugar in her tea, stirs thoughtfully. "I nearly made it, too. A couple of roles in community theater, staged readings, that sort of thing. Once I auditioned for an important role I hoped would launch my career." Her sigh is long and slow. "I didn't get it."

"I know how that goes."

She pats my hand. "I know you do. I so admire the way you hang in there, never give up. I wasn't nearly so brave. My year ended. I married Ralph, settled down and made a life. I'm sorry you won't get a chance to know him. He's a sweetie. Like Annie's Walter. My life's been a good one, all in all. Working at Equity has been my way of staying in touch with theater all these years."

Annie drives up, her hair freshly cut, nails manicured. "You needn't have waited for me," she says, obviously delighted we have.

In Rosie's kitchen, we open containers of fabulous Thai food, decide to eat on the sunny porch. These two ladies are gifted gossips, funny, irreverent. While I shovel in dish after scrumptious dish, they slice, dice, and dissect half Chicago's theater community. Funny stories. Secrets I can't wait to share with Beth.

Hamlet climbs onto Annie's lap. She feeds him tiny bites of satay. I feel the connection between them. This seems a perfect time to present my idea. "I was thinking," I say, "that you might like to look after Hamlet."

"Are you going away?"

"No. I mean keep him." She looks puzzled, as if I'm offering to give up a child. "I'm not really a dog person."

Hamlet tilts his head at me. He knows what I'm up to. I hope he understands, approves.

"What about Beth?" says Annie. "As close as she was to Lily. Doesn't she want Hamlet?"

"Her boyfriend's allergic."

She nuzzles Hamlet's left ear. "This was Lily's dog, you know," she tells Rosie.

"Don't I remember? Always carrying him into our office in that bag of hers. I can't look at him without thinking of her."

"I know what you mean," says Annie. She peers over her glasses at me. "You're sure about this?"

"Only if you promise to let me come visit from time to time."

She hoists Hamlet, holds him nose to nose. "Well, young man, it looks as if you have a new home."

A huge boulder of responsibility rolls off my back. Slugs crawl out from under. I'll miss the furry rat. This comes as a huge surprise.

"I'll drop off his things on the way to the theater."

"No need," says Annie. "I have plenty of dog things here. Besides, I have a million errands this afternoon. It will be nice having Hamlet along for company. If you like, you can bring a few of his favorite toys to the theater tonight." She slips him another piece of satay. "You'll want to be sure to keep a few things at your place. He can stay with you when I go out of town."

"I'd like that." Never thought I'd hear my voice say those particular words about a creature of the canine persuasion.

FORTY

GROCERY STORE. Shoe repair. Watch repair. Dry cleaner's. Post office. Flowers to bring to Mom and Dad tomorrow. A Pez container with refills by way of a peace offering to Sylvia. Errands, like laundry, have an annoying way of piling up. For some perverse reason, I prefer tackling chores all at once, in one exhausting rush. Strange behavior for a woman descended from a long line of compulsive list-makers.

I am nearly home, my mind on cruise control, thoughts of Grandma Belle loving me again, Sylvia and Adam walking down the aisle, daydreams about Roblings, trying to imagine his interview with Harold—

Harold!

I promised to bring him Lily's box of mementos. Annie forgot to give them to me when I left her and Rosie, and I forgot to ask.

Old Selfish Morgan: This can wait until tomorrow.

New Un-selfish Morgan: No, it can't. Harold is fanatic about dressing Junque and Stuff's windows. I promised him the box and I should bring it. Now.

Old Me: I don't have time.

New Me: Annie lives ten minutes from here.

Will I do the selfish thing or the right thing? The specter of Grandma Belle and my sandbox looms large. "All right, all right," I say, swinging around, driving back.

Annie's car is gone. She and Hamlet must still be out running errands. A hollow place opens in my gut. I can't help it; I'm jealous of their good time together.

Old me: Well, I tried. Let's go home.

New Me: I'm sure Rosie has Annie's key, can let me in, help me find Lily's stuff.

I ring Rosie's bell. Knock. She must be busy with Ralph. I try the front door. It opens.

"Rosie?" I ease inside, moving slowly as my eyes adjust to the dark. "Rosie?"

A grandfather clock ticks in the corner of the living room. The collage Rosie made for Annie sits propped in the center of the dining room table. She's tied a large red bow around it and tented a card, which says: *For Annie. My dear sweet friend, for making these last months bearable. Your friend forever, Rosie.*

A voice drifts in from the kitchen. I move toward it.

"Rosie?"

I stop in the doorway. Rosie, her back to me, stands at the sink wearing a long red gown and Spanish mantilla. She is speaking to the window over the sink.

"Yes," she says, "they told me you were fools. That I was not to listen to your kind words, nor trust in your charity." She stops, swigs water from large glass. "You think," she tells the window, "life is nothing more than not being stone dead."

She's doing Joan of Arc's speech from Shaw's *St. Joan.* It is practically law that every beginning actress commit these impassioned lines to memory. She said she'd been a starstruck girl. I'm impressed she still remembers. I waver. Is it better to cough, make some noise so she knows I'm here? Or to wait, let her finish? Rosie's reading is powerful, moving. She has wonderful inflection and timing. Curiosity gets the best of me. I decide to wait.

Sequins glitter. Sunlight from the window filters through the mantilla lace. Considering Rosie's depressing circumstances, it's amazing that she's summoned enough energy and sense of fun to play-act. She pauses, swigs more water. She refills the glass. With a gin bottle? Isn't it a bit early to be tippling? Well, why not? With all she's had to face.

"Bread has no sorrow for me," she says, "water no affliction."

I suddenly feel the voyeur. If I can tiptoe away, she'll never know....

"But to shut me off from the light of day, from the sight of the fields and flowers..."

She chugs the rest of the gin.

"Rosie!" I rush in.

"Wha—?" She whirls, her eyes wide with shock. It takes a second for my presence to register.

"I...I'm sorry. I didn't mean to startle—"

"You mustn't be here!" she says.

"I knocked. I thought you were busy with Ralph. The door was open and I—"

She rushes toward me, chiffon gown billowing, back lace flowing. I hardly recognize her. Her makeup—mascara, eyeliner, bright red lipstick—creates a younger, healthier Rosie than the one I left two hours ago.

"How long have you been spying on me?"

"I'm not...wasn't— That is, I didn't mean—"

She backs toward the kitchen table as if shielding something. "I want you out."

Lily's box of mementos lies on the table behind her, its contents strewn about. "What are you doing with Lily's things?"

"Nothing."

She tries to block me. I duck around the other side of the table. She's lined up all the old photos of Lily. Lily in rehearsal with the actors. Lily in a director's chair next to Wexler. Lily in full costume with the company. Except—I shudder. Lily's face has been gouged out of every photo. Another face has been pasted in their place.

I pick up the *Stagebill*. Cringe at the stabbed, jagged hole where Lily's face used to be. At the cute pixie of a girl now smiling out at me. At first I don't recognize her. Then, I do.

Rosie.

Rosie who longed to be an actress.

Rosie who lost her big chance to no-talent Lily London.

I look across the table. Rosie's eyes are wild, frantic. She gasps erratic breaths. Suddenly, she lunges for the scissors on the table, the ones used to gouge Lily.

I throw myself on the table, grab her wrist.

"Don't," I say.

"You shouldn't be here."

"Let go of the scissors."

"Get out of here. You'll spoil everything. Just get out!"

She has an iron grip, strength built from months of lifting her dying husband. I have trouble holding her hand down. But I have youth on my side and a powerful will to live. I hold tight until, at last, her hand relaxes. Slowly, carefully, I take the scissors away.

She slumps into a chair, buries her face in her hands. "Stupid, stupid woman."

At first I think she means me.

"Stupid." She grabs Lily's head shot, holds it in shaking hands. Both of Lily's eyes are gouged, the lips slashed to shreds. "I accepted what happened," says Rosie. "For forty years, I accepted."

Tear-streaked mascara blackens circles around her eyes. Eerie effect. Like eye sockets in a skull. Her face is a hard lifetime away from the bright-eyed girl pasted over Lily's photos.

"You were the actress Harold told me about," I said. "The talented one he saw audition for Daughter."

She manages a small smile. "He really said 'talented?' "

"Yes." What else, what else, what else? Come on, Morgan. Think. "Harold said he thought—Lily was wrong for the part. That Wexler gave it to her to help distract her from her grief. Harold said the part should have gone to you."

"Really?"

"Really."

The effect is magical. Layers of gloom peel away. A small calm settles in. "We watched each other audition that day," she says.

"You and Lily?"

Rosie bites a piece of skin from around her thumb. A small drop of blood appears. "I thought her performance was weak, uninspired. I, on the other hand, was at the top of my form, full of piss and vinegar. Oh, my dear, you should have seen me back then." She blots the blood on Lily's photo. "When I left that audition, there was no doubt in my mind whatever. The part was mine.

"That afternoon, that poor young boy died. The next thing I

heard, Wexler had given my role to Lily." She lifts a corner of her gown, wipes away fresh tears.

"It was so painful. You can't imagine the pain. All my dreams, the only thing I ever wanted, snatched away in an instant." She grips my arm with tremendous strength. "But you see, I understood. After all, what was my pain compared to Lily's? To a mother experiencing the death of a child? Except…" She lets me go, beats a fist against her chest. "Except…"

It hits me full force. I reel at the horrible magnitude of Lily's selfishness. "Except," I say, "Lily London never had a child."

"Never."

"A young boy died, and she used that."

Rosie nods. "Stupid, stupid woman. Mailing me those insurance forms." She crumples Lily's photo, hurls it across the room."

Her voice grows husky. Words slur, come out slow. All that gin must be kicking in.

"I thought," her voice a whisper, "I'd buried my rage years ago. But it's been festering under the surface, putrid and rancid and awaiting resurrection. Lily stole my life. It's only fair I repay her in kind."

Her head lolls forward. Her sequined bodice rises and falls in deep breaths. She's passed out. Thank goodness. What do I do now? I need to call Roblings. There's a phone in the dining room. I tiptoe out of the kitchen, find the phone. No dial tone. Must be unplugged so as not to disturb Ralph. I trace the cord down the wall, under the desk.

Something sharp jabs my neck. "Get up!" She jabs again, harder.

"All right," I say. "All right."

She steps back, lets me stand. "Rosie—"

"Not a word!"

She presses the point in my spine—butcher knife, midnight special, can opener?—leading from behind, prodding me toward the basement door.

"In," she says.

I open the door. An automatic light goes on. The steep wood

stairs lead straight down. She pokes harder. I arch my back. Walk down a few steps. She pulls away her weapon. I whirl around, catching a glimpse of the "knife" she'd stuck in my back. I've been captured by the jagged stem of a banana. The door slams shut.

Locks click into place. Hurried footsteps shuffle away.

"Rosie!" I slap my hands against the door. "Rosie. Please. Let me out. Rosie!"

I am still banging on the door when the light goes out, sealing me in total darkness. The only way to turn it on is to open the door. And that's not likely to happen anytime soon.

The smell of the basement creeps up the stairs. I know the smell. It is the same dank chill I slept in all those years my grandfather was dying upstairs in my room. Creepy crawly things live in this smell. Evil seeks comfort here.

The wood railings wobble as I inch my way down the stairs. At the bottom, I slide my feet, one in front of the other, along the damp cement. I wave my arms in full sweeps in front of my face, feeling for crumbling walls or splintery beams or sticky webs of spiders.

There is a click. A whoosh. The furnace kicks on. Blue flames cast sudden light, enough for me to make out shapes. I find an outside wall. The small, high windows are boarded up. To keep out thieves? To hide other bodies stashed in the basement? The acrid taste of fear rises in my throat. Stay calm. Don't panic. There is a faint chemical smell. Dusty plastic trays and an enlarger sit on a table. This was once a darkroom. That's why the boarded windows.

If I can pry off the plywood, I can break the window and... And what? Am I going to climb through jagged glass? Not bloody likely. I still have the mean scar, wrist to elbow, from when I was a little girl and ran through a sliding glass door. But, with the plywood off at least I'll have light. And with light, I'll find a way out.

The floor creaks overhead. I freeze. Is she coming back? Panic rises. The half of me that feels sorry for Rosie gives way to the half that says: She's killed Lily for sure, probably Diana, and possibly tried to poison her best friend. Why wouldn't I be next on her hit list?

The footsteps move around a while. I think she's in the bedroom. After a while longer, the footsteps stop midroom. Silence.

Tools. I need something to pry the plywood off the windows. I search the wood shelves mounted over the darkroom table. Push aside piles of supplies, disintegrating boxes of chemicals. A crystalline ooze coats my hands. There's nothing here of use.

The furnace clicks off. The room goes black. For an eternity, I listen against the dark for sounds of Rosie coming to get me. Silence. Total. Absolute. I jump when the furnace finally clicks on again.

No time to waste. I need a prying tool. In the flickering furnace light, I see where the top of one of the long metal shelf standards has pulled away from the wall. I sweep away the photographic supplies, throw off the shelves, rip the standard from the crumbling concrete.

The U-shaped metal's too thick. Won't fit under the plywood. I grab some thin shelf brackets, wedge them under the plywood, pry up. They bend. Useless. The furnace will go off soon. I pick up the metal standard, use an end to hack away at the concrete around the plywood. In minutes, I've dug a hole deep enough to force the standard under the plywood and pry up. Little by little, the anchoring screws give way. By the time the furnace clicks off again, a beautiful stream of sunlight shines in through the window. The window is made of glass bricks cemented in place. I couldn't break out if I wanted to.

I race through the two rooms of the small basement. The only way out is through the door Rosie locked. Both rooms are immaculate. No bodies lying about, no piles of boxes or papers or racks of old clothes. They are, in fact, too immaculate. Floors and walls scrubbed. As if the owners have cleaned in preparation to move. Only the photography equipment has been left.

Pungent chemicals ooze from a couple of the boxes I threw to the floor. Don't want to die from noxious fumes before Rosie has a chance to hack me to death. Death by banana. I pick up the boxes, set them on the table. Something rattles. I shake out bottles of medicine hidden inside two of the boxes, hold them up to the light of the window. Prescriptions for Walter Andrews. Annie's dead husband?

Some of the bottles are for crystodigin. Easy enough for Rosie to steal while visiting Annie. Or maybe she found them when Annie was throwing them out. One way or another, Rosie took them and hid them. Ironic. Lily was murdered with heart medicine she would have taken if she really did have the heart trouble she claimed.

A cork board near the window overflows with yellowed pieces of paper. Old news clippings, mostly, some theater programs, articles detailing highlights and lowlights of various plays, actors, directors. Poor Rosie's Almanac. How painful it must have been to keep such careful track of the last forty years of Chicago's vibrant theater community.

She's tacked a pink piece of paper front row, center. It's stamped with a Priscilla's Produce logo. I shudder as I take it down, move to the window to read it. It is delivery paperwork for "one gift basket of fruit to Martin Wexler." The basket was delivered to the Equity office the day before auditions began, to be messengered over the following day.

"Oh, Rosie," I say. I don't need to look at the signature to know who signed for the basket. The same person who scheduled Lily first on the Equity audition sheet. Who knew Lily always arrived early to warm up her voice, knew Lily's grapefruit-eating ritual. Murder takes motive and opportunity. Rosie certainly had motive. But, if Harold had never ordered the fruit basket to be delivered to Wexler via Equity, would Rosie's rage have gradually faded, played itself out? Or would she have found another way to kill Lily?

The point's moot. Rosie brought the fruit basket to the Heartland Theater, was waiting when Lily arrived. What fun Rosie must have made it seem. A little lighthearted larceny, a harmless theater prank played on the great director. One old friend helping another liberate a beautiful grapefruit from Wexler's basket.

Barking! Hamlet! Annie's home! I stand on tiptoe, peer out the glass brick into the backyard. I can make out a small form frolicking in the grass. How Rosie must have hated seeing him in her yard, this living reminder of Lily. It was Hamlet Rosie meant to kill. Not her friend, Annie, who doesn't eat cold cuts.

I rap gently on the window. Don't want to alert Rosie. I rap again, a little louder. Hamlet runs over, begins turning in circles. He starts barking. I hold my breath. No sounds upstairs. A bigger form moves into the yard. I grab a metal bracket and knock on the glass.

"Annie. Here!" The form comes to the glass, bends down. I keep my voice low. "Annie, it's me, Morgan."

"What on earth are you doing down—"

"Be careful."

"What? You'll have to speak up."

I have to risk shouting. "Call the police. Rosie's the killer. She's in the house. Hurry. Be careful."

Thank God she understands. She leaves. I hear her run up the stairs into her house. What if Rosie heard? I pick up the metal standard, clutch it like a weapon in case she comes for me. She can't let me leave. I know too much. Everything. I'm the only one who can put it all together.

Minutes drag by. Hamlet dances outside the basement window enjoying our new game. Rosie moves across the room overhead, walks around, leaves. She's coming for me. I clutch the standard tighter, press myself against a far wall, well out of sight if she opens the door. She's moving around, now, room to room. She stays in the kitchen a long time. More gin? What's she up to? Where are the police? Why don't they come?

Locks click, echo against the cold cement. I flatten myself against the wall as the basement door creaks open. "Morgan?" Annie's voice. "It's all right. You can come up now."

I move to the bottom of the stairs. "Where's Rosie?"

"You're safe. It's over."

I don't let go of the standard. Annie looks down from the top of the stairs. "They're in the bedroom," she says. "You go look. I'll call the police."

"You haven't called yet?"

"In a moment. There's no hurry."

I ease up the stairs. I've seen enough bad movies to be terrified that Rosie will jump out, slash at us with a huge butcher knife, send us plummeting down the stairs to the concrete below.

"It's all right," Annie says softly. She's crying. "I'd like you to go see."

The civilian part of me longs to go someplace safe while we wait for the police. The actor needs to push the edge, confront the nervousness knotting my gut. I move through the kitchen. A bowl of fruit sits on the table where the mutilated photos used to be. The empty gin bottle is gone from the sink. Annie has cleaned up after her friend. I walk down the hall to the bedroom. The door is closed. I push it open.

Bizarre tableau.

Pink bulbs in the nightstand lamps cast warm light over the two forms stretched out in the bed.

The chiffon skirt of Rosie's gown spreads gracefully to either side. Her hands clasp a beautiful Spanish fan to her chest.

Ralph, too, has been transformed. Somehow—I don't know where she found the strength—Rosie dressed him in a tuxedo. The ancient jacket dwarfs his wasted body. The shirt collar stands away from his neck. His black bow tie is askew. Gone is the ashen skin, replaced by a healthy bronze foundation, a touch of rouge, a bit of mascara. Here lie a lively couple, taking a short rest before their big night on the town.

An array of empty vials sit open on his nightstand. A nearby pestle and mortar are dusted with a telltale coating of powdered pills. How long did it take her to crush them, to coax them down his throat?

I would rather put my hand in fire than touch them, but I force myself to press the back of my hand against Ralph's cheek.

Cold. He was dead, no doubt, the whole time I was with Rosie in the kitchen. The gin I saw her chugging was all about her getting up the courage to kill herself.

I touch Rosie.

Not yet cold. But no less dead.

They are so peaceful, these two, their faces calm, untroubled. Probably for the first time in months. I back out of the room and close the door behind me.

FORTY-ONE

"YOU...WERE RIGHT," says Roblings, leaning against my door-jamb, catching his breath from the climb up.

"About your need to exercise?"

He winces. "Sure. Hit a guy...when he's down." A vein pulses in his neck. I give in to a strong urge to reach out and touch it. He smiles. It does something wonderful to his eyes. "Wouldn't you rather...live on the first floor?"

"The long trek up weeds out the weaklings."

"I'll bet." He comes in, handing me a bottle of Chianti Classico to go with dinner.

"So," I say, "what am I right about?"

"The fourth set of fingerprints on the kugel foil."

"Rosie's?"

"Rosie's."

After dinner, we take our coffee into the living room, settle next to each other on the sofa.

"Do you think Rosie intended to poison me?" I ask.

"No. She was definitely after Diana. I think they saw each other at the theater the morning Rosie killed Lily. Maybe passed each other as Rosie was leaving."

"Queen Tut wouldn't have noticed Rosie. She treated most people like old wallpaper, something you look at but don't really see."

"Rosie couldn't take that chance. What if Diana remembered? So when Wexler hired Diana as your understudy—"

"Rosie came prepared, laced a piece of my mother's kugel with old Walter's medicine, and gave it to Diana as a present."

"From what you say, Diana sounds like a woman who expected people to do things for her. I think Rosie was a great student of human nature. She understood people's strengths and weaknesses, knew exactly how to play them."

"I can't help feeling sorry for her," I say.

"Murderers are frequently pitiable people." He drizzles a finger up my arm.

"If Rosie had starred in that play forty years ago," I say, "who knows how her life might have turned out."

"We are all faced with life-altering choices every day. Should we wake up or stay in bed? Go to work or stay home? Try out for another play or give up acting? Rosie had a choice."

"She didn't see it that way."

He reaches into his jacket pocket and takes out a thick bar of chocolate. I watch, enthralled, as his large hands delicately unwrap the outer paper, peel back the gold foil. He breaks off a small piece, holds it to my lips. "A choice," he says.

I lean forward, take the chocolate and bits of his fingertips in my mouth. "Mmmmm," I say. Then it is my turn. We feed each other until the chocolate is gone.

THE THOUGHT wakes me during the night. Keeps me awake. I toss and turn until he's up, too.

"What?" his voice groggy.

"When Lily died," I say, "we all believed it was a heart attack. The killer was home free."

"Right."

"Then, why did Rosie call the police and tell them Lily was murdered?"

"I doubt she did."

"Who, then?"

He slips his arm around me, pulls me close. "My money's on Wexler's daughter."

"Evelyn?"

"Mmm-hum." He nibbles my ear. "She's a publicist. Needs to draw attention to your play. An elderly woman's heart attack is hardly big news. But murder? That's front-page stuff. Spread the rumor to a few reporters, start the police investigating, get people gossiping, and pretty soon you've got yourself the kind of publicity money can't buy. So what if an autopsy eventually shows the old woman died of natural causes?''

"Except, in this case, the old woman really was murdered.''

He pulls me closer. "Now can we go to sleep?''

"In a minute,'' I say, kissing the tip of his nose, his eyes, his mouth. "In a minute.''

Celebrate
Silhouette's 20ᵗʰ Anniversary

with *New York Times* bestselling author

LINDA
HOWARD

and the long-awaited story of
CHANCE MACKENZIE

in

A GAME OF
CHANCE

IM #1021
On sale in August 2000

Hot on the trail of a suspected terrorist, covert intelligence officer Chance Mackenzie found, seduced and subtly convinced the man's daughter, Sunny Miller, to lead her father out of hiding. The plan worked, but then Sunny discovered the truth behind Chance's so-called affections. Now the agent who *always* got his man had to figure out a way to get his woman!

Available at your favorite retail outlet.

Silhouette®
Where love comes alive™

AILEEN SCHUMACHER

A TORY TRAVERS/ DAVID ALVAREZ MYSTERY

AFFIRMATIVE REACTION

Tory Travers planned to spend her afternoon crawling through a storm drain in an unfinished housing development project. She was looking for a leak. Instead she found a corpse.

When Detective David Alvarez arrives on the scene, romantic and political tensions heat up. The victim is Pamela Case, a county commissioner who has a tainted political history with the abandoned housing complex. Her murder exposes a life—and death—entangled in graft, corruption, suicide and blackmail.

Available July 2000 at your favorite retail outlet.

WORLDWIDE LIBRARY®

Visit us at www.worldwidemystery.com   WAS355

WINNING CAN BE MURDER

BILL CRIDER

A SHERIFF DAN RHODES MYSTERY

It's been a while since Sheriff Dan Rhodes's football days, but things haven't really changed. But the excitement of the upcoming state play-offs is short-lived when coach Brady Meredith is found shot to death.

His murder leads to rumors concerning illegal betting and black-market steroids. Then the sheriff's old nemesis, a biker named Rapper, reappears, causing too many coincidences for Rhodes's comfort.

Another corpse makes it a second down for a killer determined to lead Sheriff Rhodes into a game of sudden death.

Available July 2000 at your favorite retail outlet.

W(O)RLDWIDE LIBRARY®

Visit us at www.worldwidemystery.com   WBC354